Chapter

1

"I think I'm ready," Lucille said.

"Ready for what, Miss Lucille?" For the first time since she entered the room, Katie stopped going through her mindless motions to focus on Lucille. Lucille was staring toward the corner of the room.

"Yes, dear, I'm sure. I do think I'm ready."

Katie bit her bottom lip and paused. "Who are you talking to Lucille? What are you ready for?"

"Yes, honey. I am a little afraid. But I s'pose that's just part of it." Lucille continued to ignore Katie.

Katie looked at Lucille and then followed her gaze to the chair that was sitting in the corner of the room.

Katie snapped her head back to Lucille. "Lucille, I think maybe you need to close those eyes and take a little nap. Here, let me fix your pillow."

Katie reached under Lucille's head and adjusted her pillow – it had slid to the left a little bit.

"That is such a pretty red dress," Lucille offered, her facial muscles barely moving to make a smile.

Having worked as a nurse for five years, Katie heard enough nonsensical talk out of her patients that it rarely fazed her. Although the palliative care unit had only been open for six months, Katie had been around dying patients long before that. However, this time Katie looked at Lucille with a dumbfounded awe. Lucille was so intently staring at the corner of the room, and despite the irrationality of her words, they also carried a weight of lucidity that most things in Katie's recent life didn't seem to hold.

Katie stared at Lucille, whose eyes began to moisten. A tear rolled down Lucille's cheek as she stared at the chair in the corner of the room and said, "I understand. OK."

Katie took a step back from Lucille and felt like she was invading an intimate moment. Katie looked over at the chair in the corner, looking again for someone she missed when she entered the room. Katie didn't see anyone.

Lucille kept her head on the side of her pillow facing, the chair as she slowly closed her eyes. Her breathing was labored – both shallow and heavy at the same time. Katie looked down as Lucille's newly trembling hands inched their way toward each other and gently, yet with great struggle, folded across her stomach.

2

Taking an out-of-the-ordinary deep breath, Lucille whispered out the word, "blue," and then exhaled deeply. Only this time she did not breath back in.

****

Earlier that morning…

Katie missed the alarm clock with her poor aim the first time she flung her hand toward its incessant beeping. After a second, successful attempt, she rolled away from the alarm clock, fixed her half-twisted pink nightgown, and laid a hand on Kyle's upper arm.

"Why do we have to go to work, anyway?" Katie moaned as she scooted closer to Kyle, running her hand down his arm and interlocking her fingers into his fingers under his pillow.

Kyle groaned something incomprehensible, not opening his eyes.

Katie, already next to Kyle, made one last scoot to verify there was no space left between them and raised her head a few inches to whisper into his ear, "I mean, wouldn't life be a lot more fun if we could just lie in bed all day?"

Katie pulled her husband tight with her arm as she snaked her other arm under Kyle's body and wrapped it around his stomach.

Kyle scrunched his nose as Katie's breath wafted across his face. Like the lazily illuminating lights when he first turns on his equipment in the morning, Kyle begrudgingly opened his right eye and then his left. He let out a short exhale and considered turning to face his foul-breathed wife, but instead let loose of her fingers and re-closed his eyes.

"I don't know Katie. If no one worked, then nothing would ever get done."

Like an inner tube freshly released of its air, Katie's grip on Kyle went limp. Her wrapped-around arm retreated back to her body as her other hand fell free from his stomach, now trapped under the boulder of her unreciprocating husband. Katie rolled onto her back and used her free hand to pull the covers up to her neck.

Kyle, frustrated in himself, lifted his body a little bit to turn to face Katie. As he turned over, she retracted her trapped arm and turned away from Kyle. She didn't see him wince as he finished turning and faced her back.

Making amends, Kyle wrapped his arm around Katie, who felt warm by his embrace but didn't grab onto his outstretched hand.

"I had a weird dream, Katie."

Katie, not in much of a mood to talk about weird dreams, could only manage a soft, "Yeah?"

"It was like none of it ever happened. It was like today was still today, but life was like it used to be."

"Wouldn't that be nice?" Katie more stated than asked.

"Yeah, it would," Kyle replied softly, caught up in his own incoherent thoughts of what has been versus what could have been.

Katie didn't want to get up, secretly savoring her husband's rare embrace. She closed her eyes and wished that she too could dream of what life could have been like.

She clinched her eyes tightly, trying to replay images of their last trip to the beach, their nights playing cards with her parents, and their weekend days spent riding Kyle's motorcycle through the fall trees.

The alarm clock went off a second time, rudely interrupting Katie's mostly unsuccessful attempt at having a good dream. Katie reached over and turned off the alarm on her first try. Kyle took back his arm and let out a deep exhale as he gingerly retreated onto his back. Katie sighed, threw back the blankets, and rolled out of bed.

"I'm working another double," Kyle called out as Katie stood up beside the bed."

"Oh yeah, I nearly forgot."

"You don't need to stay up for me."

"OK – I might not be able to. We have a few patients who've been harder for me to deal with. There's one or two that I'm just not quite ready to let go of and I'm afraid that I don't get a say in the matter."

Kyle didn't know how to respond. Katie went into the bathroom to get ready for work. While she was in the shower, Kyle came in, brushed his teeth, told her bye, and left for work.

About the same time, Lucille was awakened by a newly familiar voice.

"What color do you dream in?" asked the little girl who was wearing a red dress.

Lucille turned her head toward the girl who was sitting in the corner of the room. Lucille's eyes lit up as she let out her distinct laugh – a chuckle that came mostly through her nose, accompanied by a smile that slowly overtook her wrinkled face. "What did you say, child?"

"What color do you dream in?" the little girl asked again, unfazed by Lucille's laugh or seeming disparagement of her question.

"Well, I s'pose I've never thought of that before. Of all the questions you've asked me these last few days, this one beats them all!" Lucille paused and then answered the little girl's question. "All of them, I s'pose."

"I do not think so," replied the little girl. "Dream colors come from within us – deep within us. They come from a place that we know is there, but we are not quite sure how to find it."

Lucille thought about it a minute and then spoke slowly and deliberately. Her southern drawl and choice of words led people to mistake her for dumb. She was not dumb.

"Well, my dreams these days are hard to remember, child. I used to dream of picnics with my children and grandchildren. I used to dream of Sunday dinners after church. I used to dream of sittin' by the fire, workin' on some crochet, and actin' like I wasn't interested when Harold was listenin' to his ballgame on the radio. But, I s'pose those dreams have long passed." As Lucile spoke, she slowly turned her head up toward the ceiling. It looked like she could see the scenes she described playing before her eyes. The wide eyes that shone brightly when Lucille discovered the girl's presence in the room now moistened as she reminisced about times long gone.

"Those sound like very good dreams," replied the little girl.

Lucille didn't immediately respond, caught up in her own world — a world of pleasant memories and thoughtful appraisals. Lucille continued staring at the ceiling.

Unfazed by the little girl's approval of her dreams, a few moments later Lucille said, "They were the best dreams, my dear. And they all came true. I got to have my family dinners and my time with Harold, bless his heart. I got to see Leo married and have his kids. I got to see Mauve married and have her kids — she looked so beautiful in that weddin' dress. I wish her marriage would have lasted, but I made peace with that years ago."

"It sounds like you lived some very good dreams," the little girl responded, sensing Lucille's spirit of peace with the life she was blessed to live.

"I did have some good dreams honey — and they all were real. I didn't dream them in my sleep, I dreamt them in my awake." Lucille smiled with her eyes wide open. "I lived those dreams."

Lucille continued looking at the ceiling, lost in her own world of memories. Over the next several moments, her face provided a window into the emotions that her memories supplied. The little girl watched as Lucille alternated between smiling and frowning, and then drifted into an awake-like sleep, staring at the ceiling and deep in thought.

Lucille, having temporarily forgotten that the little girl was with her in the room, snapped out of her catatonic state and turned her head back to the girl. Lucille studied the little girl like one might study the details of a High Renaissance painting. She was a pretty little girl — long blond hair tied into two braids that rolled down her back. The little girl's hair reminded Lucille of the way she used to fix Mauve's hair when Mauve was about her age. The little girl had on a crisp, short-sleeve red dress that extended just past her knees. It had a Peter Pan collar trimmed out in white stitching with three white buttons down the front at the top. The little girl was swallowed up by the big chair in the corner of the room — certainly too big for her small body. She had her legs crossed at her ankles and her black and white Saddle Oxford shoes swayed front and back, missing the floor by a couple of inches.

Lucille appreciated the visits she had with the little girl. Despite her pleasant memories of a full life, these last several weeks felt lonely, regardless of who came to visit. She had a lot of time to think — a lot of time to remember. She enjoyed most of that time, despite being lonely. However, these last few days her thoughts were begrudgingly leaning more forward than backward. Like the alarm clock rudely awakening Katie away from her attempted dreams of what might have been, Lucille's apprehensive thoughts of what is to come often rudely interrupted her pleasant thoughts of what used to be.

Lucille stared at the little girl. She wrinkled her nose once, pursed her lips together, and for no reason that seems logical to share with a little girl, confessed, "I'm afraid of what's to come."

"Not knowing what is to come can be exciting," replied the little girl, unfazed by Lucille's transparency. "Like the moment before you unwrap a present — that is a most exciting time."

8

"I don't know if this is a gift that I want to unwrap." Lucille paused for a second, looked up at the ceiling, and continued. "I mean, I know that we all gotta' do it. I understand that it's just part of life. But that doesn't mean I have to *want* to do it, does it?"

"You do not have to *want* to do it," replied the little girl, speaking matter of factly, yet warmly. "But, you do not have to fear it either."

Lucille didn't respond. She continued looking up at the ceiling, deep in thought, trying to process her fears and uncertainties.

"I mean, I have faith. I've trusted Jesus my whole life. I know there's a heaven. I know there's a mansion for me. It's just... I've never ever been face-to-face with the idea that I'm gonna find out if it's all true. I'm gonna find out pretty soon. I'm gonna know – or not know – and that's a little scary."

"When I am scared," said the little girl, "I just fold my hands like I am praying and close my eyes." The little girl closed her eyes and demonstrated for Lucille by folding her hands across her stomach. "I just kind of drift away – I do not have to be in the scary place anymore. I can be somewhere nice, like in a field with pretty flowers or on the floor playing with a puppy."

Lucille looked back at the little girl and the little girl opened her eyes and smiled at Lucille. It was a warm smile and it made Lucille feel lucky to have the company of such a sweet, innocent creature with her on this lonely morning.

Cocking her head to look at the little girl, Lucille grimaced and touched her forehead. Laying her head back down, Lucille slowly, and with a bit of pain, moved her hand to a button on her bedrail and raised the head of her bed.

"There, that's better," Lucille said. "Now I can see you and it doesn't hurt so bad." Lucille squinted as she looked at the little girl – the low, morning June sun blinded Lucille as it pierced through the tinted glass.

Even a reasonable person might have thought that Lucille could just keep on going forever, never lacking energy or enthusiasm. However, reality set in two years ago when she found out she had cancer. At first it was a growth in her neck that was dangerously close to her spine. After a successful operation and a fierce round of radiation treatments, she thought she was healed.

Then six months ago, Lucille's doctor found more cancer after she started getting bad headaches. This time it was all over her body and her doctor began to speak more in terms of months rather than in treatments.

Lucille, with her bed raised up, began to feel lightheaded.

"I think I'm going to rest now, honey... if you don't mind. Leo is supposed to come later – Mauve too. And I'm just kind of tuckered out."

"That is fine with me. I will just sit here in this chair while you rest."

Lucille tried to take a deep breath, which caused her to cough and spit up a little blood.

"I don't think I'm ready, honey. Though I don't think I've got much use here," Lucille paused. "I'm going to rest now."

Lucille closed her eyes and fell asleep.

A few hours later one of the two machines beside Lucille's bed started to beep.

Katie, with her ponytail held by a pink hair tie, bound into the room.

"Hey there, Miss Lucille. It looks like we need to turn up your oxygen," Katie called to Lucille, who had her eyes closed and either didn't hear Katie or just couldn't respond. Oxygen wasn't usually part of a treatment plan, but Lucille's case was special.

Katie walked to the side of Lucille's bed and made a couple of adjustments that made the annoying sound go away. Katie reached to the handrail and pressed the down button to return the head of Lucille's bed to its lower position.

Leaving the room, Katie ran into Trish, who was exiting the room beside Lucille's. Katie, Trish, and a small team of others, were selected six months ago to create Southwest Ohio Medical Center's first palliative care unit – a special unit for patients whose hospital care has moved from trying to fix the problem to only managing the symptoms. Day after day it proved to be an emotionally taxing job.

"I don't think she has much time left, Trish," Katie said. Trish was also a nurse and usually worked the same shifts as Katie.

"Ahh, I'm going to miss that sweet, little lady," Trish said kind of quietly. It wasn't the best idea to talk out loud about a patient's impending passing.

"Yeah, me too," Katie replied. "They just don't make women like that anymore."

"You can say that again," Trish replied as she gave Katie's arm a squeeze and walked away.

Katie took a lot of joy in caring for Lucille these past few weeks. Each morning when she arrived at work, Katie checked the schedule to see if Lucille was on her load. The dependable kindness and positive outlook that Lucille exuded every day was exactly what Katie needed in this most trying time of her young life.

One year ago, in the midst of their jealous-inducing happy marriage and plans to soon start a family, Kyle had an accident riding a dirt bike. He broke four ribs, his right femur, and a couple of vertebrae. He was hospitalized for a few weeks and in a lot of pain.

When he came home from the hospital, Kyle wasn't sure he wanted to use prescription painkillers as part of his treatment plan. However, after some long talks with Katie, they decided that his recovery would happen quicker by using pain medicine and that they could both keep a sharp eye on its use. They believed it was a blessing that Kyle had a nurse for a wife and were confident Katie could help Kyle monitor both his pain and his prescription drug usage.

Unfortunately, neither of those things worked out. Recovery was slow and frustrating. Despite the medication, physical therapy caused Kyle great pain. And, despite Katie's best intentions to keep an eye on her husband, Kyle first justified taking an extra half of a pill a couple of times a day, which soon led to an extra whole pill a couple of times a day.

After four months of being home from work and trying to recuperate, Kyle was fully addicted to his pain medicine, eventually using a guy at the machine shop to get him extra pills.

Things came to a head two months ago when Katie found more pills than Kyle should have had. After a long talk and a few tears, Kyle resolved to attack his problem. He started attending 12-step Narcotics Anonymous meetings to work through his newfound addiction. Both he and Katie even attended a family meeting on Saturdays – at least most Saturdays that Katie didn't have to work.

Kyle never had addiction issues before the pain pills and he didn't have anyone in his family who he knew struggled with addiction. His struggle brought him great emotional pain and an overwhelming feeling of powerlessness. It was a strain on their marriage, though attending meetings together these last two months was helping.

Despite the turmoil, Katie was confident the worst was over. She was proud of her husband's strength in overcoming his newfound addiction, and Lucille's short impact on Katie's life restored Katie's faith and positive life outlook. Kyle, however, didn't have a Lucille in his life. Though abstinent from pill use, Kyle inwardly fell apart, doubtful that he could ever live a life in pain without medication.

Unfortunately for Katie, Lucille's impact on Katie's life would have to be brief like so many of the other Lucilles in Katie's life of the last six months. This was the most difficult part of Katie's job.

A few hours after falling asleep and after Katie adjusted Lucille's oxygen, Lucille woke up and half opened her eyes.

"Are you still there, child?" Lucille asked, not able to lift her head while trying to look toward the chair in the corner.

"I am still here."

"I want to see you," Lucille said, summoning all of the strength she could just to reach her hand over to the button on the side of her bed.

Lucille's bed raised about eight inches and Lucille leaned her head on its side so that she could see the little girl in a red dress without lifting her head.

"I'm afraid," Lucille said with small tears starting to run down her face.

"You will be fine, Lucille. Very soon, you will be fine," the little girl spoke, reassuring Lucille and speaking with a maturity and authority that most little girls do not possess.

Lucille smiled at the little girl.

"Just keep your eyes on me, Lucille, I will not leave you."

Sometime later, nearing the end of her 12-hour shift, Katie walked into Lucille's room with a little less spring in her step.

"All right, Miss Lucille. It's time to change your bags." Despite the weariness she felt from working two 12-hour days in a row, Katie tried to speak to Lucille with energy and a high pitch. It was the same voice Katie uses to speak to young children who visited the hospital.

Lucille didn't look at Katie and Katie barely looked at Lucille. Lucille stared over at the little girl, wearing a red dress, sitting on the big chair in the corner of the room.

Katie saw that one of Lucille's tubes was pinched under her arm. "OK, Miss Lucille, I need to get under your arm here to make sure that the tube isn't pinched." She lifted up Lucille's arm and pulled the tube out from under it.

"There, that should help a little bit. We don't want anything to keep you from getting your fluids!" Katie was used to talking to Lucille and other patients without receiving much of a response or even a thank you – the way people talk to their pets or even their cars.

"Isn't she just so pretty?" Lucille softly asked. Katie jumped and nearly pulled Lucille's tube out of her arm when she heard Lucille speak.

"Why, Miss Lucille, thank you very much!" Katie said, her face blushing while making sure that she didn't mess up Lucille's tube.

"No, darling. I mean the little girl," Lucille breathily said.

Katie continued inspecting Lucille's equipment and responded, "Oh yes, she is quite pretty." Katie said, continuing to watch Lucille's oxygen. Katie's tone sounded like she was talking more to a four year old than a lady nearly three times her age.

"I think I'm ready," Lucille said….

And then it was just moments later, after having taken an out-of-the-ordinary deep breath, Lucille whispered out the word, "blue," and then exhaled deeply. Only this time she did not breathe back in.

Chapter

2

. . . .

Katie stood there, frozen.

Lucille wasn't even the first patient Katie witnessed die this week; however, this felt different. It felt both peaceful and sad. It felt both warm and cold. The lifeless Lucille, hands folded across her stomach, looked like she was gazing over at the chair in the corner of the room, even though her eyes were closed.

Katie buzzed the nurses station to call for the physician on duty. Just a moment later Trish came into the room.

"Oh, man. I'm sorry, Katie," Trish said as she extended her arms out. "Bring it in and let me give you a hug."

Definitely in need of a hug, Katie stepped toward Trish and accepted the comfort from her new coworker of just the last six months.

"I don't know, Trish. Maybe it's everything going on at home, but this one just kind of hits me hard."

"She was a sweet, sweet old lady, Katie. She's the woman I wish I had for a grandma."

"Yeah," Katie said. "She would have been a nice grandma to have."

It's not like Katie needed nicer grandmas than the two she was blessed with. Though one passed away while Katie was in college, both of Katie's grandmas – and all of her family for that matter – were what most people considered perfect. Katie's parents had a good, long marriage. Both sets of grandparents had good, long marriages. Both sides of her family grew up in church and passed along that faith to their own children.

Trish, on the other hand, didn't have the stability in her life that Katie had. When Trish said she wished she had Lucille for a grandma, that was because Trish would have been happy with even one stable person in her family. Trish could name each person – one by one – and tell an hour-long story about each and their trouble with the law, trouble with relationships, trouble with addiction, trouble keeping a job – you name it. As she grew up, Trish's life had no sense of stability – sometimes she had to spend weeks at a time at an aunt's house or a second cousin's apartment, all because her parents (and even their parents) couldn't figure out how to properly adult.

Katie and Trish walked over to the nurses station where Sue was busy working on tomorrow's schedule.

Sue, not meaning to sound quite so matter of fact and oblivious to a patient's death, said, "Well, I hate to say it, but her passing will make tomorrow's schedule a little easier to figure out." Sue rarely made an effort to evaluate how other people might react to what she said.

"Sue! How can you say something like that?" Trish shot back.

"Well, Trish," Sue began with her condescending, lecture-like tone, "When you have beliefs like I have – and it certainly seems like Lucille had, then you don't quite worry about death. You've got nothing to worry about."

Trish rolled her eyes and said, "Well, I'm glad you've got it all figured out. Though I don't know how you plan to live forever in heaven if you can't even figure out how to live like a normal human being here!" Trish tossed down the papers she was carrying and walked away from the desk.

Trish and Sue rarely got along. Sue let everyone know she was a Christian and wore the light of that witness more as a police car's search beam than a lighthouse near a safe harbor. Trish, while not necessarily eschewing Christianity, wasn't quite sure things were so cut and dry and never appreciated Sue's condescension and arrogance.

Katie found a way to get along with both women. While she recognized Sue's faults, she admired Sue's unwavering faith regardless of the challenge or issue. On the other hand, Katie also admired Trish's zest for life and willingness to judge everyone individually, without labels or presuppositions.

Katie said down next to Sue. "Sue, something weird happened in there," Katie confided, speaking softly to Sue.

"What's that, Katie? Did the monitor act up again?" Sue didn't look at Katie, but was busy rearranging tomorrow's schedule.

"No, it wasn't anything like that. It was something different – something kind of spiritual."

Sue stopped writing and looked up at Katie with a bit of judgmental curiosity. Sue was more comfortable with religious discussions rather than spiritual ones. "What do you mean, 'kind of spiritual?'"

"I don't know, Sue. Miss Lucille kept looking over at the corner of the room, like someone was there."

"Katie, you know how they get at the end. You can't really trust anything anyone says or does in their last moments." Sue looked away from Katie and back to her work.

"I know. I've definitely heard some pretty crazy things come out of patients' mouths, but this was different." Katie paused. "It's not just like Lucille believed she was talking to someone. It's more like there really was someone else there in the room."

"It's a good thing this shift's about over, Katie. I think working two 12s in a row is about to do you in."

"I totally agree with that, but I just can't shake it. She was saying that the little girl looked so pretty."

Sue stopped writing, sat down her pen, and looked intently at Katie. Sue looked a little pale and looked like she might throw up. "Little girl?" Sue asked, this time speaking with a hint of shock and genuine curiosity.

"Yeah," Katie paused, looking off to the side and not noticing Sue's reaction. "Lucille said something about her dress. It was red or blue or something."

"Red," Sue whispered with authority, nearly inaudibly.

"Yes, I suppose it was red," Katie said before catching herself and fixing her eyes on Sue. "Wait, were you asking me if it was red or telling me it was red?"

Sue asked, "She was talking about a girl in a red dress?"

"Yes, apparently a pretty little girl who was wearing a red dress. Why, Sue? Did you see the little girl? Was she really here? You're kind of freaking me out."

"I can't believe it. I don't know what to think..." Sue stood up from her chair, not having anywhere to go, but no longer able to stay seated.

"What is it Sue? Was there a little girl here? Maybe I missed her. Are her parents looking for her?"

Katie waited in silence as it appeared Sue wasn't going to answer any of her questions. She begged, "Sue?"

"A long time ago," Sue began, "when I first started working here, we had a few patients who talked about seeing a little girl. They always described her as pretty and sweet. She usually had on a red dress and shoes that sounded like they were plucked out of time from decades ago."

"That is really weird," Katie said, not really sure what to think. For the first time ever, Katie was witnessing a break from Sue's usual judgmental, no-nonsense personality.

"Yeah, and it gets a little weirder. Everyone who saw this little girl ended up dying — not by some tragic unexpected death, but nevertheless dying. I never quite believed it. Honestly, I didn't want to believe it — it always sounded like some kind of made-up ghost stuff. And then...."

Katie looked at Sue, wide-eyed and eager to hear the rest of Sue's story. Sue didn't speak, so Katie shifted her weight and said, "And then what, Sue?"

Sue bit her lip, paused, and said. "And then nothing. She went away. But, for you to say someone saw her — all these years later — I just don't know what to think."

At that moment, Trish, now recomposed and letting Sue's condemnatory attitude slide off her back, walked back up to the two women at the nurses station and said, "Now that's the first honest thing I've ever heard you say, Sue. You 'don't know what to think.'"

"Very funny, Trish," Sue shot a nasty look at Trish and her normal grumpy demeanor washed back over her face.

Katie, not quite ready to release this moment and allow the two women to fall back into their usual ways, interjected and said, "Hey Trish, Sue was just telling me about how all these patients they used to have would see a little girl in a red dress before they died. The thing is, apparently there wasn't really a little girl there — they just saw her or something without anyone else seeing her."

"It sounds like a ghost hunters show or something to me," Trish joked. "Let's call TLC or somebody and have them come out here and shoot a couple of episodes." Trish

21

looked at Sue and raised her eyebrows. "Besides, that doesn't sound like something you'd believe, Sue."

Sue rolled her eyes.

Katie swatted at Trish and spoke softer. "And get this, right before Lucille died – when I was in the room – she looked like she was talking to someone in the corner of the room. And she told me there was a little girl… IN A RED DRESS!"

"Oh stop it!" Trish exclaimed. "Either you both are deliriously tired or you need to share with me whatever it is you are keeping for yourself, if you know what I mean!" Trish chuckled and slapped Katie on the arm.

"No, Trish," Katie replied. "We aren't trying to pull anything on you. It was the weirdest experience in the room with Lucille when she passed away and I was telling Sue about it. Then Sue, without me giving her all the details of what Lucille said, told me about similar things that used to happen several years ago."

Trish looked at her coworkers in disbelief – not disbelief that they were trying to trick her, but disbelief that they could both be so far out of it. "OK, ladies. Believe what you want, but I know what I believe, and I believe it is time to go home! So, goodnight."

With the next shift of nurses having already arrived and having been caught up on each patient, Katie looked up at the clock and agreed with Trish. She also said her goodbyes and walked out to her car.

The drive home wasn't a far one – she only lived about 20 minutes from the hospital. Katie was glad that today was Friday and that she actually had the entire weekend off.

Tomorrow morning she and Kyle planned to attend the family meeting – they missed last Saturday because of Katie's work.

During the ride home Katie thought about the oddness of the evening. She actually thought less about the specific events and more about how it made her feel. She felt like she was off – like she had seen a ghost, even though she never actually saw anything. On one hand she felt very spiritual – very in touch with her own spirit and with God. But, on the other hand, she felt like she was trapped in a mysterious cloud – there was no certainty in her emotions, only a lot of doubting and questioning and wondering.

During the last few minutes of her drive, this evening's events led her to think about her own spirituality. Katie grew up in church. When she was a kid, her family would go to Sunday morning service, Sunday night youth, and even Wednesday night missions study. Katie didn't jut grow up going to church, she was in the building practically every time it was unlocked.

But, growing up in church isn't the same thing as having your own faith. Katie had that too. When she was 13 years old Katie went to a summer church camp and made the decision to believe in Jesus. It was a real, honest decision. Oddly enough, despite being a well-behaved child, having all of the correct Sunday School answers throughout childhood, and always volunteering when they needed help at church, Katie was actually one of the last children in her age group to come to faith in Jesus. Many of her friends "asked Jesus into their hearts" when they were only five or six years old. Katie liked the idea of it, but always felt like her faith meant more to her because she was older when she decided that she truly believed.

Katie's faith guided her decisions throughout high school, keeping her from making both inconsequentially immature decisions and life-altering dumb decisions. When looking at colleges during her senior year of high school, Katie was determined to go to a Christian college to protect her faith and hopefully even find a good, Christian husband.

Katie didn't attend a Christian college, but was nevertheless successful on both counts. She more than protected her faith – it blossomed. After graduating high school, she chose to stay local and go to the University of Cincinnati. It was while at UC, that despite all of its opportunities and temptations, she made the faith of her childhood into the faith of her adulthood. While not always perfect in college, her faith still grew as she matured into adulthood. And, Katie also met Kyle at college. He was actually a year behind Katie in school, though only about four months younger. She met Kyle at the beginning of her sophomore year when he stopped by a club booth she was working during Welcome Week. Thankfully he acted quickly when he met her, wasting no time asking her out. He only stayed at college that one semester, but they continued their relationship and married the year after she graduated.

Katie and Kyle's wedding was like one from a fairytale, though Katie's parents made sure it didn't have a fairytale budget. Ever since Katie was a little girl she could envision the church's pews outlined with pink roses. She envisioned her pink bridesmaids dresses, her pink bouquet, and even her white wedding dress trimmed out in pink lace. Like a five year old who obsesses over her favorite color, Katie had a deep, almost spiritual connection to pink. Kyle quickly learned to tolerate her obsession, not even objecting to purchasing a house they found a couple of years after they married whose brick contained the faintest tint of pink.

Continuing the example of her parents and their parents before them, Katie and Kyle started their marriage in church and got quickly involved with a group of other young married couples. But, things had not been the same the last several months ever since Kyle's accident. When it first happened, so many people in their church visited them, provided meals for them, and helped with things around the house. Unfortunately, once Kyle's rehabilitation fell into the depths of addiction, Katie and Kyle both stopped attending church – partly out of shame and partly out of a general confusion about life and faith and God's role in all of it. Katie would never admit it out loud, but everything added together – Kyle's addiction despite her always doing all the right things, their not going to church, and even the repulsive attitude of the ultra-conservative Sue – caused Katie to doubt her faith in a way that she had never experienced before.

Pulling into the driveway, Katie didn't see Kyle's truck and briefly forgot that he was working a double shift. Usually she would wait up for him, but tonight she was too exhausted – physically, emotionally, and spiritually.

Katie went inside, dropped her purse on the table, took a quick shower, and fell right to sleep. Her exhaustion erased the memory of the little girl and Katie slept deeply that night. Sometime – it must have been a few hours later – Katie barely heard Kyle in the shower after he got home from work. She glanced at the clock – it was a half hour later than she expected he'd be home. A few moments later she groggily heard Kyle open a pill bottle – he usually ached after working a double shift. There was no need to worry because Katie made sure the hardest drug they had in their house was extra strength Tylenol. A moment later, Kyle came to bed and Katie didn't even stir. They both slept solidly that night.

A few hours later, but not long enough for Kyle, Katie's alarm went off.

"Kyle, it's time to get up," Katie said softly as she reached over and wrapped her left arm around him.

Barely speaking loudly enough to hear, Kyle scoffed, "Oh, man, it can't be time already." Kyle took his right hand and used it to hug Katie's draped arm. "Maybe we can miss this one and just get some more sleep."

"There's nothing more that I want right now but to stay in bed," Katie agreed, "but that isn't what we need. We've already missed too many meetings because of my work."

"I know, but I've been going to my NA meetings. This one is just like extra credit or something."

"Yeah, maybe so. But it's the only meeting that I can go to with you. And, honestly, it's been good for us."

Katie squeezed Kyle a little bit with her arm. He turned around and faced her. He slid one arm under her head and outstretched the other one toward her. She buried herself into his shoulder.

"Yeah," Kyle said. "It has been good for us. These last few weeks or so have been better. I'm trying to get better, Katie."

"I know you are, and I love you for it. Well, I don't just love you because of that – you know what I mean." Katie paused. "I know it has been hard for you. I'm so proud of the progress you've made."

"Yeah, I'll be getting my 2-month chip soon."

"I'm so proud of you, honey. I think that you're getting yourself out of this."

Kyle didn't respond and Katie laid in his arms for the next few minutes – secure and at peace. The last year had been such a roller coaster and on this morning her mind was at ease.

Despite his best attempts to keep her in bed, Kyle and Katie both got up and ready for the family meeting. It was located in a local recovery center. Kyle hadn't been to treatment or anything, but Ralph, a middle-age man who Kyle met at his regular NA meeting in a local church, invited Kyle to bring Katie and join him and his wife at the recovery center's Saturday family meeting six weeks ago.

At first Kyle wasn't sure he wanted to go. It was already hard enough for him to attend the NA meeting and acknowledge that he had a problem. He really didn't identify with most of the people at his regular meeting. Some of them had dealt with addiction issues for nearly their entire lives. Some of them had terrible childhoods and abusive adult relationships. Some of them had trouble with the law, spending time in and out of jail. Some of them had deep-seated mental health issues and struggled with depression, anxiety, and even schizophrenia and suicide. And, just about all of them dealt with harder drugs than he did. After all, he just got hooked on painkillers because of a surgery that he had to have because of an accident that was out of his control.

Kyle's didn't think that his addiction was like their addictions. He felt like he was a "normal" person. He didn't have all of those lifelong issues. His family life growing up was normal — at least what Kyle thought was normal. Kyle felt out of place at the NA meeting, yet he kept going. Despite his hesitance to identify with the other attenders, he slowly started to glean nuggets of truth from the strangers in those meetings and realized that even his addiction shared some common principles with their addictions.

Kyle met Ralph at his very first NA meeting at the church. Ralph welcomed Kyle to the group and spoke with him over coffee at the end of the meeting. Ralph offered to be Kyle's sponsor, which seemed like an unnecessary and foreign idea to Kyle, but he politely agreed. Since then, Ralph had been checking in on Kyle and Kyle actually looked forward to Ralph's phone calls. Lately though, they hadn't talked in about a week. Kyle was actually relieved when Ralph didn't make the last NA meeting.

After Kyle attended a few NA meetings, Ralph invited him to bring Katie to the family meeting. Kyle was really uncomfortable with that idea. He was always used to telling Katie everything — exposing his deepest fears and most embarrassing secrets, but this was different. His addiction made him feel dirty and inhuman in a way that he knew Katie couldn't understand. Obviously she knew that he struggled with pills, but he was afraid to let her hear his most vulnerable insecurities about life and faith and marriage and even his own identity.

Nevertheless, Ralph's stubbornness coupled with Kyle's newfound respect for his new sponsor convinced Kyle to acquiesce. He told Katie about the meeting and she jumped at the chance to be a part of this experience that seemed like such a private journey for Kyle. She deeply wanted to understand him and his addiction, naively thinking that she could figure it all out.

They had been to three family meetings now and Katie found Ralph and the others in the meeting to be warm and inviting. She was shocked to hear other people talk so intimately about their personal struggles and even more shocked to hear their loved ones share the sacrifices and pains they'd gone through with their family members in recovery. As shocked as Katie was, Kyle recognized even in his young recovery that the stories that shocked Katie were actually watered-down versions of the same stories he heard in his regular NA meeting. And, he supposed, the stories he heard in his regular NA meeting were probably watered-down versions of what was really going on in each person's life.

"Kyle and Katie, it's so nice to see you both!" Ralph practically yelled across the room when they walked in. He made a straight line toward them, abandoning his wife at her chair, and hugged them both like he had known them for years.

Ralph leaned over to Katie and said, "I need your help with something. I've been trying to get Kyle to share more at our meetings." He gave Kyle a playful shove. "I know it can be hard to open up, but it's part of the process."

Katie looked at Kyle, able to tell that Kyle was a little uncomfortable and embarrassed.

"Hey, maybe that's why you haven't been answering my calls or texts the last week or so," Ralph joked.

Katie looked again at Kyle, this time with a slight puzzled look on her face. Kyle didn't see it because he was looking at his feet.

Before Ralph could say anything else or Katie could ask Kyle why he hadn't been answering Ralph's calls, the leader of the meeting instructed everyone to find a seat in the circle of chairs.

Everyone introduced themselves. Katie had not gotten used to hearing her husband identify himself as an addict out loud. It actually still sounded foreign to Kyle as well.

Katie, taking her cue from other family members in the circle, called herself a "supporter of people in recovery." This too was a phrase that sounded foreign coming out of her own mouth.

A few moments later the leader spoke. "I want to introduce you to Trudy. She is a supporter of people in recovery." The group leader motioned to Trudy who was sitting beside him. He continued. "Her husband overdosed and passed away last year. She wants to share part of her journey in the hope of encouraging other family members here today.

Trudy started to stand up, but then changed her mind and stayed in her seat. "Jimmy was my husband for 27 years," Trudy started. "We got married pretty young – I was just 18 and he was just 19. We didn't have any money and we didn't care – we both worked hard for the little we had and we were pretty happy with it."

Trudy's clothes looked old and tattered. Her hair was out of place and it looked like it hadn't been washed in a few days. She was more Eliza Doolittle than Dolly Levi. Katie tried not to judge, but found that her focus on Trudy's outside delayed her ability to hear from Trudy's inside.

"Jimmy's father was an alcoholic – he died a couple of years after we were married. Jimmy wasn't an alcoholic at the time – we both drank – you know with friends and at parties. In fact, if anyone occasionally drank too much, it was me. There was this one New Year's Eve that Jimmy, God bless him, had to practically carry me to the car, drive me home, and put me in bed. I don't remember much about it.

"But, the problem was, I could drink like that – you know, have a good time – and then that was it. I liked it. I had fun – but I didn't need it and I could go on forever after a fun party and not drink for a long time.

"Not my Jimmy though, he had to drink every night – though it was more like just one or two beers. He rarely got drunk, but he did get pretty mad if we ran out of beer and he couldn't drink.

"Well, as time went on, he drank more and more. After a few years, it seemed like Jimmy would drink his supper instead of eat it. One night – he had been drinking like all the other nights – our little boy knocked Jimmy's high school baseball trophy off the shelf and it broke. Jimmy just lost it. I really feared for our son's life. I think Jimmy would have thrown him across the room if I hadn't 'a stepped in, picked up the boy, and locked ourselves our boy's room."

Katie reached over and grabbed Kyle's hand.

"Well, you all know how it went from there. He got worse and worse. He started missing work. He started lying about where he was going. I already told you we didn't have much money, and he eventually started stealing money from my purse – and even his own mother's purse – just to buy booze.

"Finally, one night he got pulled over and ended up with a DUI. I was so relieved because I thought that this was going to be it – Jimmy's big wake-up call. He went to jail for a night and then he went to treatment. We couldn't afford it – we took out a second mortgage on the small house we had and sold off our boat – the only nice thing we owned.

"Jimmy came out of treatment and I was so happy. We were happy... for a little while at least. A few months later he started drinking again behind my back.

"Well, long story short, three trips to treatment later and more 30-day chips than I can count, and Jimmy was back at his old ways. Our son, now an adult, didn't talk to Jimmy any of the last five years of Jimmy's life."

Trudy paused and started to cry. "Jimmy got so sad and depressed. I didn't know what to do. I threatened to leave him more times than I remember but never could do it because I was so afraid for him — who he was and what he might do.

"It didn't matter, though. I guess he just couldn't take it no more. He took his own life about eleven months ago."

Trudy wiped her nose with her sleeve as her tears ran down her face.

"I don't understand it and I never will, but Jimmy's not here anymore. I'm happy he's not drinking, but I wish he was here."

Judy sniffled her snot back to its place and wiped her eyes with her hand.

"I suppose the reason I'm telling you all this is because I want you to know that we all feel the same. If your husband or wife or mother or father or kid or anyone struggles like my Jimmy did, then I know how you feel. It's a terrible feeling and it's terrible to go through it all alone. So, if I can come here and say something that you understand or identify with or anything, then I guess that's the best I can do with losing my Jimmy."

Most people in the room choked back tears as Trudy finished her story. Katie felt an odd connection to Trudy, now looking past Trudy's exterior as Katie's heart broke. While Kyle and the other addicts didn't need more guilt in their lives, Trudy's story was a good reminder of the pain and confusion that their loved ones experience as a result of their addiction.

After the meeting, Katie and Kyle talked with Ralph and his wife for a few minutes. Kyle promised to answer Ralph's calls and texts. Saying goodbye, Katie and Kyle drove home.

During the drive, Katie reached over and took Kyle's hand. "I just can't believe what some people have to go through."

"Yeah," Kyle responded.

"I mean, I know we've got it tough. But look at you — you're getting through this. We have a strong marriage and good family members and our faith. I just can't imagine going through some tough struggles like that and *not* having what we have."

Katie kept talking while Kyle listened.

"I mean, I count my blessings and I thank God — I really do — that we don't have to go through what other people have to go through. I mean the pills were bad enough, but now you're over that and your physical therapy is good and you're healed and everything." Katie paused. "I'm just so proud of you, honey."

"Thanks, Katie," Kyle tried to say out loud, but only whispered.

"And you know," she continued, hardly even caring if Kyle spoke, "I know you've been working extra shifts to pay off those hospital bills. I bet I can find some extra shifts too. I want to help us get out of this financial mess from the surgeries and therapy and get this part of our life behind us."

For the rest of the drive home, Katie kept talking — her mood was good and her outlook on life was even better.

She was determined to work hard for Kyle and she was so grateful for how they were blessed. Kyle, however, drove in silence, listening to his wife's cheery optimism and wondering deep inside if he could really do this.

Chapter

3

. . . .

The same morning as Katie and Kyle's family meeting, George Marshall got out of bed at 7:15 like nearly every other day of his life for the 14 years of his retirement. He put on one of his red, button-down flannel shirts, a pair of black pants, and his black shoes that had special arch support. George turned on the coffee pot, grabbed the paper off the front porch and sat down to read it at the kitchen table like nearly every other morning these last several years. Unfortunately for George, today wasn't going to be another Saturday in an endless line of daily

Saturdays. Today was his birthday, and like it or not, his wife was having the family over to "celebrate."

Celebrate might not be the best word to represent how George's family intended to mark his birthday. By this point in his life not too many people celebrated the fact that George took up any space on this earth. Sure his wife, Louise, loved him, but if you could corner her into a moment of pure honesty, then she might even admit that her life would be better if George just found a way to stop existing. Be that as it may, Louise planned to throw George a party, and she invited her son and his family, as well as their neighbor, Phil.

George's lack of loving affection from his family and acquaintances merely reflected back the same lack of loving affection he gave them throughout his life. Only 75 years old today, you might look at George and think he was 90. His childhood was marked by an emotionally absent, though physically present father, who, when he did make his presence known, was harsh and unbearable. George left home as soon as he was old enough and found work in the local rail yard. That's where George worked all of his adult years – it was a tough job that was hot in the summer and cold in the winter.

People who knew George were actually most fascinated to learn more about Louise. On the one hand they questioned the sanity of a woman who put up with such an unlovable man for so many years. On the other hand they expected that she must be some type of mean creature as well, the Bonnie to George's Clyde or the Jezebel to George's Ahab.

On the contrary, Louise was a calm, peaceful woman. A woman of deep faith and devotion to both God and his institutions, Louise never once considered leaving George. She was his wife and God blessed them with one child, Tom. Over all these years Louise learned how to navigate George's moods and found herself more like Abigail to George's Nabal than anything else. Unfortunately for Louise, though, God never struck down George and never gave her the chance to become the wife of a king.

Nevertheless, Louise loved George and remained devoted to him. Their son, Tom, however, was a different story.

Tom found plenty of reasons to hate his father. In fact he could name many without having to think much about it. There were the long hours George spent away from home after his shift at the rail yard. There was George's constant belittling of Tom's ability to hit a pitch or make a free throw, though George never took an interest in helping his son learn either of those skills. There was George's criticism of Tom's love for art and his ability to sing. There was also George's unflattering critiques of Tom's wife, Rachael. Tom learned from a young age that he wasn't going to get anything positive from his father, so without consciously thinking about it, Tom didn't give George anything positive in return.

"There's the birthday boy," Louise said as she entered the kitchen where George had the newspaper sprawled across the table and a cup of coffee in his hand.

"I don't want a blasted party!" George shot back, usually skipping the pleasantries of "Good morning" or "How'd you sleep?"

"I know, George," Louise said in a whiny, soft voice, "but I think it's important that your family spends a little time with you." Louise paused. "You know… you just never know…"

George interrupted, "You never know what!?" George wasn't just grumpy, he was mad. "Go ahead and say it, Louise. You never know if I'll be around for another birthday!"

"George, that's not exactly what I meant."

"That is too *exactly what you meant*! What else could you mean?" George ruffled his paper like he was trying to scare a dog. "Well, I'm sure that the day I'm put six feet under will be the day you and Tom and Rachael and their kids will all be singing and shouting and praising the Almighty." George mocked, *"Ding dong, the witch is dead!"*

"No, George. I don't want you gone. We don't want you gone. We just know that it's been a tough year."

"Yeah, well we don't have to have a birthday party just to remember how bad of a year it's been and how bad of year this one is going to be. If they want to remember me, then get out your phone and take a picture!" George sat down his newspaper, looked up at Louise, and smiled the biggest fake smile he could stretch across his old face. George could barely hold it for just two seconds before his muscles retreated to their normal positions.

"Well, like it or not, Tommy and his family are coming today at noon. We intend to celebrate your birthday, whether you do or not! Phil's going to stop by too."

George angrily shot back, "Well, maybe you can celebrate it on your own. I don't have to be here for my own party if I don't want to!"

Saying that, George stood up, slammed down his coffee which splashed on the table, and pushed his chair back from the table with his legs. He took a step away, then stopped and reached back for what was left of his coffee. Picking it up, he stormed out the front door.

You would think that Louise would be immune to George's outbursts, but her eyes moistened with tears as she grabbed a paper towel and cleaned up his mess.

Louise was well-intended for planning the party. After all, George had a terrible year of health and it wasn't too far of a reach to guess that he didn't have another birthday left to celebrate.

It would be partly accurate to say that George's serious health issues started when he was 60 years old and had his first heart attack, though George's lifelong anger and bitterness were probably just as much to blame. Luckily, all the surgeon had to do was put in a stint to fix his first problem. That was a scary time, and while most people who survive a heart attack use it as a great awakening to make changes in their lives, George did not. If anything, George acted like he was more mad that he survived the heart attack than if he had died from it. Nevertheless, the heart attack and subsequent recovery forced George into retirement just a few months after it occurred and a few years earlier than he planned.

Then three years ago, George had his second heart attack. This one was accompanied by a coronary bypass surgery and strict instructions for George to reduce his stress (which Louise knew meant his anger), make healthy eating choices, and exercise. Despite the evidence of George's long walk around the neighborhood after storming out of the house, he failed at all three instructions.

The natural result of that failure was an ever-weakening heart. The worst news came about five weeks ago when George passed out at the grocery store. After an expensive ride in an ambulance (which George never wanted and felt betrayed that he had to pay for), George and Louise learned that his heart was beyond repair and that his next cardiovascular event – big or small – would probably be his last.

About an hour and a half after angrily leaving the house, George walked through the front door, thoroughly exhausted from his unusually long walk. George didn't say anything to Louise, who was in the kitchen preparing food for the party. He went into the living room and watched TV.

At twelve o'clock sharp exactly no one had yet come to George's party.

"See, no one wanted to come to this stupid party!" George called out from the living room, the first time he spoke to Louise since returning from his angry walk.

"They'll be here," Louise called back softly. And, just as if she knew someone was at the door, the doorbell rang.

"Howdy, neighbors!" exclaimed Phil, coming into the house on his own after ringing the doorbell. Phil and his recently deceased wife, Ruth, lived next to George and Louise for the last 35 years. Ruth and Louise were good friends, playing cards together and going to ladies events at the church. They even talked George and Phil into joining them for a few card games over the years, but those games usually ended with George getting mad and quitting, which led everyone else vowing to never try it again.

"Hi, Phil," Louise said smiling as she walked over to meet him. "It's so nice of you to come."

"I wouldn't miss it for the world! I thought today might be the first time I ever saw George crack a smile!" Phil joked. He knew George and Louise long enough that he didn't mind joking about George's generally irritable demeanor.

"Don't count on it Philip," George shot back. Though George was a grumpy old man, he knew how to be mildly sociable when necessary. He and Phil occasionally exchanged tools or helped each other around their houses with broken tree branches or moving furniture. But, in some desire to maintain faux power and superiority, George always called him Philip, not knowing whether that was even his full name.

"Oh, come on George, it's not every day that someone turns 75," Phil said, smiling and trying to lighten George's mood.

"Well if we're all lucky, there will be no day that this old guy turns 76," George shot back.

"George," Louise turned around toward him and scolded, "don't say that."

Phil sat down on the couch that was beside George, who was in his usual lazy chair. The two men sat in silence watching the noon news on George's old, but surprisingly resilient box TV.

With Phil's wife having recently passed, he was extra aware of the short time George might have left. In a way true to his own personality but contrary to George's, Phil tried to talk about it.

"So, George, you had quite a scare a few weeks ago, huh?"

George groaned, not interested in talking about his health with anyone, let alone Phil.

Phil unabashedly pressed on. "I mean, it's enough to make one think. You know, take stock of everything in life."

George rolled his eyes and tried to look like he was engrossed in the TV.

Phil leaned toward George and continued, "If you think about it, none of us really knows how much time we have or anything like that. I suppose we just have to be ready for whatever might come."

At this point, George wasn't sure if Phil was going to force him to think backward about his life of mistakes or think forward about eternity and heaven. George's face turned red and he was about to tell Phil to shut up, when just then, the doorbell rang again. This guest didn't barge in like Phil, so Louise came from the kitchen where she had retreated and walked over to open the door. She looked through the partially open door, turned her head around and looked at George, and then went onto the porch and pulled the door closed behind her.

"Oh, look who it is! Elyse you're looking so old! And Brynna, my, how much you've grown!" Louise reached out her arms to her two grandchildren and hugged them while giving Tom and Rachael a loving look. Louise mouthed "Thank you" to Tom as she hugged the girls who were 15 and 11 years old.

"Hi Mom," Tom exclaimed, reaching in to join the group hug.

"Hi, Louise," Rachael added, smiling.

Louise, not releasing her grip on her squirming and barely reciprocating granddaughters, said, "It's so good of you to come. George has been looking forward to it."

"I doubt that, Mom," Tom paused. "Does he even know that we're coming?"

"Yes, he knows, he knows. And you know what, deep down I think he's happy that you're here."

"Well it's been awhile. Here's goes nothing."

Tom opened the door and led his family into the house. Tom hadn't seen his father in about a year and a half – even though George had the scare in the grocery store a few weeks ago. Three years ago, when George had his second heart attack, he and Tom rekindled their relationship and it seemed like it might be on its way to healing. Tom visited the hospital every day and George was briefly cordial and even warm. But after some time, George said a few rude things to Tom – about Rachael, about Tom's job, and even about Tom's children. That was all Tom could stand and he hadn't seen his father since. He and his family still visited with Louise, but she would have to go to their house alone to see them or meet them at a park or the mall.

"Dad," Tom nodded as he spoke deeply and directly. He took two steps toward George. "It looks like it's your birthday. Happy birthday."

"Happy birthday!" Elyse shouted out.

"Happy birthday, grandpa!" Brynna echoed.

"Well I don't know what the fuss is about," George shot back gruffly. "Another old man has gotten another year older and the world is no better for it."

Rachael, usually unsuccessful, stepped forward to try to break the tension. "Hi, George. You look good today. Happy birthday."

George, who forgot his ability get along socially, shot back, "You wouldn't know what good looked like if it hit you between the eyes," George nodded toward Tom. "Look what you once thought looked good."

Tom rolled his eyes and muttered something under his breath. Louise was thankful that George didn't hear Tom do that.

Louise ushered the family into the dining room. George resisted at first, but realized that he wasn't going to win. On the table Louise had set out tiny sandwiches — chicken salad and turkey salad. She had cubed cheese and crackers on one of her best plates, as well as freshly cut watermelon in a bowl. In the middle of the table was a German chocolate cake with 75 candles crowded on top of it.

Louise positioned George in front of the cake and motioned everyone else to gather on each side. Then she grabbed a candle lighter from the table and starting lighting the candles.

After lighting a dozen candles, of which only ten remained lit, George called out, "Come on, Louise. We don't have all day."

"I'm sorry, George. I'm trying."

Tom and Rachael both reached in and grabbed two lit candles and helped Louise light the other candles.

Several seconds later and with candle wax dripping all over the cake, Louise led everyone in a half-hearted and out-of-key rendition of "Happy Birthday." Tom, who was a good singer, snickered at how bad it sounded. He sang even louder out of tune, making the song more unbearable to hear.

Mercifully the song was over and everyone grabbed a plate of food, took a piece of cake with half of its waxy icing scraped off, and headed to the living room to eat. George insisted that they eat in there so that he didn't miss even more of the 12 o'clock news.

After everyone was settled, Brynna asked her grandpa, "So, how does it feel to be 75 years old?"

George, unamused by the question, replied, "I suppose about as miserable as you must be living with both of your parents." George chuckled.

Tom, who couldn't believe the vitriol, even from his father, again mumbled something angrily under his breath. Tom didn't want to be heard, but he didn't exactly mind not being heard either and probably spoke louder than he normally would have intended.

George looked at Tom, shot up out of his chair, and aggressively asked, "What was that, son? Did you have something to say?"

"No sir," Tom said, patronizingly.

Phil looked on, uneasy of what to make of the suddenly tense situation. In more of an anticipation of what might come, Louise started to cry, which made Phil grow really uncomfortable.

"Well, I didn't ask you to come here and if you don't want to be here, then you can turn around and leave," George said to Tom, puffing up his chest just a little bit, standing in front of his chair.

"Boys, boys," Louise interjected while sniffling, staying in her seat and waving a tissue that she seemed to produce out of midair. "I wanted Tom and Rachael and the kids here. They are our family and they should be here to celebrate your birthday."

"Well it's my birthday," George shot back, "and I didn't ask anyone to come. It's my birthday – I should get a say. I didn't want anyone to be here."

"Just like the rest of my life," Tom sneered back. "You never wanted me around when I was little either."

Rachael reached up, laid her hand on Tom's shoulder and whispered, "That's enough Tom. It's not worth it."

"Yeah, Tom," George sneered, "listen to the man in your family. It's not worth it."

Tom shook off Rachael's hand and walked up to his dad, standing directly in front of him and pointing at him in the face. "Listen here old man. Don't talk to me that way or my wife that way. You've never been anything but mean and heartless."

George smacked Tom's finger out the way. George's face was beet red and he yelled, "Yeah, well you've not ever been anything worth having a heart for! You and your nonsense, artsy-fartsy junk. What a disgrace as a man!"

"That's it, we're leaving!" Tom exclaimed. "I'm sorry Mom." Turning to the girls he said, "Girls, tell your grandma goodbye."

"Tom, don't go," Louise pleaded.

Tom turned toward Louise while pointing at his dad. "I can't do it, Mom. Not with him acting like that." Tom looked at his dad and said, "Not that I should have expected you to act any different." Tom reached for his girls and began corralling them to the front door.

Phil continued to sit motionless on the couch, thinking that maybe he should get up and go as well, but too afraid to move.

George took a step toward Tom and his family. He began heavily sweating and hollered, "As far as I'm concerned, you don't ever need to come back!" George held up his finger at Tom, shaking it violently as he yelled.

Tom turned his head to look at George while he pushed his family toward the door.

"And another thing...!" George continued.

George was shaking his hand violently back and forth. He tried to finish the sentence, but he couldn't. He tried again, "And another...!"

This time George took his shaking hand and clenched his chest. He looked over at Louise and said, "I..." before he collapsed to the floor.

"George!" Louise hollered! "Are you having a heart attack?"

"Dad!" Tom yelled out as well, dashing back to his father and kneeling beside him on the floor.

George groaned. "Ohhhh." He slowly talked, "I just need to lay here and rest."

"I'm calling an ambulance," Louise exclaimed.

"No..." George softly shot back. "If I go there, I'll never come back home."

"That's nonsense, Dad," Tom said, raising his eyebrows and taking a deep breath. "Call the ambulance, Mom."

Seven minutes later an ambulance and fire truck pulled up to the house. Wasting no time and afraid he might be having a heart attack, they loaded up George in the ambulance and took him to the hospital. Tom followed the ambulance, driving his family and his mother.

"It's going to be OK, Mom." Tom said as he reached over and laid his hand on top of Louise's hand. She took her other hand and grabbed ahold of Tom's hand with both of her hands.

"I don't think so, Tommy. They said that the next one would probably be the last one."

"Well he wasn't gone when they put him in the ambulance, and now he's with people who can help. And, who knows, maybe it's not anything to do with his heart, anyway."

Louise appreciated Tom's optimism, but she understood that he was just trying to help her feel better. She stared out the window as Tom darted in and out of traffic.

They arrived at the hospital just a few minutes after George arrived. Tom helped Louise fill out papers while George was put through a series of tests and given a variety of medicines.

George spent that evening in the emergency room where they determined that he had a mild heart attack. Stabilized, yet knowing his heart health was precarious, they moved George to the cardiac intensive care unit where he stayed that night and through the rest of the weekend.

Thanks to the medication, George slept most of the time in the cardiac ICU. When he did occasionally wake up, George knew that things weren't good. He didn't feel good himself and he could tell by the look on Louise's face that the prognosis was bad.

That same evening and after their morning meeting where they heard Trudy pour out her heart, Katie and Kyle had bowling plans with Katie's parents. Katie had been pretty anxious about the plans ever since her mom insisted that they do it about a week ago. Reluctantly, Katie finally agreed and found herself wishing she never would have.

Katie and Kyle hadn't seen her parents much the last several months, even though Katie's parents still lived in the Cincinnati area. Before the accident, Katie and Kyle attended Sunday dinners at her parents' house nearly every weekend that she didn't work. Kyle's accident and his recovery took them out of that habit and they never started it back up again. Then, Katie began completely avoiding her parents altogether after Kyle's addiction issues surfaced a couple of months ago. Instead of leaning on their love and wisdom, Katie's embarrassment and pride kept her from divulging what was going on.

As for Kyle's parents, they moved to Arizona shortly after Katie and Kyle were married. Katie found it easier to manage how much they knew about Kyle's addiction, though both she and Kyle knew that it wasn't wise to keep them in the dark as well.

On the drive to the bowling alley and after a few minutes of silence, Katie spoke up. "We can still cancel if you want to. I don't want you to have to go, with your back and all."

"I'm sure it will be fine," Kyle replied. "This will be a good test for it, to see if it's really healed. Besides, the therapist said I can do what feels comfortable."

"Yeah, well it doesn't feel *comfortable* to me! But anyway, I don't want to set you back. You know... I'm not just talking about your back...." Katie was always careful not to say anything about Kyle's addiction that sounded like she didn't think he had it under control. Truthfully, she believed that he was different from the other addicts at the family meeting. The family meeting always pulled at her heartstrings, but Katie never really identified with the other family members at the meeting and also didn't associate Kyle with the other addicts.

"I know," Kyle said sheepishly. He was embarrassed when Katie said anything that made it appear that she didn't think he would be able to stay clean.

"And," Katie continued, almost oblivious to his obligatory comment, "this will be the first time that you've really tested it. Maybe your back's not ready."

"I'm sure it'll be fine. Let's just go and try to have a good time."

Kyle was eager to change the subject or just end the conversation altogether. He had actually been testing his back quite a bit at work, not always following his physical therapist's suggestions.

A few minutes later, Katie and Kyle pulled into Sunset Lanes where Katie's parents were parked and waiting for them to arrive.

Diana practically skipped to Katie's car and nearly pulled Katie out through the window as she reached in for a bear hug.

"Oh, I've missed you. It seems like you live on the other side of the country these days."

Katie, normally warmed by the embrace of her parents, got out of the car and re-hugged her mom, only half-reciprocating her mom's embrace. "It's been really busy."

"I know, I know," Diana replied, letting go of her grip and shooting Katie a half-disapproving, half-puppy-dog eyes look.

Katie's dad stretched his hand out to Kyle and gave him a hearty handshake. "How are you doing, Kyle? It's good to see you guys."

Kyle returned the firm grip. "Fine, Stephen. It does feel like it's been awhile."

"Oh, Stephen," Diana chided Stephen like she was his mother. "Don't shake the boy too hard. He just had surgery, you know!"

Stephen released his grip on Kyle's hand and gave Kyle a private eye roll and then a wink. Stephen turned to Katie and gave her a hug. Speaking softly in her ear, he said, "Hey there, baby doll. It's so good to see you."

"It's good to see you too, Daddy."

The four went into the bowling alley, picked up their shoes, and started bowling their first game. They laughed and had a really good time. After a few frames, Katie's anxieties dissipated and she began re-experiencing the joy she used to feel when hanging out with her parents. Occasionally at first, Katie flinched when she watched Kyle hurl a ball with all of his strength down the lane, but she never saw him wince in pain. By the middle of the evening, Katie forgot all about Kyle's back.

After their first game, Diana said, "I think I need to visit the little girl's room. I'll be right back."

"I'll go with you, Mom," Katie called out to her mother who was already walking away.

After Katie caught up to her, Diana grabbed Katie's arm and walked with her daughter, arm-in-arm.

"So honey, what's been keeping you guys so busy?" Diana asked.

"Oh, I don't know. Kyle has his physical therapy. I like to go when I can." Katie freely talked. "A lot of it, too, is work — we are trying to pay off those medical bills. And then you throw in the occasional meeting, and…" Katie paused. She realized she slipped up and she just hoped that her mom didn't process what she said.

Demonstrating the ears that only a mother seems to possess, Diana asked as they walked into the bathroom, "Meeting? What meeting?"

Katie panicked, and stayed silent to buy some time as they both went into separate stalls. Katie was happy to not have to look at her mom.

"Well, you know," Katie was trying to think of what to say while talking stall to stall. "We… have…," Katie paused a little awkwardly between her words before blurting out, "a type of physical therapy group session." Katie, sitting on the toilet, recoiled and held her breath. Her palms were sweaty and she suddenly felt hot.

"Oh yeah, I've never heard of that. What's that all about?"

Katie was annoyed that her mom pressed her about it, so she stuttered and then continued, "Uh…, it's like for people who are trying to regain things after accidents. It's like a little support time to share successes and challenges and stuff like that."

"Oh, that sounds like a good idea, dear. Though, I can't imagine that Kyle needs too much of a pick-me-up from other people. He's always been pretty positive."

Katie finished going to the bathroom but wasn't willing to give up hiding in her stall. She said, "Yeah, he is tough, but it's still hard sometimes. He's had a lot of stuff to work through."

With that, Diana was happy to move the conversation on to something else. Katie felt terrible. She tried to reassure herself that she managed to tell at least a half-truth; however, there was no way she was going to go into everything about Kyle's addiction. Katie felt like they had already gone too long without telling her parents and that it would be a lot worse to open up and say something now. She really hoped that she and Kyle would be able to put all of this behind them soon and actually forget about it themselves, never having to tell her parents or his parents. Leaving the bathroom, Diana took Katie's arm again. Katie felt really uncomfortable in her mom's loving embrace, having just told one of the only lies she had ever told to her mom.

When the evening ended, Katie felt terrible about hiding everything from her parents and remained silent the entire ride home. Kyle was quiet too. He had a good time and genuinely enjoyed spending time with Katie's family, but he thought that maybe he had overdone things tonight. His back didn't quite feel right.

Kyle reasoned to himself, "It's just sore – it's not painful. I think I've always been sore after bowling in the past. It's probably not a big deal."

Chapter

4

. . . .

Not quite bright, but very early on Monday morning, Katie rolled into work a little tired and not ready to start a 12-hour shift. She was grateful to have had the weekend off, and she probably slept in too late on Sunday, which made it hard to go to bed on time last night. Before Kyle's accident they would go to church on Sunday mornings, which made Monday mornings easier to bear. But they hadn't attended church very often lately.

"Morning, Trish." Katie said, holding her purse in one hand and her tall coffee in the other.

"Girl, you look like death warmed over," Trish exclaimed as she watched Katie try to take a sip out of the wrong side of her coffee's lid.

"Yeah, I couldn't fall asleep last night."

"Well, I didn't get much sleep either, but you don't see me complaining!"

Actually, Trish usually got less sleep than Katie. 29 years old and single, Trish liked to spend her Friday and Saturday evenings at a bar or at a country music concert. She considered it a bonus if she could find a bar that had live country music.

Trish was never in a serious relationship and wasn't even sure if she wanted to be in a relationship. She lived with her roommate, Jennifer, for the last three years and the situation fit both of them well – they could split the cost of the apartment and utilities, but mostly live their own lives.

Trish started nursing a little later in life than Katie. She spent her first four years out of high school in the Navy and then used the GI Bill to pay for her degree. A first impression would not lead you to believe that Trish made a good palliative care nurse, but despite her occasional snarky attitude and general demeanor of not caring what other people think, Trish made a very good, compassionate nurse. In fact, she often scored the highest on patient satisfaction surveys. That's the reason she was hand-selected along with Katie to be a part of the new palliative care unit just a few months ago.

A couple of minutes later Sue sauntered her way to the nurses desk.

"Four minutes late, like usual," Trish shot.

"I clocked in right on time," Sue sneered back. "There's a time clock right by the parking garage entrance and I clocked in one minute early, if you really want to know."

"Well," Trish egged her on, "I just think that it's our job to be at our station on time, not to clock in on time."

"If the hospital wants me to be at my station at a certain time, then they are going to have to change my shift to four minutes earlier!"

Sue didn't intend to come across mean, but that's how most people took her. Ever the rule follower, Sue never clocked in late. But, just like most things in her life, she chose to take clocking in at 7:00AM quite literally and didn't bat one eye at the idea that she should arrive earlier to actually make it upstairs to the palliative care unit by 7:00.

In her late 40s, Sue and her husband had two children who were both in college. Sue was very outspoken about the things she believed in and made sure that you knew if she thought you were wrong. She was a devout Christian, but for her the word "devout" meant strict, unmerciful, and not really caring if someone was going to heaven or to hell. Her faith was more of a set of rules and expectations and less of a compassionate, feed-the-world kind of faith.

Her holier-than-thou attitude and patent disregard for others' opinions made her a less-than-ideal candidate for the new palliative care unit. It only took a couple of days after meeting her that Katie, Trish, and practically everyone else wondered why she was asked to join the group. They were stumped for a few days, until they got to know Dr. Zachary Moore.

Dr. Moore was hired to be the main physician in the palliative care unit. In fact, palliative care was his only duty at the hospital. The other physicians who visited the floor were stationed elsewhere in the hospital and only came to pronounce deaths, cover shifts when Dr. Moore didn't work, or consult. After Dr. Moore completed his residency, he attended a one-year post-residency studying palliative care at the University of Washington.

Originally from Illinois, Dr. Moore found his way to Cincinnati because first, SOMC was starting a new palliative care unit, second, he was one of the few qualified applicants, and third, Sue is his mother's cousin. She informed him of the position and when he was offered the job, he convinced the hospital that the unit would need an experienced nurse as charge nurse. He practically made including Sue on the team a demand of accepting the job.

31 years old and single, Dr. Zachary Moore didn't have much use for settling down because he enjoyed being a rich, young, single doctor and all of the perks that you might guess accompanies that position. Zach, as he liked people to call him, was a flirtatious man who made no qualms of his interest in whomever was the most attractive woman in the room regardless of her present relationship status. Unfortunately for Katie, she was often the most attractive woman in the room.

It's not that he was ever really inappropriate to her. He wasn't necessarily her supervisor and she never felt intimidated or harassed by him. He was just a nuisance in her mind and she always made sure to speak loudly about her marriage when he came around.

A couple of hours into the shift, Katie, Trish, and Sue had already made their rounds and were settling into the rest of their day.

"We have a new arrival coming up from CICU," Sue announced. I'm going to put him in 227 – he's going to be yours today, Katie."

"OK," Katie replied. Then she joked, "I knew I wasn't going to make it all day without a full load."

"His name is George Marshall," Sue continued, ignoring Katie. "He is a heart patient. He had hypertrophic cardiomyopathy several years ago and he suffered from diastolic heart failure on Saturday. It looks like his heart is too weak to operate on."

"Poor guy," Katie said. Even after six months, her heart still broke every time a new patient joined the palliative care unit.

"Yep," Sue replied, unable to offer very much more empathy than that. Always down to business, she pointed her finger down the hallway and said, "There he is now."

Having just come around the corner, an orderly pushed George's bed past the nurses station and on toward his new room.

"Not so fast!" George sneered. "I know I came here to die, but you don't have to be the one responsible for it."

"I'm sorry sir," the orderly replied, probably just a year or two out of high school.

After the orderly wheeled George around another corner, Trish leaned over to Katie, patted her on the back, and laughed while she said "Good luck with that one, ma'am!"

Katie rolled her eyes, "Yeah, it looks like I'll need it!"

"Just don't be the one *responsible* for his death!"

"Yeah, I'll try not to kill him if he gives me some of that attitude," Katie joked back.

"That's inappropriate, girls," Sue spoke demeaningly. "Stop fooling around and go be real nurses."

Katie and Trish shot each other a glance and on cue they rolled their eyes at the same time.

"I'm going to run to the bathroom," Katie said and she left the nurses station.

More looking for a reason to take a break from Sue and also putting off her impending introduction to George Marshall, Katie chose to walk to a bathroom that was a few halls over instead of the one closest to her.

A couple of hallways into her journey, Katie heard a voice call out behind her. "Hey there. You look nice today."

Katie didn't have to turn around to know that Zach was speaking to her. Already needing an escape from Sue, Zach was not the person who Katie wanted to run into.

Katie stopped in her tracks, took a deep breath, and turned around. She didn't mean to sound flirtatious, but she didn't quite know how to handle the attention from the young, handsome doctor who she worked so closely with.

"Hello, Dr. Moore. So, I look nice today? What does that say for all of the other days?" Katie asked. She actually couldn't believe the words that were coming out of her mouth. Her goal was to make conversations with Zach go away as quickly as they could, not invite him to turn on his charm and continue his nauseating onslaught of flirtation and pursuit.

"Oh, Nurse Thurston, you know you're supposed to call me Zach," he said as he smiled from ear to ear. "And I could honestly say 'You look nice today' any day of the week. I could close my eyes, not see you all day, tell you that you look nice, and confidently know that I'm right."

Katie slipped out of whatever demon previously possessed her and jabbed back, "Oh, Dr. Moore, I have no doubt that you always confidently know that you're right."

"Touche, Nurse Thurston."

"Well, fencing is my specialty." Katie really didn't know how to talk to Zach. She definitely didn't want to flirt with him, but she was intimidated by him.

"Really?" Zach responded surprised. "I did some fencing in undergrad."

"Oh gosh," Katie laughed and snorted once. She blushed and looked down at the floor. "I was just kidding. I don't know the first thing about fencing."

"Oh, that's a shame," Zach replied. "You know, I'd be happy to show you sometime."

"Oh yeah? I don't know if I have much interest, but I think my husband, Kyle, would love to learn to swing a sword." Katie was proud of herself, remembering to bring Kyle into the conversation and hoping to stop Zach's pursuit.

"Ha, well if I was your husband, I think I'd learn to swing a sword and shoot a gun. You know, to fend off all the creeps."

Katie thought to herself, "Like you?" Slightly uncomfortable and ready to leave the conversation, Katie said, "Yeah, well, I've got to go." Katie turned to walk away.

"Where are you going? I can walk with you," Zach offered as he stepped into action behind her.

"I'm going to the bathroom, Dr. Moore." Katie said, not stopping and relieved that she had a legitimate reason that he couldn't go with her.

Walking beside her, Zach said, "Well, I'm afraid the hospital would frown on my accompanying you to the women's restroom, so I guess I'll see you later."

"It depends on how lucky I am!" Katie replied - knowing in her heart that she meant that she hoped she wouldn't see him again, but knowing in her head that he probably didn't take the hint. Zach peeled off from her side and Katie walked down the last hallway quickly and alone.

Finishing going to the bathroom, but afraid to leave its sanctuary, Katie tried to drown out the creepy feelings created by her encounter with Zach. She tried to think about Kyle, but those thoughts were clouded by the recent struggles they'd had.

Determined to push those negative thoughts out of her mind and think of her husband positively, Katie closed her eyes and replayed how she first met Kyle.

Katie was getting ready to start her second year at the University of Cincinnati and moved in to her dorm room a couple of days early to represent UC Dance Marathon at the club fair for incoming freshmen. The club raised money for Cincinnati Children's Hospital and despite any intrinsic reason Katie had to help lead the club, she also figured that it would look good on her future nursing resume.

About twenty minutes into the club fair, Kyle walked by Katie's table. Kyle wasn't much into anything that had to do with dancing, but his instant attraction to Katie made him stop at the booth anyway.

"Hey there," Katie called out as Kyle slowed down, who was acting like he was checking out the club's banner, but really just checking out Katie. "Are you interested in joining UCDM?"

"Uh..." Kyle stumbled, a little lost for words and suddenly nervous. "Sure... maybe." Kyle really didn't know anything about dancing. "Tell me, what is UCMD?"

"That's *UCDM* – University of Cincinnati Dance Marathon."

"Oh." Kyle was embarrassed but tried to play it cool. He smiled as he spoke. "So, you said 'U. C. H. D. M. H. D?'"

"No, University of Cincinnati Dance Marathon – U. C. D. M!"

"Oh!" Kyle exclaimed. "Why didn't you say so? UCDM."

"Wow!" Katie joked. "If this is what the freshman class looks like, then UC is in trouble!"

"Who says I'm a freshman?"

"Uh," Katie motioned toward the rest of the room behind Kyle. "If you're on that side of the table, then you're definitely a freshman!"

"So, what does that make you?"

"A sophomore."

"And what does that make us?" Kyle smiled as he asked, feeling like he was reciting lines from one of his mom's Hallmark Christmas movies.

Katie blushed for a moment and said, "That depends. Can you dance?" In spite of her flirtatious question, a moment of panic overtook Katie. She was afraid that maybe he really could dance. She wasn't much of a dancer herself – you didn't exactly have to be a good dancer to be a part of the UCDM.

"Oh I can dance," Kyle took a step back and started imitating a ballroom dancer.

"Not that kind of dance, you idiot!"

"Oh yeah, well, this is my kind of dancing. I guess I'm just too good for your club."

"I don't know," Katie replied, stepping way out of her comfort zone. "Your expert dancing might just be the kind of help our club needs. Why don't you sign up right here."

Katie picked up the clipboard and pen and shoved it in front of Kyle.

"I don't know. It sounds like a scam to get my phone number," Kyle joked.

"There's not even a place on there for your phone number!"

"Yeah, well maybe there should be. I'll give it to you anyway – just in case you need it. Maybe you should give me yours too. You know, just in case."

That two-minute spoken conversation led to a two-hour texting conversation later that night, which in turn led to lunch in the TUC Food Court two days later and an actual date a few days after that.

Katie smiled as she sat in the bathroom, thinking about her husband and happy that their marriage was starting to return to the joy of its earlier days. Taking a deep breath, Katie figured it was time to get back to work. She poked her head out the bathroom door. Not seeing Zach around, she made a beeline for the palliative care unit. She stopped at the nurses station and logged into a computer to learn a little bit about her new patient.

Before she could start reading, she felt her phone buzz. Katie didn't normally answer texts while at work but that didn't keep her from looking at her watch to see who it was so she could determine if she needed to sneak back to the bathroom to have a quick conversation.

Katie glanced at her watch and saw a message from her mom: "Hey, we missed you at dinner yesterday. Love ya."

Even though they bowled with her parents on Saturday, Katie and Kyle still didn't go to dinner yesterday, just like they hadn't attended Sunday dinners for the last several months. Katie really wasn't ready to be around the entire family, thinking somehow that someone – probably her sister – would be able to look right through Katie's facade and know something big was wrong. Deciding that her mom's text didn't warrant a stealthy return trip to the bathroom and not wanting to reply to begin with, Katie ignored the text and got back to reading about her new patient.

"George Marshall," she read in her head. "75 years old, retired, wife Louise, first heart attack, second heart attack, and now heart failure."

After George's first night in the hospital, the cardiovascular surgeon met with Louise. During the meeting, the surgeon told Louise that George's heart was too weak to operate on and that they should plan on him not getting better. He told her, in fact, that George would need 24-hour supervision and care, and that George would not likely ever go back home.

Finishing up her preparation, Katie brushed up on George's meds and headed toward room 227. On her way, she walked by Lucille's old room and a chill ran down Katie's back, causing her to shiver. She stopped and looked in the room – now occupied by Peter Smith. He was asleep, so Katie decided to walk partway into his room. Katie closed her eyes and thought about Lucille's odd little girl for a moment. Katie shivered again and thought about how weird it all felt. Shrugging it off, Katie left the room and continued on toward George's room. She practically forgot about it all when she reached George's door. Pausing at his doorway, Katie took a deep breath, put on her best smile, and confidently bounded into the room.

"Good morning, Mr. Marshall, my name is Katie. I'll be your nurse today."

As Katie walked into the room, George turned his head to look at her. His face was cold and uninviting. Katie waited for his response, but instead he just stared at her and studied her for a couple of seconds.

After a brief, awkward pause, George snarled, "The only thing good about this morning is that I'm one day closer to not having to watch dumb, head-in-the-clouds, kids like you come into my dying room and telling me that it's a *good morning*."

Katie's forced smile slowly lost its grip on her face and she shot George a blank look. Shaking it off, she replied, "You're right, Mr. Marshall. This probably isn't a happy place for you. But, I want you to know that it's my job to try to make it as good as it can be."

"If you want to make it 'as good as it can be,' then you'll give me a new heart and knock fifty years off my life. Either do that, or you can just hold a pillow over my face and save us all the trouble."

Even in her short time in the new palliative care unit, Katie had seen many different reactions from her patients as they dealt with their impending deaths. Some were really depressed and upset. Some were angry. Some were regretful. Some were even full of joy and at peace. She had not encountered, however, someone who was just mean.

"Well, Mr. Marshall..."

"Call me George," he interrupted.

"OK. Well, Mr. George." Katie caught herself, blushed, and cleared her throat. "I mean..., well *George*, I am here to help you. I want you to be as comfortable as you can be. I want to help you with your pain. If you're hungry or thirsty, let me know."

George just gruffed at her and turned toward the window.

Katie walked over to George and took his vitals. She examined his IV and made notes in his chart on the computer. Normally she made small talk with her patients, but every time she started to speak to George she stopped herself.

After a few moments of silence, Katie finally decided to speak up.

"So, George, I see you're married. Should I expect to see your wife today?"

"Only if your eyes work and you're looking for her. Neither you nor I could be so lucky as to miss her coming here today." Then George spoke in a patronizing voice, "She'll try to tell me everything is going to be OK." George grunted at the thought and turned his head away from Katie.

"Well, I'll be sure to keep a look out for her."

"If you see her, tell her I'm in a different room. Make up a number. Maybe she can go bother someone else for awhile."

Katie ignored George's silly request and tried to quickly finish typing her notes in his chart. She was eager to get out of his room.

"All done," she said, breathing a sigh of relief. "If you need anything, just hit that button right there." Katie pointed to the call button on the side of George's bed.

"What I need is for you to get out of my room and leave me alone," George shot back.

Katie got up and headed toward his door. "Remember," she called out, barely slowing down and not looking back as she continued her way out, "just hit the button if you need something."

Katie didn't wait for George to respond. She kept walking out of his room and straight to the nurses station where Trish was looking at her phone.

"Well, that one is something else, Trish!"

"Yeah? You got a real winner there, huh?"

"I've never met someone so mean and angry in my life!" Katie said, perplexed. "What do you think makes someone get to that point in their life? Someone who's so mad that they don't really want to live or die?"

"I don't know," Trish replied. Then she shot Katie a look and said, "I bet if we hang around Sue for a few years, then we'll find out!"

Trish and Katie laughed at Sue's expense, who thankfully, wasn't at the nurses station.

Katie visited George's room a couple of more times that day, though she felt a knot in her stomach each time she had to go into his room.

Thankfully, the first time she went back into George's room, Dr. Moore was there talking to both George and Louise. For once in her life, Katie was happy to see Zach. She was able to do the tasks she had to do and avoid talking to either George or Zach. She considered that a win on both counts.

The second time (and last time) he was asleep. "He even looks mad when he sleeps," Katie thought as she checked his vitals. George was restless while he slept – he looked quite uncomfortable. Katie thought he looked more than just physically uncomfortable – he looked like he was uncomfortable on his inside – like he was wrestling within his soul. George's body jerked a couple of times in his sleep and he groaned each time. "Poor old man," Katie continued thinking. "And, more importantly, what a poor wife he must have."

Chapter

5

. . . .

About a week later, Kyle was working at his station in the machine shop early in the morning. He bent over to pick up a tool off the floor and grimaced as a quick, yet sharp pain shot through his back.

"Hey there, buddy, that doesn't look like it felt too good."

Kyle looked up and saw Rick walking toward him from across the shop. Rick was the guy who hooked up Kyle with all of his extra pills a few months ago. Rick never set out to become a dealer, but was more of an opportunist. At first, Rick took advantage of his grandparents' unnecessary prescriptions and their refills, finding a few buyers in his neighborhood. Once he got a taste for the money he could make, Rick partnered with his cousin who stole pain pills from the patients in the rehabilitation home he worked in. Kyle never knew where Rick got his pain pills, and Kyle decided that the less he knew, then the less guilty he would feel about it. He later learned he wasn't exactly right with that logic.

Kyle took a deep breath when he saw Rick approach and spoke, "Hey there, Rick. Yeah, I guess I felt a little pain a second ago."

"Well, a little pain usually leads to a lot of pain. So tell me, are you back in the market?"

Kyle grew immediately uncomfortable and looked all around him to make sure that no one could hear them talk. Annoyed, Kyle whispered, "Hey man, keep it quiet. And no, I'm not in the market. I'm done with all of that."

"Hey take it easy," Rick held up his hand and was a little offended. He whispered, "I'm a careful guy. Besides, you're just taking them for your back. It's not like that's a bad reason."

"Well, good or bad, I don't need any part in it. Those things messed me up and I'm doing everything I can to not need them again."

"Clearly that's working for you," Rick said sarcastically as he pointed to Kyle's back.

"Things aren't perfect, but they're getting better. I tweaked it a week ago while bowling. It'll be OK. Thanks anyway."

"A week ago? Suit yourself," Rick shrugged his shoulders and turned to walk away. "I don't have that many anyway."

Rick left Kyle alone and Kyle stood there nervously. He thought, "What an idiot I was for buying pills from him – right here at my work! I wonder who else at work he sold them to and if they know about me."

When Kyle first started buying pills from Rick, he didn't think much about the potential consequences. Kyle felt justified in his need for extra medicine and didn't figure that what he was doing was really all that wrong. However, now that he'd been clean for nearly two months, Kyle's stomach hurt practically every time he saw Rick. He didn't figure that Rick would ever rat him out, but he also wasn't too sure either.

Nervous, Kyle tried to forget about his conversation with Rick. Kyle turned up his music and got back to work. While working at his station, it seemed like even the smallest movements radiated into his back and sent a pain all the way down his leg. For a moment, Kyle contemplated what it might be like to ask to Rick for a couple of pills – just to help him get through right now.

"It wouldn't be a bad thing," Kyle thought. "After all, they are pain pills and I'm in pain."

Kyle mulled it over some more. "I mean, really, I've been clean long enough. Certainly I could take one or two pills for the pain and not get re-addicted or anything. I could even tell Katie."

Kyle had been standing at his work station and now sat down in his seat. As he squatted into his chair, another sharp pain shot through his back.

Subconsciously, Kyle battled with the decision to get more pain pills. He couldn't formulate clear thoughts as he wrestled. Then, like a lightbulb flicking on, Kyle had some clarity. "There's no way Katie would go for it. She doesn't understand my pain and she would never think that even just one or two would be OK."

Kyle was frustrated, realizing that getting new pain pills would require going behind Katie's back, and that wasn't something he was willing to do. Kyle determined to get back to work and push his pain and their pills out of his mind. He tried really hard to focus, but felt distracted all morning anyway.

That morning at the hospital, Katie practically skipped to the nurses station as she arrived at work.

"Hey there!" Katie attacked Trish with a tap on Trish's shoulder and an extra dose of morning cheer.

"Ahh!" Trish jumped and screamed, turning to Katie. "What's gotten into you? Did someone forget to tell you that it's morning?" Trish turned back around and traced her finger on today's schedule.

"Nope, I'm just in a good mood!"

"Crap!" Trish exclaimed.

"Well, I'm sorry that my good mood's not good for you!" Katie snapped back, a little annoyed, but still nearly floating on air.

"No, that's not it." Trish looked at Katie and pointed to the schedule. "I've got him again today – George Marshall!"

"Oh, that is not good," Katie snickered.

"No, it is *not good*," Trish annoyingly mocked back. "I knew it when I woke up this morning – I had a feeling in my stomach. I knew that I was going to have him today."

"Well, the rest of the staff thanks you!" Katie said as she half-bowed to Trish.

"Well, the rest of the staff can kiss my butt," Trish shot back, rolling her eyes.

Katie chuckled and said, "I was actually on my way to do the same thing – to look at the schedule to see if I had Mr. Marshall today."

"Nope, I'm the one cursed today."

"It'll be OK, Trish," Katie patted her on the shoulder. "Maybe that means you won't have him tomorrow."

"Maybe he'll die this morning and I won't even have him this afternoon!"

"Trish!" Katie smiled and playfully slapped Trish. "Shame on you!"

Trish rolled her eyes again and gave Katie a curious, yet odd look. "What's gotten into you anyway? Why are you so happy?"

"Well, if you must know, I have a meeting with Charlene this afternoon."

"Charlene? Ooo. Either you're in trouble or you're getting a raise. I don't want you to be in trouble, but you better not be getting a raise either!"

"No, it's neither of those tings. I emailed her and asked her to meet."

Trish lowered her voice and pulled Katie in close, "Is it Dr. Moore. Did he cross the line?"

Katie pulled away. "No! It's nothing like that."

Trish looked at Katie, expecting her to continue. Frustrated, Trish asked, "So what is it?"

"Well, there's nothing official yet, but I'm going to talk to her about scaling back my hours."

"Scaling back your hours? Why? I thought you had a lot of medical bills or something."

"We do. I don't mean scale them back yet. I just mean sometime in the near future."

"Why?"

"You know…"

"Are you pregnant?!" Trish's face lit up and she shrieked. "Oh my gosh! You're pregnant!"

Katie whispered, "Shhh…. No, I'm not pregnant. Let's not start any rumors, but we probably will get pregnant soon, and I want to start thinking about moving to part time – you know to be a mommy and all."

"Can't you be a mommy and work full time?"

"Yeah, of course. But, Kyle and I always talked about me being at home more when we start having kids. I'll still work – just not full time."

"So, Kyle's ready to become a dad, huh?"

"Well…."

"Wait, what do you mean, 'Well…?'"

"Kyle doesn't exactly know yet."

77

"Huh? I would think he would have to know if he's having a baby. The way I understand it, he's an active participant in the process."

Katie rolled her eyes. "Yeah, I just mean...." Katie paused, searching for her words. Her smile dissipated and she spoke matter-of-factly. "Listen, our plan was always to have a baby after we've been married about four or five years. Now is that time. His accident almost threw things off a bit, but it was always our plan. I'm going to talk to him about it soon, but I thought I would get some answers from Charlene so that I'm better prepared for my conversation with him."

"OK, my friend. If that's the way you see it. I just think that you might want to have your husband fully on board before you go setting things in motion."

"Oh, I'm not setting things in motion. Consider this a fact-finding mission."

"OK, Double-Oh 7. Good luck."

"Ha-ha," Katie stuck out her tongue at Trish.

"Well then, I guess it's time to go see if Mr. Marshall died in his sleep."

"Then good luck to you, too!"

Trish rolled her eyes still yet again and left the nurses station. As Trish walked a few steps down the hallway, she turned around to Katie and whispered loudly while she pointed down the hall, "Psst...!"

Katie looked up at Trish who was pointing at Dr. Moore coming around the corner. Katie saw him, mouthed "Thank you" to Trish, and then snuck out the back of the nurses station and into the supply closet.

Later that afternoon, Kyle was busy working and had finally forgotten about his back and Rick's pain pills. His music was turned up loud and he was was lost in his own world – doing his work and nearly oblivious to the people around him.

Out of the corner of his eye, Kyle saw a blue light flickering against the shop's wall. He turned his head to inspect it. When he looked at the wall, he saw the light more brightly coming through the window. Turning in his chair a little bit farther, Kyle saw flashing blue lights outside the window.

"Oh my gosh, did someone get hurt?" Kyle thought. He got up from his chair and walked over to the window.

Getting close to the window, he saw another coworker standing at the window and looking outside. "Hey, Bill. What's going on? Did someone get hurt?"

"No man, it's the police."

Kyle turned white when he saw two police cars parked outside with their lights flashing.

"What's going on?"

"I don't know, man."

Kyle's palms became sweaty and he started breathing quick, short breaths. He tried really hard to not look nervous, but everything inside was exploding. He burst through a set of quick thoughts. "Did they find pills here?" "Do they know that I used to buy?" "Are they here for Rick?"

Just then, Samantha from the front office walked up to the men who were gazing out the window. "Hey guys, guess what. A couple of cops just showed up and asked for 'Richard Stevenson.' Bob went to get him and now the cops, Bob, and Rick have been shut up in the conference room for about ten minutes."

"No way!" Bill replied. "I wonder what's going on."

"I don't know,"Samantha replied. "But I bet he hasn't been paying his child support. I've always thought he was a deadbeat like that."

"Yeah, maybe," Bill said. "I don't know. Maybe he's been skipping out on paying tickets or something."

"They wouldn't send police to his job for that, ding dong," Samantha said.

"Yeah, well they wouldn't send police to his job for child support either, you dumb blonde," Bill shot back.

"Hey, it's not even natural!" Samantha stuck out her tongue and then turned to Kyle, "What do you think it is?"

"I…, I…" Kyle paused for a second and then composed himself. "I don't have any idea. Rick always seemed like he was OK to me."

Just then, the trio looked out the window and saw the officers lead Rick out of the building in handcuffs. They put him into one of the cars and drove away.

"I"m going to go talk to Bob!" Samantha said as she darted off.

"Well, the show's over," Bill responded, leaving the window and going back to his station.

Kyle stood there alone, staring out the window. He was scared. A flurry of thoughts went through his head. "Why was Rick being taken to jail? Certainly it was for selling pills. Am I going to get in trouble? I'm clean now, that has to count for something, doesn't it?"

Unaware that he was alone and staring out the window at nothing in particular, Kyle snapped back to reality and walked back over to his station.

Sitting down and not feeling any tweaks or pain in his back, Kyle prayed in his head. "Dear God, I've really messed up. I didn't mean to. I don't deserve to get in trouble and Katie doesn't deserve it either. Please protect me. I'm trying to do the right thing."

Kyle tried to concentrate on his work the rest of the afternoon, but his thoughts were constantly invaded by doomsday scenarios. He nervously played out storylines in his head of being arrested or even just suffering the humiliation of being outed as an addict.

A couple of hours after lunch, Katie walked back to the palliative care unit after her two o'clock meeting with Charlene. She walked up to Trish and the other nurses who were all hunched over a piece of paper at the nurses station.

"So, what did she say?" Trish asked, already reading the answer on Katie's bright, smiling face.

"She said that although she needs more full time nurses than part time nurses and that although there's a nursing shortage right now, she doesn't want to lose me and would accommodate me going to part time when I'm ready."

"Oh, good for you!" Trish did a good job of showing excitement for her friend, but didn't really see the point in Katie reducing her hours.

"Thanks, Trish." Katie smiled and then realized that she walked in on the group of nurses intently studying a piece of paper. Katie asked, "So, what are you guys doing?"

"We *guys*" Trish harshly emphasized "guys" and gave Katie a sideways look as she continued, "are making a chart of how many times we've each had George Marshall as our patient. And look," Trish tapped twice on the hand-drawn table, "I'm leading the pack!"

"And we all thank her," Amy, another palliative care nurse exclaimed.

"You're welcome," Trish sarcastically replied. "I'm not taking it. This isn't a contest I want to win. I'll tell you what, the next time I have George Marshall on my load, I'll buy someone's lunch if they'll trade me."

"That would have to be a pretty nice lunch!" chimed in another nurse, Brian.

"That wouldn't work for me," Amy interjected. "I would need a nice lunch and something else – like maybe a bottle of Jack."

"You guys are impossible!" Trish exclaimed.

"Oh, I'll do it, Trish!" Katie called out. "The next time you have him, I'll trade you. I'll happily take a lunch, but you can keep the whiskey."

Trish looked at Katie and smiled. "For you, Katie, I'll buy you lunch and the Jack Daniels. I think we'd all like to see how the perfect Katie Thurston handles a couple of shots."

"Ha ha. Well, that's not going to happen. Don't push your luck or my offer's off the table!"

Amy and Brian left the nurses station. Alone, Trish asked, "So, everything went well with Charlene?"

"YES! It went really well. You know Trish, things just seem to be working out right now. It was rough for a while, but now I think things are getting back on the right track."

Annoyed, Trish snidely commented, "Well, I'm glad that things are getting back on the right track for your perfect little life. I sure hate that you had some adversity."

Unfazed, Katie replied, "My life isn't perfect, but things have been kind of tough."

"OK, well I've got to go check on America's number one patient." Trish turned around from Katie, rolled her eyes yet again, and walked away.

Katie sat down at the nurses station, counting her blessings. She pulled out her phone and opened a note she kept of her favorite baby names. She said out loud to herself, "Addison... Addison..., Hmmm.... I'm not sure I'm a fan of that name anymore." Katie backspaced over the name in the list that previously contained exactly ten boy names and ten girl names. Then typing, she said out loud, "I wonder what Kyle would think about Isabelle?"

Chapter

6

Another week later, Katie's alarm clock jerked her out of her deep sleep to wake up for work.

"Ohhhh," she groaned. Katie reached over and turned the alarm clock off.

"Kyle, it's time to get up. I'm going to jump in the shower."

"Ughhhh," Kyle let out a similar moan.

After her shower, Katie went to the bedroom where Kyle was still in bed.

"Hey, aren't you going to get up? You're going to be late."

"Yeah, I'm working on it."

"Well, maybe you should work on it a little bit harder."

Kyle forced himself out of bed and into his work clothes. He groaned as put on his pants and shirt. He barely could bend over and put on his socks.

Kyle was in a lot of pain this morning. He didn't know why. His back really hurt him in a way that it hadn't hurt in a while. This was different than when he bowled a couple of weeks ago. His back hurt then too, but then it was more like sore muscles and it mostly went away. Kyle went to the bathroom and looked through his approved medicine – Tylenol, Ibuprofen, and Advil. He turned his head over his shoulder and saw Katie with her back to him. He took two from each bottle and swallowed them with a cup of water.

A minute later, Katie was getting her things together when she saw Kyle wince.

"Are you OK, honey?"

Kyle shrugged it off, not wanting Katie to know he was in pain – mainly because he didn't want her to know that he just took six pills from three different bottles. "Just a little stiff this morning. I must have slept on it wrong."

"Oh, poor baby," Katie said as she came over and gave him a hug. "How about tonight I'll draw you a nice, hot bath, followed by a good back rub? Then we can catch up on our shows."

"Sounds good," Kyle responded, returning her hug with the best embrace he could manage without causing more pain.

Katie headed out the door and Kyle stood in the foyer, looking at the his truck keys that were hanging on a hook by the door.

"I just can't do it," he thought. "I can't do any of it."

Kyle's head began racing with thoughts that spiraled deeper and deeper. At first he kept telling himself that he should call off work and rest in bed. His back hurt so bad and he hadn't missed any work since he started getting clean. Of course he didn't have any sick days to use — his sick day balance was negative. It wasn't a normal thing for his shop to allow employees to go negative on sick days, but they valued Kyle and were willing to loan him the days to keep him as an employee. Putting Kyle in the hole with sick days probably did more damage than it helped. On this particular morning, Kyle reasoned that it might have been better to have gone without pay for those couple of months because now he couldn't take the day off.

Even though it made his back hurt worse, Kyle paced around the living room. He needed to call in, lie in bed, and rest today. That wouldn't magically make his back feel better, but it would be the best coping mechanism that he had to get through this pain. There was no way he was going to be able to work an entire day feeling like this.

Knowing he couldn't really stay home from work and not feeling any effect from the pills he just took, Kyle had a thought that scared him, but also seemed like the only logical choice.

When Kyle was abusing pain killers and taking extras each day, he stashed them in groups of four or five in different places around the house. He hid a bag of pills high up in an old bowl in the kitchen cabinet – that was the one Katie found first. He hid a bag in his old boots that were in the closet. He hooked a bag on a nail under the house in the crawl space. He stuffed a bag in his old suit pocket in the bedroom closet. He even put a bag on a shelf in the living room behind some books. Kyle had about a dozen hiding spots all around the house and both cars. After he came clean to Katie, they went through the spots one by one, finding whatever pills that remained and flushing them down the toilet.

Kyle figured that there had to be pills that he forgot about and he was determined to find them. After all, it's not like he wanted to abuse them. He just wanted to take one or two for what they were actually intended for – to help him with his pain in his back.

Kyle went through the entire house looking for pills. He went through every pocket in every shirt, pair of pants, and jacket in each closet. He picked up every shoe in the house and shook them upside down, hoping something would fall out. He got a chair and, despite that it made his back feel worse, he climbed up and down, looking in the kitchen cabinets in every cup, every bowl, every pitcher, and every pot and pan for pills.

"Dang it! There've gotta to be some around here somewhere!" Kyle yelled out loud.

Kyle was getting more impatient and more frantic in his search. Barely having the sense to not make a mess that Katie might later discover, he went room to room, through all the drawers, all the clothes, all the shelves, and all the boxes. He even went into the attic – again despite making his back feel worse – and looked in the plastic tubs of Christmas decorations, Katie's childhood trophies, and his old baseball cards.

Fraught with despair, Kyle gingerly sat down on the couch in the living room and cried. His back hurt so bad and he wanted to find pain killers – even just one – to help take the pain away and give him a few moments of peace.

Now firmly late for work but justified in his determination that he couldn't work like this anyway, Kyle thought, "I bet I still have some refills left at the pharmacy. I'll drive there and get a new bottle. I don't have to take more than I'm supposed to. I'll just take one or two and flush the rest down the toilet."

Kyle picked up his keys and headed to his truck.

"Just one or two," Kyle replayed over and over in his head as he started the drive to the pharmacy that was only five minutes away.

Stopping at a red light, Kyle grew impatient. "I have to get those pills!" he actually said out loud waiting at the light.

The green light was almost like a drug itself – the light turning from red to green provided its own high to Kyle. It reinvigorated him as he peeled out and continued driving the last block to the pharmacy.

"You know," he thought as he pulled into the pharmacy's parking lot," maybe I should take a couple now and then put a few in a bag to keep in case I have another day like this. Then I'll flush the rest down the toilet. I've hardly ever had a day like this, and who knows, I probably won't have another bad day like this ever again."

Kyle barely got his truck put into park when he opened his truck door and flew through the front door of the pharmacy, straight to the back of the store.

"My name is Kyle Thurston. I'm here to get a refill on my pain medication."

"All right, Mr. Thurston, let me take a look," said the pharmacy attendant – a young woman who looked barely out of high school. "What's your date of birth?"

Kyle gave his date of birth and then handed over his ID when she asked for that.

"Give me just a second, Mr. Thurston. Let me go check something with the pharmacist."

Kyle grew impatient and worried. He thought, "'Check something with the pharmacist?' What could that mean?"

A full minute later the young lady came back to the front counter. "I'm sorry, Mr. Thurston. You don' t have any refills left. You'll have to talk to your doctor."

"That's crazy!" Kyle shot back, a little annoyed and a little too aggressive toward the young employee. "I know I have refills left."

"I'm sorry, Mr. Thurston. We don't allow refills on prescription pain killers to stay active longer than 60 days. You'll have to talk to your doctor."

"That's a bunch of crap!" Kyle yelled, slamming his fist down on the table. "My back is killing me and I need this medicine!"

The pharmacist, a middle-aged man, came walking around the corner and said, "Hold on there, sir. I need you to calm down."

"I can't be calm. My back is killing me — it's been good for so long but it hurts today. I'm not some druggie. I just need some pain killers to get me through today. I've got a prescription and everything!" Kyle continued speaking with an agitated tone, though a little less aggressively.

"Look," the pharmacist said firmly while staring directly into Kyle's eyes, "nobody's calling you a druggie. But, your prescription has expired." Then he spoke each word deliberately, "There's nothing I can do. You have to talk to your doctor."

Kyle, realizing this was a battle he wasn't going to win, grabbed his ID off the counter and turned and hurried out the door. He pulled out of the parking lot and started to cry out of frustration and anger.

He only got about two blocks down the road, when he decided to pull over and find his doctor's phone number on his phone. He looked for it online, found it, took a deep breath, and dialed the number.

"Dr. Klyn's office, how can I help you?" a cheery voice answered on the other end. Kyle was startled to get a live person on the call.

"Hello, my name is Kyle Thurston. I am one of Dr. Klyn's patients. There seems to be a mistake." Kyle spoke quickly without hardly taking a breath. "I went to the pharmacy to get a refill of my pain medication and they said it has expired."

"OK, let me take a look." After collecting the information she needed, the lady placed Kyle on hold. Spending some time on her computer, the woman on the other end came back on and said, "It looks like your refills are in fact expired. And, it also looks like the pain management part of your treatment is over. I'm afraid there's nothing we can do over the phone. Would you like to schedule an appointment?"

"Would I like to schedule an appointment?" Kyle asked back incredulously. "Yes, I'd like to schedule an appointment. I can be there in fifteen minutes."

"Oh, I'm afraid we can't get you in that soon. It's actually your lucky day. I just had a cancellation and I can get you in on Friday."

"Tomorrow!? I can't wait until tomorrow. I'm in pain now!"

"Actually, I don't mean tomorrow," the receptionist replied. "I have an opening next Friday, in eight days."

"No way! I can't wait that long!"

"Well, I'm afraid that's all we have. If you're in need of immediate medical attention, please hang up and dial 911. Otherwise, I can have the nurse call you back in a couple of hours and talk to you about ways to manage your pain in the meantime."

"Yeah sure, that'd be great!" Kyle said, mockingly. He hung up the phone without saying "Bye" and sat there in stunned disbelief.

"I can't wait until next Friday!" he thought. "What good are they if they can't help me? Aren't they supposed to help me?"

In the midst of his anger and loss for what to do next, Katie texted him.

"Hey, honey. How's work so far this morning?"

Kyle read her text, remembering for the first time since he left the house that he was supposed to be at work.

"Fine," was all he texted back.

"OK. Well, I was thinking..."

Katie sent that part of the text without typing the rest. When she had some crazy idea, she liked to tease Kyle by sending only part of a sentence. It was a cute game they played with each other, but Kyle wasn't in the mood today. He could see the text bubbles bouncing, so he knew that she was typing more. He was annoyed by her text and wasn't really in the mood for one of her grand ideas.

"I was thinking," Katie continued in the next text, "that now that things are going well, we should go ahead with some of our big-picture plans."

Kyle read those words with his mind out of sorts and desperately not wanting to have this kind of texting conversation with Katie right now.

He didn't respond – he knew that Katie would think he was just busy at work.

"Anyway, I'm thinking that now we can start to try to have a baby. And..."

Katie sent that message and then started a new one. "Maybe it's time for us to get involved at church – with the youth or something. And..."

Another break.

"Once we get our bills paid off in a few months, I can go down to part time. You know, like we talked – to get ready for the baby."

Kyle read every text that Katie sent, but his emotions wouldn't let him process her bold statements. Kyle didn't respond, but stared at the phone screen while thinking about how badly he wanted to get ahold of some medicine.

"Anyway," Katie continued, "I don't want to bug you. I know you're busy. Have a good day. I love you!" Katie texted.

"You too – talk later," Kyle was able to force himself to reply, knowing that she'd just think he was busy at work.

Kyle sat in the parking lot beside the road for two minutes, unable to put his thoughts together. As big as the things were that Katie had texted, he practically forgot about them as soon as she stopped sending him texts. He actually didn't even feel his back hurting – he only felt an intense desire to take some medicine. Instead of needing to take the pills for his back, now he needed to take the pills because the thought of taking them totally consumed him.

Kyle thought through a list of people he worked with, trying to remember if any of them or their family members had any bad accidents or surgeries in the past that might mean they have extra pills around the house. He couldn't think of anyone. On top of that, Rick was picked up by the police a week ago and Kyle wasn't too convinced that he wouldn't be next. It would be really dumb to ask people at his work about drugs. Frustrated, Kyle even went through a mental list of coworkers a second time, trying to guess if any of them might be seedy enough to have a stash of pills they could sell him – even if it it was only a half dozen or so.

Kyle couldn't think of anyone at his work who might be able to provide him with the pills and certainly no one who he wanted to take a risk and approach them about it, so then he started thinking through people he went to high school with. "Jeff... no. Bryan... no. Tony...." Kyle paused and let his brain rest on Tony. "Tony.... Hmm.... I bet Tony can help me out."

Tony was neither the best student nor the best person in high school. While in school, he was never rumored to be involved with drugs, but he always got in trouble and was once caught running a scheme where he charged freshmen money for fake English test answer keys. After graduation, Kyle heard through some friends that Tony had gotten mixed up in the wrong group of people and was in and out of jail for drug-related charges.

Kyle searched social media for his old classmate. It didn't take too much digging to find a common friend and eventually find Tony's profile. And, much to Kyle's surprise and joy, Tony listed his cell phone number in his public profile.

"Here goes nothing," Kyle thought.

"Hello, this is Tony," Tony said with his New York accent. Tony's family moved to Cincinnati from Brooklyn when Tony was eight years old.

"Tony, this is Kyle Thurston. We went to high school together."

"Hey, Kyle! How's it going buddy? To what do I owe the pleasure of this call?" Tony spoke with exuberance, like a used car salesman.

"Hey, I'm glad you remember me. Listen, I don't know how to say this…," Kyle stumbled. For the first time since he left the house, he had a moment of lucidity and realized he was about to make the decision to head down a dark, unknown road. And, for the first time since he decided to search for Tony's number, Kyle realized that he didn't have a good way to ask his former classmate if he had access to illegal drugs.

"Well," Kyle continued, "I'm in a bit of a bind and I wanted to see if you could help."

"Hmmm. It's interesting that you called me."

"Yeah, I don't know. I'm probably barking up the wrong tree here, but I was wondering…," Kyle paused.

"Spit it out, buddy."

Kyle vomited out his request in one long, run-on sentence. "I had a back surgery last year and then they gave me some prescription pain killers to help with the pain and then I stopped taking them and now I need them again and I can't get them. Do you know where I can get some?"

"Wait a second!" Tony feigned offense. "Are you saying that you reached out to me – a guy you haven't talked to in years – and you think that I might be able to get you some drugs? What kind of person do you think I am?'

Kyle was embarrassed and he stuttered, "I…I'm sorry, Tony. I didn't mean anything by it. I'll hang up."

"No, no! Wait a minute," Tony laughed. "I'm just pulling your chain! Of course I can help out an old high school buddy. You need the stuff now?"

"Yes, that'd be great," Kyle replied. He was relieved that he didn't offend a shady guy like Tony and he was also relieved that it was beginning to look like he was going to get his pills.

"OK, well then, lucky for you, I'm free right now."

Tony gave Kyle his address and Kyle plugged the address into his phone. The house was about a twenty-minute drive away and it wasn't in a great part of the city – not quite inner city but not quite far enough away from the inner city either for Kyle's taste. Nevertheless, Kyle went straight there.

When Kyle arrived, he pulled up to the rundown, two-story row house that was in a string of similar houses. The house's paint was chipping off and it only had one of four shutters hanging properly beside its front first floor windows. A porch ran across the length of the front of the house and a cracked, uneven sidewalk welcomed visitors from the road to the porch. Kyle parked his truck on the street in front of the house and he walked up the cracked sidewalk and onto the porch. The porch had a couple of pieces of wood flooring that were missing, a few beer bottles lying around, and one of the missing shutters broken in half lying on its floor.

Kyle tried the doorbell, but didn't hear it make a sound, so after a pause he knocked on the door.

"It's open!" a woman's voice yelled out.

Kyle tried to turn the handle to open the door, but felt the door push open when he first applied pressure to the handle.

Walking in, Kyle saw that the small foyer opened into a living room with an old, dirty brown couch off to the left, a coffee table in front of the couch, a green sofa chair beside it, and a big flatscreen TV sitting on top of a folding table on the other side of the room. Kyle should have been knocked over by the bad smell in the house, but he hardly noticed it being so intent on getting his pills.

Kyle scanned the room looking for the voice who called him in and didn't see anyone. A couple of seconds later a woman walked through an entryway into the living room. She looked like she must be in her mid-twenties and all she wore was a t-shirt and underwear. Her eyes were sunken in and she carried a lit cigarette in her hand as she walked through the room. She was very thin – unhealthily thin. Kyle wondered if she could weigh even 100 pounds.

"Who are you?" she asked in a deep, raspy voice.

"I'm… I'm Kyle." Kyle stuttered, a little shocked by her appearance and sound. "I'm looking for Tony."

The woman yelled, "Tony! Some guy's here to see you!"

Turning to Kyle, she said, "What did you say your name was?"

"Kyle."

She yelled again, "His name is Kyle!"

A moment later Tony walked into the room. He didn't look quite as rough as the woman, but he didn't look all that great either.

"Thanks, Becca." Tony said as he gave her a kiss on the cheek. "Why don't you go back to the room and let me talk with my buddy, Kyle, here."

"Whatever," Becca said, giving Kyle a suspicious scan, then turning around and leaving the room.

"So, Kyle. How are you doing, buddy?"

"Not so good, Tony. I really need some help. The pharmacy won't give me any more pills and the doctor won't see me until next week. I had a bunch left over but Katie, my wife, made me flush them all."

"Oh, that's no good! I don't know who this Katie is, but I don't think I like her!"

"Nah, she's not bad. She's my wife. Anyway, I really need some pain killers. Do you have any?"

"Kyle, Kyle, Kyle," Tony walked up to Kyle and put a hand on his shoulder. "Yes, I have some pain killers I could give you, but they're hard to come by. That means they cost a lot of money." Tony paused. "You know, there's a better way."

"A better way? What do you mean, a better way? My back hurts really bad and I just want to make it stop hurting."

"Oh man, I'm sorry." Tony poured out the empathy. "Yeah, listen. I could get you some pills – and I have some. But like I said, they're expensive. That's a rich man's game, Kyle. Tell me, are you a rich man?"

"No, I guess not," Kyle responded, a little dejected that he might not get what he came for.

"Listen, there's a better way to do it." Tony walked over to the coffee table and picked up a syringe. "I knew you were coming, so I got some all ready for you, right here."

"What is that, Tony? I only want a dozen or so pain pills."

98

"This is better than pain pills. One dose of this does more than five pills! And it's about twenty cents on the dollar too! It's a win-win situation."

"I don't know, Tony. What is it?"

"What are you talking about? Were you born under a rock?" Tony laughed. "It's heroin."

Kyle shrunk back from Tony and a look of fear washed over his face.

"Whoa there, buddy!" Tony reassured. "You look like you've just seen a ghost."

Tony sat down the syringe, walked back over to Kyle, and put a hand on his shoulder.

"Heroin gets a bad rap," Tony explained. "A few bad people have messed it all up for the rest of us and made us all look bad. Listen, those big pharma companies make all this medicine and then charge us way more than we can pay – all so they can live in their big houses and send their kids to fancy schools and drive nice cars. Well, we've taken the power away from them. Heroin is cheaper and easier and much more effective. And you don't need a pharmacy or a doctor to tell you that you do or don't need it. Who are they to tell you what you need, anyway?"

Kyle squirmed. He was trying hard not to be influenced by Tony's pitch. "Yeah," Kyle said, "I guess they shouldn't be the ones to tell us what we need."

"Exactly! Why let them have the control?"

Tony looked at Kyle, waiting on him to respond.

"I don't know, Tony. Is it safe? I mean, not that I know a lot about this stuff, but I thought people were ditching this for, what is it…, fentanyl or something."

Tony gruffed and was a little annoyed. "Fentanyl! Fentanyl? Are you kidding? Who knows what's in that stuff! Besides, do you want to support some Mexican drug cartel? Haven't you seen Narcos? No man, no fentanyl here. I can't control it and, let's be honest, there's not much money for ol' Tony in that."

"Speaking of money," Kyle interjected, "how much is this going to cost me,... the heroin?" Kyle could hardly say the word.

"Think of it like a sample at Costco," Tony said, now smiling and no longer annoyed. "If you like what you try, then maybe you'll become a paying customer." Tony laughed as he slapped Kyle on the back. Kyle didn't even notice any pain from the playful slap.

Kyle thought for a second. Tony, growing a little impatient, said, "So what will it be? Are you ready to take care of that back?"

Kyle stalled. Remembering his unanswered question, Kyle asked again, "So, is it safe?"

"Of course it's safe! I've got a pack of brand new needles and I've done this a million times. I've got just enough here so that you can get the relief that you need. And, I'll be here the whole time."

Kyle stared at the syringe on the table. His instincts told him everything about this was wrong. He couldn't believe that he got himself into a place where he had to make such a crazy decision. But, then he thought about how both the pharmacy and the doctor's office were failing him. They weren't interested in helping him feel better and get better – they were only interested in getting his money.

Standing there, agonizing over his decision, Kyle felt his phone buzz.

"Hey there, how's it going?" It was a text from Katie.

Kyle just stared at the phone. He wasn't sure how to answer her or if he should answer her at all. Finally he decided to shoot back, "Fine. Really busy today."

Immediately, she wrote back, "No problem. Have a good day. I love you."

Kyle put the phone back into his pocket.

"So, it's cheaper and better than a pain pill?"

"Absolutely. I wouldn't steer you wrong!"

"I don't know, Tony. It seems like a bad thing."

"That's just because everyone tells you it's a bad thing. Listen, you can pay a lot more money for something that's going to work a lot less, or you can take one shot of this and your back will feel like you just left the spa or something."

Kyle agonized in silence. Tony stood there and let his old classmate mull over his decision. Finally, Kyle said, "Let's do this."

Tony motioned Kyle to roll up his sleeve. Tony wrapped a rubber strap around Kyle's arm and Kyle could see his veins rise to his arm's surface. Tony reached for the syringe, flicked it a couple of times, and stuck it in Kyle.

"Shoot!" Tony exclaimed. Kyle's arm immediately bruised around the inserted syringe.

Deciding his stick was good enough, Tony pressed in the syringe's plunger and Kyle could feel the liquid go into his arm and run through his veins. A moment later, Kyle felt an intense euphoria wash over his body and he had no consciousness of pain in his back or much feeling of anything anywhere. Kyle's entire body felt warm and his arms and legs started to get heavy. Tony led Kyle to the couch, where Kyle sat down and smiled in relief. Kyle took in a big breath and tried hard to generate saliva to moisten his newly dry mouth. That was all that Kyle remembered of the afternoon and he soon fell asleep on Tony's couch.

Chapter

7

. . . .

That evening Katie didn't get off work until 8:30 – a full hour after she was supposed to leave. It was a difficult day – Sue was her typical condescending self and Trish went on a daylong, nonstop rant about politics and the religious right. So, neither of those women could hardly stand to be around each other. In addition, It seemed like every time Katie turned a corner she ran into Zach, and on top of it all, two patients passed away during her shift. Katie was selfishly thankful that they weren't hers.

"Too bad George wasn't one of them," Katie actually found herself thinking. As soon as the thought entered her mind, she was embarrassed of herself. She didn't want George to die, but he had been a handful for her and the other nurses over the last two weeks. Today she was lucky enough to not have him as one of her patients. In fact, the first thing every nurse on the floor did when they came in to start their shifts was look at the patient list to see if they had George. Sue and the other charge nurses tried to even out the burden, though Trish was certain that Sue gave George to her more than to anyone else.

Driving home, Katie looked forward to the escape of her cozy home and the embrace of her loving husband. She texted some with Kyle earlier in the day, but she hadn't heard from him since his short response earlier. She knew his work kept him from being able to text her much, and she really hated to bother him when he was at work anyway.

"Maybe I'll pour a glass of wine, put on some music, and take a bath," she thought as she drove home. "Then Kyle and I can cuddle on the couch and watch some TV." She allowed herself to sink into her fantasy of relaxation and escape, barely even conscious of driving her car.

"Oh, shoot," she thought, her fantasy skidding to a halt, "we don't even have any wine."

Katie and Kyle decided to remove all the alcohol from their house when Katie first discovered Kyle was taking extra pain pills. She had seen enough addicts in the hospital in her short five years of work to know that they should remove everything that might be an addictive substance. Katie even got rid of their hand sanitizer after she read an article online about middle school kids trying to get high from it.

It's not like they had much alcohol to begin with — neither of them were really drinkers. They had a half-drunk bottle of champagne left over from their third anniversary, an unopened bottle of wine Trish gave her one day out of the blue, and a couple of flavors of hard cider that she bought after she heard some people at work talking about them. Throwing out the alcohol wasn't a big sacrifice for Katie, but on today's drive home it did disappoint her a little bit.

Katie considered stopping by the grocery store to buy a cheap bottle. She went back and forth, trying to decide if Kyle was long enough away from his addiction to really matter if she bought it. She mostly decided that it would be OK, but found herself too lazy to make the left turn into the busy grocery store parking lot and instead drove past it to continue home.

Pulling into the driveway, Katie noticed that Kyle's truck wasn't there.

"Maybe he worked a second shift this evening," she thought. Katie got a little emotional and even had to rub her eyes, thinking about how her husband was fighting so hard these last couple of weeks. He was attending meetings, paying more attention to her, and now, apparently working another shift to help pay off his medical bills.

Katie walked into the home, threw her purse on the dining room table, and drew a hot a bath. Sufficing with a cup of hot tea instead of a glass of red wine, Katie actually dozed off for a moment in the bathtub before she summoned the energy to move her lifeless body out of the tub, into her favorite pair of pink sweatpants and an old college t-shirt, and to her bed where she quickly fell asleep. Katie didn't think Kyle would mind forgoing her preplanned evening of cuddling and TV. She was exhausted from work and satisfied by the hot bath, her comfortable clothes, and the improvements Kyle was making.

Katie didn't even remember going to bed when she woke up in the middle of the night to the sound of the shower running. With her eyes half open and her mind barely catching up to her eyes, she saw that is was 3:30 in the morning.

Katie's brain woke up a little more. "Gosh, he must have just gotten home," she thought. "Poor baby, it's so late. He's got to be exhausted. And I bet he has to turn around and be back to work in a few hours."

Filled with a depth of warmth for her husband that she hand't felt in months, Katie started to cry and was overcome with gratitude.

"Thank you, God," she whispered. She pushed off the covers and got out of bed.

Katie walked into the bathroom, slipped off her clothes, gently pulled back the shower curtain on the side away from the running water, and stepped into the shower behind Kyle, who was turned away from her, facing the water.

Katie was so happy to see her husband and was filled with the same feelings she had on the day they were married — believing that there was nothing else in the world that mattered, believing that she was safe, believing that no obstacle would ever be too great, and believing that she was loved and was with the right person that God made her to be with.

Kyle barely noticed Katie enter the shower, or at least he didn't turn around and acknowledge her. Katie reached around his chest and gave him a big hug.

"Hey, there, honey. I love you so much."

Kyle just stood there. He didn't say anything and he didn't reach up and grab Katie's arms as they wrapped around him.

Unfazed and not even noticing his lack of reply, she released her grip and grabbed ahold of his upper arms, which lifelessly dangled to his side.

"I'm so sorry you had to work late tonight. We will get out of this financial mess soon and then we won't have to take these dumb second shifts," Katie said as she started running her hands down his arms, intending to take ahold of his hands, intwine her fingers with his, and hold onto Kyle for the rest of her life. This was her husband — the man whom she gave all of herself to — her fears and her dreams, her love and her devotion, and her very life.

As she slid her fingers down his forearms, her hands froze in place.

"What's this? Did you get hurt" she asked softly as she took her left thumb and rubbed the bruised area on Kyle's inner forearm. Katie couldn't see what she was touching.

"Ouch, that hurts! Cut it out!" Kyle said, speaking for the first time.

"What is this?!" Katie asked, a little more determined and a little more curious. She ran her index and middle fingers along the bruise and felt the tiny place where the needle had pierced his skin.

"Kyle, what is this?" she said again – this time with a tone that demanded an answer. Katie grabbed Kyle's left arm and pulled it awkwardly backward to inspect it.

"Quit, that hurts!"

"Turn around here."

Katie practically spun Kyle around to face her. Water that previously hit his hair now dripped down his cheeks, nose, and chin. She pulled his arm up closer to her face.

"Kyle! What is on your arm?"

"I got hurt – it's nothing," Kyle said as he jerked back his arm and turned off the water. He swung open the shower curtain and grabbed a towel that was lying on the toilet.

Katie followed him out of the shower, not grabbing a towel and dripping all over the floor.

"Kyle! Did you shoot up? Is that a syringe mark?"

"No, it's not a syringe mark." Kyle wrapped his towel around his body and walked out of the bedroom and into the kitchen. He didn't need anything there – he was just trying to get away from Katie.

"Where were you today?" she shot back – not accepting his answer and following him into the kitchen dripping everywhere she walked.

"Work," Kyle said as he made it to the kitchen table and started to walk around it.

"Why did you get home so late?" Katie pursued Kyle as he walked around the table and back toward the bedroom.

"Leave me alone. I had to work."

"You've never gotten off work in the middle of the night. Second shift ends at 11:30. Where did you go after work?"

"Leave me alone, Katie."

"Or, did you go to work at all? I've been texting you all day. I didn't want to bug you, but you hardly texted me back. Where did you go, Kyle? Who did you shoot up with?"

"I didn't shoot up with anyone Katie. I'm tired – I want to go to bed."

Kyle's aimless flight around the house led him back into the bedroom. He inadvertently walked himself into the corner between the bed and the wall. Katie got right in front of him, grabbed his arm, and screamed, "Kyle, I know what this is! How long have you been shooting up?" Katie took Kyle's arm in her hand and waved it around like evidence in a courtroom.

"Leave me alone, Katie!" Kyle said as he pulled away his arm for the second time.

"No, dang it. Tell me Kyle, who were you shooting up with? Did you even work a second shift?"

"No! I didn't work a second shift or even a first shift. Screw it all! I went to Tony's house."

"Tony? Who's Tony? You didn't go to work?! Kyle, what are you doing? We need the money? How long have you been shooting up?!" Katie was more yelling her questions than asking them and she seemed more interested in asking them than waiting on Kyle's answers.

"Leave me alone, Katie!" Kyle screamed. And, like a cornered animal fearing for its existence, he shoved Katie out of the way, went into the bathroom, slammed the door, and locked it behind him.

Katie fell onto the bed when Kyle pushed her. Dripping wet and naked, she sat there, head spinning and barely able to form any thoughts.

Without warning, Katie started crying uncontrollably. Her face went from tight and angry to soft and sad. And, to add to her misery, her senses caught up with the fact that she was wet, naked, and cold. She started to shiver as she sobbed, tears running down her face and water dripping off her body and soaking the bed. Katie was unable to even make the decision to get up and dry off.

After what seemed like an eternity but was really only about twenty seconds, Katie sniffled in her running nose and her face changed back from fear and hurt to anger and determination. She got up from the bed and grabbed her sweat pants off the floor, clinching them in her fist.

Speaking in a tone that was a cross between a yell and an experienced teacher's voice, Katie spoke each word loudly and determinedly through the bathroom door to Kyle.

"I can't do this anymore, Kyle!" Katie proclaimed as she dried her body with the sweatpants in her hand. Kyle didn't respond.

"I can't live like this!" she continued, moving away from the door and fumbling through her drawers to find something to wear. She slipped on underwear, a pair of jean shorts, and a t-shirt. Kyle still didn't respond.

"I CANNOT LIVE LIKE THIS!" she yelled louder, mad that Kyle wasn't talking back and hurt that he had no concern for her despair.

Kyle's silence was the perfect fuel for Katie's anger. She grabbed a bag out of the corner of the closet and yelled at Kyle while throwing random clothes into the bag.

"Do you have nothing to say?" she screamed.

There was still silence from the bathroom.

"Do you even care about me? About us?" Now Katie stopped packing and walked over to the bathroom door – her nose just an inch from it.

Katie yelled – this time the loudest of all, "ARE YOU GOING TO SAY ANYTHING?" Katie began beating on the door, pounding it with both fists at the same time. Katie was certain their neighbors could hear it, but she didn't care.

The door rattled and shook as she beat it. Its latch was never very secure to begin with. After a half dozen hits the door burst open and slammed into the doorstop on the wall.

Frozen from her anger and the shock of busting open the door, Katie squinted through her glossy eyes as she looked into the bathroom.

Much to Katie's shock, Kyle was asleep in the tub – passed out. He lied there, wrapped in his towel, snoring.

Katie began balling uncontrollably. She went the rest of the way into the bathroom, gathered some toiletries, grabbed her bag from the bedroom, picked up her purse from the table, and went out the front door.

Katie stumbled off the porch, forgetting that there was a step down to the sidewalk. Her eyes were blurry from crying and she awkwardly tried to wipe her eyes clean with the hand holding the bag.

Katie went to open her car door, but it was locked. She dropped her bag on the ground and fumbled through her purse, trying to find her keys. She unlocked her car, picked up her bag and threw it and her purse onto the passenger seat.

She screeched backwards out of the driveway, not even looking if there were any middle-of-the night walkers on the sidewalk or other cars coming down their sleepy street. Having backed out onto the road, she threw her car into drive and peeled out down the road, hoping that somehow Kyle would hear her and realize what a terrible mistake he was making.

Katie didn't know where she was going – she was just driving. She balled uncontrollably with snot dripping down her face. She had to slam on her brakes at a red light, oblivious to it at first. Too impatient to sit and wait at the light, she abruptly turned right at the light and peeled out a second time.

"Who is this man I married?" Katie asked herself, exchanging loud sobs with forceful sniffs – trying to keep the snot from running down her face.

"How did I end up in this mess? I've done everything right!"

Katie's face transitioned from a sad cry to a stiff anger. She started to seethe.

Katie began to speak out loud. "Where's God in any of this? I did all the right things!"

She took a left at the next light.

"I *saved myself for marriage*," saying those words out loud in a patronizing tone.

"I went to youth group. I didn't do drugs in college. I married a Christian. Where's God in this?"

Katie came to a stop sign at an intersection where she had to choose to go either left or right. She was too angry to even recognize where she was. On the left side, she saw a pink sign advertising something she didn't read. On the right side, she saw a red sign for something else. "Screw pink!" she thought as she turned right past the red sign.

A few minutes later Katie saw Walmart up ahead. She didn't have anywhere particular to go and wanted to just stop, sit in her car, and be mad. She pulled into the parking lot and parked toward the back of the mostly empty lot.

"Why would he do this to himself?" Katie angrily thought.

"Why would he just throw it all away? I mean, shooting up! SHOOTING UP of all things! He's done so well and fought so hard and now he's a junkie!

"He's probably been doing it the whole time. What a naive idiot I am!"

Katie stared straight ahead and turned on the radio. Christian music played for a couple of seconds and then she forcefully slapped it off.

"I'm not living my life with him! Not like this," she continued thinking – angry and hurt.

"I'm not going to be *that wife*. I'm not going to hold his hand and tell him 'You can do this – I believe in you.' I'm not going to do it!

"I'm not going to stand up at a family meeting and cry about *how hard we've worked* or *how there've been ups and downs* or how we *take it one day at a time*!

"If he can't care enough about his life to make half an effort, then I'm not going to care about his life either!"

Katie sat in the parking lot for a few more minutes, replaying the events of the shower over and over. She started crying, and then made herself stop. Then she turned angry again, before crying again soon after that.

After about ten minutes, Katie decided that she needed to go somewhere. Part of her wanted someone she could talk to and part of her just wanted somewhere to crash, to try to go to sleep, and to hope that she would wake up tomorrow with all of this being just a terrible nightmare.

She briefly considered going to her parents' house, but she really didn't want to go through all of this with them tonight. They knew Kyle struggled a little bit with his accident recovery at the beginning, but she and Kyle hadn't been honest with them about any of his addiction and about the steps they were taking to deal with it. In her heart she knew that her parents would understand and love both she and Kyle through his addiction and recovery, but nevertheless she was embarrassed to let them know and didn't want to deal with it tonight.

As a teenager, and even a college student, Katie was always the model Christian – the girl everyone knew was good and the girl that seemed to get every good break in life. She knew that she didn't have to live up to that life, but it was something she struggled with nevertheless. Obviously her parents knew she wasn't perfect, but Katie still placed a lot of pressure on herself to play that part.

Katie considered going to Margie's house. Margie was one of Katie's youth leaders when she was in high school nearly ten years ago. At the time, Margie was just the age Katie is today. Now, Margie and her husband, Justin, had a couple of kids and were still volunteering at Katie's childhood church, just not with the youth anymore.

Katie remembered that Margie always told the girls in youth group that no matter the situation, no matter how many years later, and no matter the time of day or day of the year, they were always welcome to call her in any emergency. Margie was a kind, loving person. Katie really looked up to her as a high school student and would usually take time to visit her on breaks from college. In many ways Katie tried to emulate Margie. In fact, she and Kyle had been planning to volunteer for their church's youth group because of Margie's impact on Katie's life.

Katie decided that she didn't want to bug Margie in the middle of the night and that she really didn't want Margie to see her like this. Katie knew deep down in her heart that Margie would be a good person to talk to, and Katie figured that maybe she should plan on that sometime soon. But, Katie was a little too proud to be the "perfect youth group kid" and then show up at her former youth group leader's door just after 4:00 in the morning.

Katie put her car in drive — she had never turned it off — and decided to leave. She wasn't sure where to go, but she was ready to go somewhere.

"Maybe I'll go to Trish's house," Katie thought.

This idea felt good to Katie. "Trish won't judge," Katie continued thinking. "After all, her life is one big mess after another."

It was a true statement — Trish's life always did seem like a mess. Katie usually wasn't too judgmental about it, but Katie did operate with a little feeling of superiority — confident that her faith and her wise decisions kept her away from the kinds of messes that Trish had to deal with.

"Trish won't judge," Katie thought again. She pulled out of the Walmart parking lot and drove the fifteen-minute drive to Trish's apartment.

Katie showed up at Trish's apartment around 4:30 in the morning. She knew Trish didn't have to work today, so it wouldn't be that big of a deal that Katie interrupted her sleep. Walking up to Trish's door, Katie froze. She was quickly overcome with a sense of clarity that her last hour or so had lacked. She realized that while Trish didn't have to work in a couple of hours, Katie herself was scheduled to work today. She also remembered that Trish had a roommate and Katie wondered if Trish's roommate would be so inviting of her middle-of-the-night crash. On top of that, as she reached up to ring Trish's doorbell, Katie realized that she didn't even know what she was going to say. Katie always made a habit of preparing and mentally rehearsing conversations with people — especially potentially awkward or difficult conversations. She didn't have that luxury this time. So, she pressed the doorbell and waited.

Ten seconds went by and Katie rang the doorbell again. She stood there, wondering if Trish was hard asleep and beginning to feel her own effects of being up for the last hour or so in the middle of the night.

Someone strange answered the door — Katie figured that it must be Trish's roommate, Jennifer.

"Who are you? What do you want?" Jennifer groggily asked, barely cracking the door and leaving the chain attached to it.

"I'm really sorry," Katie replied. "I work with Trish and I know it's so late. But, I just had a big fight with my husband." Much like at the family meeting, Katie's voice sounded foreign to herself as the words came out of her mouth. She couldn't believe what she was saying and she further couldn't believe she was sharing them with someone she had never even met.

"Humph," Jennifer grunted.

"Anyway, is Trish here? I know it's late. Can you get her?"

"Yeah, just a second."

Jennifer gave Katie a careful stare for a second or two, studying her over. Jennifer wasn't sure who Katie was and tried to discern if she was drunk or high or maybe just crazy. Jennifer shut the door and about thirty seconds later Trish opened the door fully and reached out her arms to Katie.

"Katie, honey, what's going on?" Trish grabbed ahold of Katie with both of her arms and pulled her in to give her a hug. "It's going to be OK, dear. Come here, come here."

Katie started crying uncontrollably. She tried to talk, but could only utter words about Kyle and junkie and hurt. Trish consoled Katie and led her over to her couch where Trish ran her fingers through Katie's hair as Katie cried and tried to talk.

"There, there, honey. It's going to be OK." Trish spoke with a motherly tone that Katie had never heard from her before. "Let me get you a pillow and a blanket. You just need to go to sleep. You can sleep right here on the couch. We can talk about all of this in the morning."

Katie didn't put up much of a fight. Trish got up to get Katie the pillow and blanket. Not even thinking to take off her shoes, Katie swung her feet up onto the couch.

"Thanks, Trish," Katie mumbled as Trish returned and helped Katie lift up her head. Trish placed the pillow under Katie's head and spread the blanket on top of her. Physically and emotionally exhausted, Katie fell straight to sleep. Before Trish went back to bed, Trish sent a text to the morning's charge nurse to let her know that Katie was sick and wouldn't be in.

Chapter

8

That same night, George tossed and turned while he slept. It's not that he ever slept well in a hospital, but after two weeks in the same bed and in the same unit, he was getting more used to it. Tonight, however, he couldn't sleep.

George's health was declining. When he first entered the palliative care unit, his health actually improved a little bit. George said it was because he didn't have to listen to Louise complain all the time. Louise hoped that his better health meant that his prognosis was wrong and that George would actually get to go home. The nurses, however, knew that wouldn't be the case and were more annoyed than grateful that his health had been mildly improving.

But now, after two weeks of better, or at least, stable health, George took a turn for the worse. His blood pressure was slowly falling. His breathing was getting worse. His appetite was drifting away. And, on this particular night, George could find neither rest nor peace.

Louise visited George earlier during the day like she did every other day. On this day she stayed a little later than normal. She could tell that he was doing worse and the false hope that she clung to over the last couple of weeks was slowly being replaced by the inevitability of what was to come.

In fact, just before she left at 9:00 — a full two hours after visitors hours were over — she tried to have a heart-to-heart talk with George. He wasn't in much of a mood to talk and so all he did was listen.

"George..." Louise paused, taking his hand in her hand. They rarely held hands, but he didn't have much energy to fight it. She took advantage of it and clutched it tightly. "George, you've got to let go of all of this anger and hurt."

Louise looked at George. He wouldn't make eye contact with her. He ground his teeth and kept pressing his lips together — moving them in all directions. He didn't feel well and he didn't have the energy to engage her with his normal, crotchety replies.

"George, look at me when I'm talking to you," Louise said sternly. She rarely had the guts to take that kind of tone with George, but she felt like he needed to hear her and she knew that he couldn't really retaliate.

Still looking away from Louise, George slowly turned his head toward her. "George, you've got to let go of all of this. It hasn't done you any good in this life and it won't do you any good in the next one either."

George's eyes caught up with his head that was already facing Louise and each eye slowly moistened. Louise thought that George might actually cry. Quick to jump to that conclusion, she started crying herself. She was hopeful that after all of these years, this was it. George was going to break.

"Go home, Louise," George muttered. He pulled away his hand and with an uncharacteristic amount of effort, quickly turned his head away from her.

Louise's tears of joy and relief turned into a small stream of hurt and sadness. She lifted her hand from his side, turned around, and walked out of the room. George never saw her leave, instead staring at the wall opposite of the door. A small tear escaped his eye, ran down his nose, and hit his lips. Instinctively he stuck out his tongue and tasted the tear's saltiness. Agitated, he tried to spit it back out, but couldn't produce enough saliva to expel it from his mouth.

As George tossed and turned throughout the night, he kept replaying Louise's insistence that he let go of his anger. His spirit was troubled, but he wasn't sorry. He just wanted rest – both physically and emotionally, though George was more concerned about finding physical rest this night. George scoffed at Louise's mention of any type of a next life. Of all of the rests George pursued, he definitely didn't think much about spiritual rest.

Sometime in the middle of the night – between his nurse's rounds – George cracked open his eyes. His eyes were well adjusted to the faintly lit room and as he looked over in the doorway of the room, he saw a little girl standing there, staring at him.

Perhaps a healthier George would have been shocked and demanded to know who the girl was and what she was doing there. A younger George would have leapt out of bed and taken a step or two toward her to scare her away. Instead, George just stared back at the little girl – not really sure if he was awake or asleep, and not sure if she was really there or just in his mind.

The little girl stood in the doorway, wearing a red dress with a Peter Pan collar and three buttons down the front. She was playing with the side of her dress between her right thumb and index finger. She slowly shuffled her left foot back and forth in her black and white Saddle Oxford shoes.

George didn't break her eye contact. He felt unusual – kind of warm and relaxed. As odd as it was to have a little girl in his room in the middle of the night, he wasn't surprised. He wasn't scared or mad or even very perplexed. It felt like she belonged there. In fact, if anything, he felt his spirit was calmed while locked in her gaze.

After a few moments, George decided to speak. Regardless of his intention, he spoke gruffly.

"Who are you? Are you lost?"

"I am not lost," the little girl in the red dress replied. "I have come to see you." She paused and then spoke again. "I have come to see *you*, Mr. George."

"Listen here, little girl. I'm pretty sure visiting hours are over. You need to go find your parents and get out of here before you get in trouble." Although harsh in tone, George spoke more easily with the little girl than he did with Louise earlier. Strangely, when he spoke to this little girl, George felt very little of the physical restrictions that lately plagued him.

"What color do you dream in?" the little girl asked, ignoring his instructions to find her parents and leave the room.

"What color do I dream in? That's a silly question. You need to leave. You're going to get in trouble."

"What color do you dream in," she asked again, still unfazed by his instructions for her to leave.

"I don't have time for this nonsense." George broke eye contact with the little girl and looked away. He wanted to say something nasty and intimidating to her, sure to make her leave, but he couldn't. He had the oddest feeling of warmth and peace mixed in with his normal cocktail of annoyance and impatience.

"You do have time," she said. "Tell me, what color do you dream in?"

George looked back at the little girl. He was at the same time confused by her question and also somewhat understanding of it. He turned to look up to the ceiling, actually deciding how he might try to answer her question.

"Red, I suppose."

"I like red," the little girl replied. "It reminds me of fresh strawberries, fragrant roses, and the color of my tongue when I eat a red sucker."

"I don't see those things in my dreams." George looked back at the little girl. "Red isn't a very nice color for me."

"What do you see that is red?" she asked.

"I see anger." George paused. He licked his dry lips with his dry tongue. "I see hurt." He paused again. "I just see a lot of hurt."

"That is very sad," the little girl replied, frowning at George.

George looked back at the little girl and let her comment soak in for a moment. He pursed his lips a little bit and then asked, "What color do you dream in?"

The little girl's eyes lit up. "Oh! I dream in many colors. I think white is my favorite color to dream in, though. It is bright. It is made of light and not darkness. It is clean like snow and innocent like a baby."

"I can't say that I ever dream in white," George said sadly while drifting his eyes back up to the ceiling. "I can't say that I see very much brightness or innocence in my dreams."

George stared at the ceiling, lost more in his feelings than his thoughts. He started to feel sad – even in the warm presence of the little girl. George didn't feel shame or disgust – just sad.

After a few moments, the little girl spoke again.

"I would like to tell you a story." She paused and George continued looking at the ceiling.

"One day I lost my doll. It was my favorite doll. I had the doll since I was a much littler girl."

The little girl continued her story, speaking softly and warmly, but also slowly and purposefully.

"I was very sad about the doll. I used to enjoy it so much. I know it is a silly thing – to be upset about a lost doll. That doll did not love me back and could not ever know how much I loved it. But, I loved it anyway and I cried when I could not find it.

"I looked everywhere for my doll. I looked in my bedroom and the living room. I looked in the car and the kitchen. I looked outside and even in the bathroom. I searched every closet and every basket. I did not want to stop until I found that doll.

"The next day I should have thought that all hope was lost, but I never gave up. I kept looking for that doll. Then, a miracle happened! I found my doll – the doll that I loved! It was underneath the living room couch. I have no idea how it got there – I did not put it there. But, it did not matter to me how it got there or why it was there. I was just happy that my doll was now found and with me once again."

"Well, I'm glad you found your doll," George said, kind of actually meaning it and offering an unusually empathetic response. Empathy didn't come naturally for George, and he quickly followed it up with, "But I bet you would have forgotten about that old doll and gotten a new one."

"Perhaps," the little girl replied, "but that doll was very special to me. I could have replaced her with another doll and I might have had a lot of fun playing with the new doll, but I always would have been sad when I remembered my lost doll."

"Well, get used to it, kid. Life is full of sadness. People disappoint you and situations disappoint you." George took a deep breath and looked back at the ceiling. "In fact, you get to my place in life and wonder what the whole point was."

"That does not sound like a very fun place to be."

"No, it's not," George paused. "Here's some advice for you, don't ever depend on people and don't ever expect to get anything out of them."

The little girl didn't have a response to George's statement. She remained quiet as George stared at the ceiling, eyes glossed over. George wasn't thinking about anything in particular, but rather was lost in his subconsciousness — lost in his feelings.

Snapping back to reality, George's eyes opened wide and he turned to look directly at the girl.

"What's that story about, anyway?" he shot at her. "Are you calling me lost or something?"

George knew that anyone in their right mind wouldn't really think that a little girl came into his room to tell him a story about a lost doll so that she could teach him a lesson. But on the other hand, George didn't have a good handle on the circumstances of this conversation with this strange little girl in a red dress.

"Are you lost?" the little girl asked.

For the first time since Louise left earlier that evening, George's anger began again to bubble up inside him. He wanted to speak roughly with the little girl, but caught himself before he could. Instead he looked her in the eyes and said, "I think you're the one who is lost. I think you need to leave."

The little girl didn't reply, but rather stared back at George. He didn't feel like she was challenging him, but rather looking deeply into him – almost like she was looking into his soul.

After a moment of uncomfortableness with her gaze, George said again, but a little softer, "I think you need to leave. Go ahead, get out of here."

"Is that what you want me to do?" the little girl asked.

"Well I said it, didn't I?"

"Yes, but we do not always say what we mean."

George looked at the girl, somewhat dumbfounded and at a loss for words.

"Do you care if I sit down?"

George didn't respond. After a short pause, the little girl sat down in a chair opposite from George's bed, with her feet dangling an inch or two above the floor.

In a moment of lucidity that evaded him for the last few minutes, George realized that it was the middle of the night and that an unaccompanied little girl was sitting in his room. George wasn't too up-to-date on children's fashion, but he was also pretty sure that he hadn't seen a dress like the one she wore in years.

George thought to himself, "I must be going crazy." He squeezed his eyes together and counted in his head to ten.

After reaching the number nine, George said out loud, "Ten!" and shot open his eyes. He looked over at the chair and saw the little girl still sitting there.

George groaned and looked away from her and toward the wall. "What do you want? Why are you here?"

"Can I tell you another story?" the little girl asked.

"Well, I have a feeling that I don't have much of a choice and there doesn't seem to be anything I can do about it. You've got a captive audience. But... I don't care much for babydoll stories."

The little girl giggled. George wasn't quite sure why. He rarely told a joke and he certainly wasn't trying to be funny now.

"I suppose you might not like babydoll stories," she said. "This one is about a dog that I used to have. Do you like dogs?"

"I can't say that I like much of anything that requires food or care — and that includes people. But, once upon a time, I used to have a dog."

The little girl began swinging her legs back and forth as she spoke, again deliberately and slowly, yet with warmth and compassion.

"A few years ago, my parents told me they wanted to buy me a dog for my birthday. I was so excited — I had wanted a dog for my entire life — at least two or three years. Instead of going to a pet store or finding someone who was selling dogs, my parents took me to an animal shelter. They said that we could find a dog that we could love from there.

"We drove to the animal shelter, parked our car, and went inside. I can still remember the smell of all of the animals and the loud barking from so many dogs living in those tiny little cages. It made me very sad."

"Do you ever get sad, Mr. George?" The little girl pushed her head forward, waiting on George's response.

"I suppose…, sometimes."

The little girl smiled and continued. "Well, we looked at many dogs that day. Some had problems — like they could only eat special food or they were missing a leg. Some of the dogs were very playful and some were very shy. And, some of them were just plain mean.

"When we got to the end of the hallway, I saw my Sparky. Sparky was a mix of black and white. My daddy said he was a mutt, which he said means that he was not one or two particular dog breeds, but just a mix of lots of them. Sparky started barking very loudly at us. He growled and ran around his kennel. He was not happy.

"My mother asked the worker about this dog, my Sparky. She told us that Sparky lived a very bad life before coming to the animal shelter. A police officer found Sparky in a house where he arrested some bad guys. She told us that Sparky did not get much food and that Sparky was beaten by those bad people.

"Can you imagine that, Mr. George? People actually beat dogs?"

It took a moment for George to realize that the little girl was asking him another question and all he could utter was a soft "Hmmm."

"Anyway, I told my mommy and daddy that I wanted Sparky. I told them that every dog needs a good place to live.

"My parents were not sure that taking home Sparky was a good idea. They told me that maybe I should consider another dog. They reminded me of the little dog several cages down with part of its ear missing and they also reminded me about the yellow dog that licked me a lot. I thought that the dog with part of its ear missing was really cute and I couldn't stop giggling when the yellow dog licked me, but I really wanted Sparky. He just looked like he needed loved.

"Do you know what I mean, George? Have you ever found something that looked like it just needed a little love in its life?"

George shifted a little in his bed and looked away from the little girl, this time quickly picking up on her cue that he should talk. "I don't know…, maybe," he mumbled.

"Oh," she said matter of factly. "Anyway, we adopted Sparky. The people at the animal shelter looked at us a little funny. It did not matter. We filled out all of the papers and took Sparky home.

"When we got home, I held my hand out for Sparky to sniff it – just like my daddy told me too. Sparky growled and growled at me. I held my hand closer and Sparky snapped his teeth at me! I jerked my hand back as fast as I could. I think I just barely missed getting bitten – I even felt his slobber on my hand!

"The next day I tried again and Sparky snapped at me again. I was sad that Sparky did not trust me, but I did not give up. My mommy asked me if I wanted to take Sparky back and get another dog, but I told her no. I told her that Sparky needed someone to love him. I told her that it was not Sparky's fault that he had been beaten up so much in his life.

"Anyway, after a lot of tries, one day I stuck out my hand and Sparky did not growl. Instead he slowly came to me and sniffed my hand. Then the funniest thing happened!" The little girl smiled and spoke in an excited, high-pitched voice. "Do you know what happened next, Mr. George?"

By this part of the story, George was just half listening. He didn't do a good job of picking up on her excited tone. Quickly replaying her last couple of phrases in his head, he cobbled together what he thought she was asking and he gruffly replied, "He bit off your hand?"

"No, silly!" the little girl giggled. "He licked it! Sparky licked my hand!"

"Hmmm," George mumbled softly, hoping that the little girl was about out of stories and deciding that it was becoming time to re-emphasize that she needed to leave his room.

"Sparky became the best dog, Mr. George. He was my best friend. He even slept in my bed! Can you believe it, Mr. George? That mean old dog ended up licking me and playing with me. He became my best friend."

"That's nice," George feigned kindness. It wasn't something he was very well practiced at – being kind or even pretending to be kind. "I think it's time for you to go home. I need to get some sleep."

Ignoring his request, the little girl continued, "Do you know what, Mr. George? I think sometimes people are a lot like dogs. They get beat up so much that they cannot help but be angry all of the time."

This time George clearly heard and processed every word that the little girl said. He wanted to be mad at her, but he also felt convicted by her observation. Although he barely moved much to begin with while lying in his hospital bed, George's muscles went rigid and he froze, staring at the little girl.

She continued. "But..., I think..., I think that sometimes people – just like my dog, Sparky – need to experience a little love. I think that all people have the chance to soften up. I just do not think that some people know how to do it."

The little girl stopped talking and looked at George. Her gaze was one of compassion, not judgement. Her gaze was a gaze of understanding, not confusion. Her gaze pierced George's soul. His eyes began to moisten. His nose got a little runny and he had to sniffle it back in.

"Well, dogs aren't people," George said slowly, a little harshly and a lot uncomfortably.

The little girl didn't reply. She simply continued her warm, affectionate gaze at George. They looked at each other for a few seconds.

A moment later, she broke the silence. "Anyway, I think I should go. It is getting pretty late. Do you mind if I come back and see you sometime?"

In George's head, he said a resounding "no," but out loud George surprised himself when he said, "Sure. Suit yourself."

"OK, then. Goodnight, Mr. George. I will see you soon."

The little girl in the red dress rose from the slightly too big of a chair, gave George a quick wave, and walked out the door.

George thought about the little girl's story. He didn't pay that much attention to it while she told it, but surprisingly he could recount nearly every word that she said as he lied in bed after she left. He thought about his own life and his own hurts. He thought about the beatings that his life took and the beatings that his life gave. He thought about his anger and how mad he was that Louise told him to let it all go. And, after a few minutes of replaying and appraising his unusual experience with such an insightful little girl, George fell asleep.

Chapter

9

. . . .

Sometime late in the morning, Katie slowly woke up. She stretched out her arms and legs. The air Katie breathed in didn't taste normal. Katie felt a spring pushing into her back. She smelled an unfamiliar odor. With her eyes still closed, Katie stretched out her arms a little farther and knocked off a lamp that was sitting on the table beside the couch.

"Hey there, easy!" Trish called out to Katie from a chair across from her. Trish was curled up on the chair under an old blanket with her phone on her lap.

Katie opened her eyes, saw the unfamiliar ceiling, and looked over at Trish. In a rush, all of the events of the previous night washed over Katie. She re-closed her eyes, brought her hands to her face, and moaned.

"Oh, Trish, thanks for letting me crash here. What a terrible night!"

"No problem, sweetie. You're welcome to stay here any time."

Katie rubbed her eyes and sat up on the couch. She looked around for a moment and then exclaimed, "Shoot! I forgot about work. Crap!"

"Easy there, potty mouth!" Trish chuckled once. "Don't worry about it, Katie. I texted the charge nurse and told her you were sick. She didn't even ask me any questions or anything."

"Oh man. Thanks, Trish." Katie sat on the couch silently, trying to process everything that happened last night and trying to figure out what she was going to do next.

"I don't even know what to do, Trish. To be honest, I'm not even sure what's going on."

"Take a stab at it, Katie. You can tell me what happened. I'll tell you what, there's a neat coffee shop just around the corner from here – it's very eclectic. I bet you've never even been there. Why don't you take a shower to feel human again. Then we can go there and you can tell me all about it – my treat!"

Katie thanked Trish, who showed Katie to the bathroom. Katie thought a hot shower would be nice, but was immediately uncomfortable when the water first hit her. Standing under the water, Katie reached around her hands and grabbed both of her arms, moving her hands up and down as she felt her forearms. She replayed feeling Kyle's bruise last night and started hyperventilating. She immediately turned the water off and burst out of the shower.

Katie dried off and went through the bag of clothes she hastily threw together last night. She discovered that she forgot to pack underwear. Putting on yesterday's underwear made her feel gross, though she didn't feel too great to begin with. After a few minutes, both ladies were riding in Trish's car and were soon sitting in Edy's Coffee Shop. Trish already knew bits and pieces of Katie and Kyle's experience from the last few months, but Katie held nothing back in their conversation this morning. She told the entire story – the accident, the pain pills, the sneaking of more pills, the meetings, and now the heroin.

"I just don't get it, Trish. Why can't he just stop? I mean, it's not that hard to stop doing something, is it?"

"I don't know, Katie. It's like an addict's brain is wired differently or something."

"Ugh! It's such a mess!"

"This all really stinks, Katie," Trish consoled. "But life's messy. It always has been for me, at least."

"I know yours is, Trish." Katie whined.

Katie didn't mean to judge Trish for the constant state of disarray of her life, though Katie did in fact think about how Trish's life was usually messy. Normally if someone like Sue made that comment to Trish, then Trish would have lost her cool. In this case, however, Trish begrudgingly let Katie's comment slide off her back.

"Well," Trish said regaining her thoughts and trying to choose not to be angry, "life is messy – for some of us most of the time and for others of us just some of the time. I've learned, over and over in my *messy* life, that sometimes you just have to leave your problems in your rearview mirror and move on to the next thing."

Katie appreciated Trish's friendship. She found it odd that out of everyone in her life, she was more comfortable talking about her messy life with someone like Trish instead of someone like her parents, her pastor, or even Margie.

"I don't know, Trish. I'm just not sure that I can, or that I should, just say 'See you later' and leave Kyle in my dust."

"Well, let me tell you Katie. Once an addict, always an addict. I could tell you stories about my Uncle Brian, or my Uncle Steve, or my cousin Marcy, or heck, even my my dad most of the time. In my experience, you have to give yourself as much separation as possible from people with those problems. They'll just suck you deeper and deeper into their miserable existence and drive you broke and crazy in the process."

In fact, Trish could have told Katie stories that would have helped Katie realize that she didn't have much to complain about; however, Trish wasn't used to being vulnerable enough to share her messy experiences. Trish learned from an early age to guard her feelings and to keep plowing through life, regardless of the adversity. Given her family history and childhood instability, most people might even consider it a miracle that Trish wasn't an addict herself – she certainly had the genes for it.

"What am I supposed to do, Trish? Just throw away four years of marriage? Just abandon Kyle when he's at his worst? If so, then what were my wedding vows all about?"

"That's one reason why you won't see me walking down the aisle any time soon!"

"Hmph. Well, I've already done that. And I don't regret it, Trish. Honestly I don't. I just don't know what to do."

"I don't know what to tell you, Katie, but you've got to make a decision." Trish paused and thought. "Actually, I do know what to tell you what I think your decision should be."

Katie ignored Trish. "I don't know – I need to figure things out."

Trish wished Katie was a little quicker in coming to her conclusion to start fresh, but she decided to give her friend a break and not press the matter. "Well, I can't speak for Jennifer, but I can ask her if she'd be OK if you stayed with us for a while. I don't think she'd mind. Of course, you'd have to get used to that old couch!"

"Thanks, Trish. It means a lot to me. I think I just need to go back home and talk to Kyle. He was a mess last night. Maybe he and I can talk this out today."

"Suit yourself, but I think you're wasting your time. You just come right back to my apartment if you need to – which you will." Trish winked at Katie, which in retrospect Trish thought might have come across too arrogantly.

"OK. Thanks, Trish."

The women finished their coffee and headed back to Trish's apartment. Katie gathered up her stuff and walked out to her car.

Katie's mind raced the entire way home.

"Once an addict, always an addict," Katie thought, replaying Trish's words in her head.

"No, that's just Trish talking. She doesn't really know Kyle. Kyle doesn't have to be like everyone else."

Like an old cartoon demon on one shoulder and an angel on the other, Katie quickly rebutted in her head, "Stop being so naive, Katie! Life's not perfect and you don't live in some fairytale, happily-ever-after story. I'm not a princess and he's certainly not some magical prince. Maybe this will never get better."

Katie argued back and forth with herself for the next minute or so. She wondered about how much Kyle loved her and if he was truly devoted to their marriage. As she wrestled within herself, she tried hard to focus on Kyle's patience and love for her over the years. When she needed to be reminded of Kyle's love, she often thought about their honeymoon. Their honeymoon didn't go off as planned, but it turned out to be a foundational time in their relationship that solidified their love and devotion to each other.

Being fairly traditional, Katie's family paid for their wedding and Kyle's family paid for the rehearsal. His family felt like they should pay for something more that just the rehearsal, but Katie's parents wouldn't let them contribute to the wedding. So, Kyle's parents gifted Katie and Kyle a trip to Maui for their honeymoon. Katie was really excited. She had never been to Hawaii before and neither of them had flown more than two hours in a plane.

Katie spent nearly as much time planning and dreaming for Hawaii as she did planning and dreaming for the wedding. They had a reservation at a nice resort, right on the beach. Katie scoured the Internet for pictures and videos of the resort practically every day. She was excited for the pools with waterfalls, the indoor-outdoor restaurants, and the sand beach that stretched for miles in front of the resort. Katie was especially excited that the resort had a unique collection of tropical birds – something that made Katie giddy like she was an eight-year-old girl.

While Katie knew that the main idea of a beach vacation is to sleep-in, relax, and soak up the sun, she and Kyle planned to fill up their days with a wide variety of once-in-a-lifetime activities. They made a daylong reservation to snorkel at the Molokini Crater. They rented a convertible for a day to drive the famed Road to Hana. They made reservations for massages and facials in their resort's spa. The reserved a sunset dinner cruise. They pre-purchased a National Parks pass and planned to spend a day hiking in Haleakala National Park.

In preparation for her honeymoon swimsuits (more so than her wedding dress), Katie even lost a stubborn, and mostly unnecessary, ten pounds. She bought new dresses and new shorts. She bought new swimsuits and three pairs of sunglasses because she couldn't decide which one made her nose look the least hideous. To say the least, she was excited to marry Kyle and start their life together, but maybe just a little more excited to see and do the sights of Maui.

Their pink wedding went off without a hitch. Afterward, Katie and Kyle spent their first married night in downtown

Cincinnati at a swanky hotel and left early that morning for a one-stop, 12-hour flight to Maui.

As soon as they arrived, they checked into their room, put on their swimsuits, and hit the beach. And, that is where Katie's dream honeymoon took an unplanned turn.

Once they laid down on the beach, physically and emotionally exhausted, they quickly fell asleep. It was only late in the afternoon in Maui time, but close to bedtime in Cincinnati. Three hours later, Katie cracked open her eyes, thoroughly confused.

"Kyle, wake up! It's like the middle of the night or something," Katie called out, lying still on her back on the beach and completely exhausted.

Katie just laid there, looking up at the near-dark sky and noticing the glow of the resort above her head just behind her.

Kyle didn't budge, so Katie mustered up the energy and attempted to roll over to give him a nudge.

"Ouch!" Katie yelled as she rolled partway over and then collapsed onto her back.

Kyle, startled by her scream, quickly woke up and said, "Hey, what's wrong?"

"I don't know. I'm so confused and I ache. It's dark – is it like the middle of the night or something?"

Kyle grabbed his phone and said, "No, it's just 7:00."

"7:00!" Katie exclaimed. "We slept all the way to the next morning?"

"No, dingbat. It's 7PM. We must have fallen asleep for about three hours."

"7PM?" Katie asked incredulously. "It's too dark for 7PM."

With that statement made, Kyle responded with an explanation of the four seasons, the tilt of the Earth, and the amount of daylight different parts of the planet gets. Katie didn't pay very much attention and instead turned the conversation to her aching body.

"OK, Kyle. I'm not too interested in a science lesson on our honeymoon. But, I am interested in figuring out why I'm so sore."

Kyle stood up and helped Katie to her feet. There wasn't much light out, but Kyle could easily see that Katie was burnt on the front of her body from her head to her toe, that is, everywhere except where her big sunglasses and uncharacteristically small bathing suit covered her body.

Katie was badly burnt even though they only had about two and a half hours of sun before it set. Katie, unlike Kyle, was fair-skinned and easily burned. In all of her preparation for their honeymoon, she regretted that tanning was not on her list.

It turned out that Katie's burn was severe. Kyle made his first of three honeymoon trips to a local pharmacy to get various medications for Katie. The next day, their first full day in Maui, turned out to be a bust. Although it really disappointed her, Katie and Kyle had to cancel that day's snorkel excursion to the Molokini Crater. Katie was doubly disappointed when she discovered that there weren't any other openings during the week to reschedule the snorkeling adventure.

Their second full day turned out to be a lot like the first, with Katie lying in bed most of the day and Kyle shuttling food and drinks to the room from the hotel's various restaurants. By that evening, Katie felt OK enough to go to dinner at a nice steakhouse in a nearby town. Katie even ventured outside of her comfort zone and tried the "fresh market catch" of the day.

Unfortunately for Katie and for Kyle, the fresh market catch wasn't very fresh. In the middle of that night, a pain shot through Katie's abdomen and she spent the next three days lying in bed again, barely eating anything at all. They had to cancel their sunset cruise, their planned day trip to Hana, and their spa reservation. Finally, by the sixth and last full day of their honeymoon, Katie felt well enough that they drove up Haleakala mountain to take in the view, but they couldn't even go on their planned hike.

With Kyle driving back down the switchbacks of the mountain on the afternoon of their last day in Maui, Katie burst into tears.

"I'm so sorry, Kyle! I've ruined every bit of our honeymoon."

"Oh, it's OK, Katie. You didn't ruin all of it." Kyle smiled and tapped Katie on the shoulder.

Katie wailed even louder. "Yes, I did!" Katie balled. "I wouldn't be surprised if you take our marriage certificate and rip it up before we can even take it to the courthouse."

Kyle didn't mean to laugh, but he chuckled a little at Katie's nonsensical talk. "Hey, Katie. I'd never do that. That ring you're wearing cost me too much!"

Katie slapped Kyle on the arm and said, "It's not funny!"

Kyle, realizing his new wife's vulnerability, pulled over at the next pullout on the side of the mountain and said, "Katie, our life is not going to be perfect. We are going to have our ups and downs — our pleasant surprises and our unexpected disappointments. But, there is nothing I can think of that I want more than to spend it all with you. I'd stay locked up in a hotel room with you every day if that's what it took. I love you."

"Really?" Katie asked.

"Really," Kyle affirmed.

"Do you mean it?"

"I do."

Katie's sobs turned to small tears of appreciation. She put her hand in Kyle's hand and said, "Those would have made some pretty good vows. I love you too." In that moment, Katie knew that what she and Kyle had was special. She knew that they could weather the storms of life. And she knew that he loved her — not because he said that he loved her, but because he showed it.

Now four years later, Katie was warmed by the memories of her near-disastrous honeymoon. Almost home, Katie turned onto her street. Her thoughts about their honeymoon and the love and commitment she felt during it gave way to her apprehension and uncertainty about their present situation. Because she spent so much time remembering their honeymoon, Katie didn't even give herself a chance to rehearse her lines and play out what she expected to happen when she got home. The reality of her lack of preparation hit her as she turned into their driveway. Immediately the memory of storming out several hours ago overwhelmed Katie and she started crying while sitting in her car.

Taking a couple of deep breaths and blowing her nose on a Chick-fil-A napkin, Katie opened the door of her car and walked up to her house.

Katie put her key in the house door and tried to turn it, but discovered that it was unlocked. She looked back for Kyle's truck, making sure that it really was there. Seeing his truck parked in its usual spot, she thought, "I doubt he walked anywhere."

Opening the door, Katie set down her bag and purse on the table and called out to Kyle.

"Kyle? Honey? Are you here?" Katie hesitatingly asked, trying hard to use a soft, concerned voice, even though her emotions vacillated between worry and suspicion.

Katie stood still beside the kitchen table, almost afraid to walk the rest of the way into the house. She didn't know what she feared, but nevertheless she trembled and put her shaking hand on the kitchen chair.

Calling again, Katie spoke with a little more confidence. "Kyle? It's me, Katie."

There was still no response. Katie took a deep breath and walked into the bedroom. Kyle was lying in bed. Katie looked at him and panicked, not sure that he was breathing. She froze and held her breath while fear washed over her body. Just a second later, she saw his chest move slowly out and then back in.

Katie breathed a sigh of relief, walked over to Kyle, and started to reach for his shoulder to gently touch him. She froze again before she touched him as her eye caught a look at his bruised forearm. Katie stared intently at Kyle's forearm with her outstretched arm still hovering in the air over him and her hand just inches from tapping his shoulder.

Katie inspected the purple and red bruise. She ran her eyes up and down his forearm, closely looking for past bruises or punctures that she might have missed over the last few weeks. She tried to look at Kyle's other arm, but it was wedged underneath his head.

Katie retreated her hand and loudly whispered, "Kyle, I'm home. Can you wake up?"

Kyle groaned and rolled away from Katie. In the process he moved his other arm so that Katie could see it – almost like he was presenting it to her, though he wasn't very conscious. Katie couldn't find any signs of past use on that arm either.

Katie reached down and laid her hand on Kyle's shoulder.

Rubbing her hand on his shoulder, Katie spoke a little louder, "Wake up, Kyle. We need to talk."

Kyle shook Katie's hand off his shoulder and brought both of his hands up to cover his face as he let out another groan.

The softness that motivated both Katie's hand and voice evaporated from inside her. Her heart began to pump harder as she forcefully spoke each word. "Kyle, get up! We have to talk."

Kyle groaned again and rolled over toward Katie. Barely opening one eye while he squinted at the daylight coming through the bedroom window, Kyle muttered, "What do you want?"

"What do I want?" Katie asked incredulously. "What do I want?" she repeated herself. She started speaking quickly and animatedly. "What I want is to talk about last night – to talk about that mark on your arm."

Kyle rolled away from Katie and mumbled, "I don't want to talk. I want to sleep."

"Sleep?!" Katie asked with a yell. "From what I can tell, you've been sleeping for nearly ten hours!"

Katie stared at Kyle as he didn't respond.

"Don't you have anything to say? Don't you care about us?"

Still no response. A moment later Kyle began to snore.

Katie lost all feeling in her limbs. Her mouth dropped open as she watched Kyle sleep. She felt her heart pumping even harder, as if it was a thundering bass speaker in a loud nightclub. Katie's entire body began to flush and her nostrils began to flare.

Breaking her momentary paralysis, Katie stomped to the closet where she grabbed their biggest suitcase. She hurled it onto the floor, unzipped it, and began throwing in clothes – work clothes, pajamas, socks, underwear (she had enough sanity to not make that mistake again), jeans, t-shirts, and even dresses. She went through her drawers and closet and kept throwing clothes into the large suitcase – not particularly paying attention to what exactly she was grabbing, but also being careful to grab samples of each type of clothing that she owned.

Katie stomped into the bathroom and turned around to see that her loud display didn't affect Kyle's slumber. She gathered toiletries and makeup to complement the items she hurriedly left with last night.

Returning to the bedroom to put her toiletry bag in the suitcase, Katie couldn't help herself anymore and hollered out loud at Kyle, "Kyle! You've got to wake up right this minute and talk to me."

Despite the seeming depth of his slumber, Kyle rolled over and this time opened both of his eyes.

"What?" he said, not very loudly but louder than a whisper.

"What?!" Katie shot back. "You tell me *what*! What's going on?"

Kyle didn't speak for a moment – he was truly trying to collect his thoughts in his foggy brain. Katie wasn't too impressed with his delay.

"Seriously, Kyle! You're not going to say anything?"

"I'm not sure what to say."

"*Not sure what to say*? How about you start with that mark on your arm. Where did you get it? How long have you been doing this? Who gave it to you? Who is *Tony*?" Katie spoke quickly, peeling off question after question and giving Kyle no time to respond.

Kyle looked at Katie as his eyes started to water, but he couldn't speak.

Katie put her hand on her hip and let out an exaggerated, "Hmph." She started waving both arms in the air. "So this is the best you can do – nothing at all?"

148

Katie turned back to her suitcase where she threw in a few pairs of shoes and then slammed it closed. She sat on it to smash it down. With her bottom firmly planted on the center of the suitcase, Katie zipped it up around her legs.

"See this, Kyle? I'm not staying here like this. I can't live in this house like this."

When Kyle saw her zipping up the suitcase, he snapped fully awake and sat up in bed.

"Come on, Katie. Where are you going to go?"

"It doesn't matter where I go. I just can't stay in this house."

"I'll do better, Katie. I really will."

"All it's been is a bunch of lies," Katie shot back. "First you snuck the pills and then you acted like you wanted to get better and now you're, what?... shooting up heroin?"

Kyle didn't know how to respond. His memory of yesterday's shoot up was pretty foggy. He was having a hard time remembering all of the events that led him to Tony's house and he couldn't really remember any of the details of last night's fight with Katie.

"We can go to a meeting," Kyle softly answered.

"Go to a meeting? Why, so you can go find other junkies to buy more drugs from?"

"I don't know what you want me to say, Katie."

"I don't want you to say what I want to hear. I want you to say something that's true!"

"I'll do better. It was just one time."

"How can I believe that? Just one time? Sure, and next time it will be just one time of cocaine or just one time of acid or just one time of something crazier."

"Come on, Katie. I've never used anything like that."

"Just like you had never used heroin before either!"

"It's hard, Katie."

"Hard? Hard is me trying to stay strong around you – to love you and support you and then to have you throw it all back in my face. I bet you have pills re-hidden all over this place. I don't even know you anymore."

Kyle was hurt and confused and very ashamed of himself. His mouth couldn't speak and he didn't know what to say if it could.

Katie, now with her suitcase fully zipped and standing upright with its handle fully extended, said, "See, you can't even fight for us. You don't even care. It's me or the drugs and apparently you're choosing the drugs."

Kyle's eyes fully teared up, but he still couldn't find the emotional strength to speak anything of substance.

Katie, herself starting to cry, said firmly yet softly, "Your silence says everything."

Katie grabbed the suitcase's handle and turned to take it out of the bedroom.

Kyle finally softly said, "I need help."

Katie, already walking out, paused, turned her head, and said, "We've already tried to get help. I can't help you. You need to get your own help."

Now more stubbornly determined than mad, Katie again turned away from Kyle and rolled her suitcase out of the bedroom and to her car. Purposefully and without the unchecked emotion of last night, she pulled her car out of the driveway and sent Trish a text that she was coming back to her apartment.

Kyle sat on the bed, dumbfounded. His thoughts and emotions were jumbled. He was sad and confused. He was ashamed and hurt. He didn't know what to think or how he was supposed to feel.

He sat there for a minute and then turned to look at the bedroom clock – it didn't provide any answers as he wasn't even exactly sure what day it was. As he rotated back around from looking at the clock, a sharp pain shot through his back. Kyle grimaced and he fell back onto the bed. Barely raising his head, he looked around the room for his phone. Luckily he found it on the nightstand beside the bed and grabbed it – it had just 3% of its battery left.

With his back hurting, his thoughts racing, and his emotions numbing, Kyle looked through his contacts until he found Tony's number. Kyle clicked on it to send Tony a message – he wasn't sure what to say, but he knew he needed something for his back and something for his emotions. Kyle typed "Hey, Tony," and then paused. He wasn't sure what to ask. Did he want another shot of heroin? Maybe all he needed was just a regular pain pill.

As he thought about what to text for a moment, Kyle's phone died. Kyle looked at his dead phone, cussed, and then threw it on the bed beside him. Frustrated, hopeless, and with an aching back, Kyle laid on his bed, staring at the ceiling. He just wanted to go back to sleep – miserable in his pain and miserable in his mind. Worst of all, he had no energy or motivation to do anything about either misery, let alone his marriage. Staring at the ceiling eventually gave way to staring at his closed eyelids, which eventually gave way to falling back asleep.

A little while later, Katie arrived at Trish's apartment. Trish met Katie at the door and gave Katie a firm, long hug. Trish grabbed Katie's suitcase out of her hand and rolled it inside. With tears in her eyes, Katie looked back at her car, as if she expected to see her husband or even her life itself watching from the car as she left it behind. Instead, seeing the same emptiness in her car that she felt inside her soul, Katie walked into Trish's apartment and shut the door.

Chapter

10

. . . .

The next morning Katie had no choice but to go into work. She missed yesterday and today was a Saturday – you pretty much needed to be near death to miss a weekend shift. Sue often joked – in a way that only she could – "You better be on your way to becoming our next palliative care patient if you're going to miss a shift on the weekend."

Trish had to work today as well, so both women rose early in the morning. Katie woke up at 5:15AM – a full half hour earlier than she normally woke up for work. She lied on the couch for a moment, listening to see if Trish was up or if it would be OK to jump in the shower. Katie regretted that they didn't plan out their morning schedule before they went to sleep last night. Hearing nothing, she got up and walked to the bathroom.

As Katie started to open the bathroom door, Jennifer walked out of her room and said, "Hey, are you just going to the bathroom or are you taking a shower, because I need to take my shower now?"

Katie, slightly confused as to why Jennifer needed a shower before dawn on a Saturday, quietly said, "Oh yeah, sorry. I can take a shower after you."

Katie let go of the bathroom doorknob and turned to walk away. Without saying anything, Jennifer walked into the bathroom, locked the door, and turned on the shower.

Katie went back to the couch where she laid down and grabbed her phone.

"Shoot!" Katie loudly whispered. Her phone was at 8%. She followed her charging cord to its end where she saw that the block had fallen out of the electric outlet.

Katie replugged in her phone and looked online for a few minutes while Jennifer took what Katie thought was way too long of a shower.

Bouncing her eyes back and forth between posts and the time at the top of her phone's screen, Katie grew more impatient. She was happy that at least she decided to set her alarm for a half hour earlier than normal.

As Katie's patience was wearing thin, she heard the bathroom door open. Katie set down her phone, grabbed her stuff, and walked again toward the bathroom. Katie saw Jennifer's door shut as she turned into the hallway and made it partly down the hall when Trish came out of her bedroom across from the bathroom. Without even seeing Katie walking toward her, Trish went into the bathroom before Katie could get close, locked the door, and turned on the shower.

Katie let out a short sigh, turned around, and defeatedly walked back to the couch where she impatiently waited once again for the bathroom. Fifteen minutes later Katie finally got a mostly cold shower, now running late for work.

A little over an hour later, Sue didn't even look up toward Katie when she curtly said, "You're ten minutes late and you don't look very sick. That is why you missed work yesterday, right? *Sick?*"

"Sorry, Sue. I got up on time — early in fact — I just had a lot going on this morning. And yes, *sick* is a very good way to describe why I missed work yesterday."

"Whatever." Sue huffed. "The last one in draws the short straw. I've reworked the schedule and now you've got Mr. Marshall. Have fun!" Sue looked up at Katie for the first time and smiled. Katie rolled her eyes and called Sue a witch in her mind — the closest thing to cussing Katie's mind would allow her to think.

Katie checked the notes left by the departing shift's nurses, asked a couple of questions about a new patient who was admitted last night, and then decided to check on George before her other patients, hoping he might be asleep or at least less awake.

Katie peeked around the corner into George's room. He looked like he was still asleep. She breathed a sigh of relief.

Katie walked as softly as she could to try and not wake him up. She tiptoed through the room and around the end of George's bed.

"I'm cold." George mumbled, startling Katie.

"OK, not a problem. I'll get another blanket." Katie's tense tiptoeing melted into slumped-over disappointment.

"Or you could pay the electric bill and turn up the heat. I swear, you'd think the amount of money this place costs me they'd be able to afford to pay the electric bill."

"I'm sorry, Mr. Marshall. I assure you that the hospital pays its electric bill. Besides, it's summer and I'm pretty sure the heat's not on. Anyway, I'll find you another blanket."

Disappointed that he was awake, but happy to have an excuse to leave George's room, Katie walked out the door, went to a supply closet, and then returned ten minutes later with another blanket.

"Here you go. This should help," Katie said as she shook it out and gently placed it on top of George's other blankets.

"It stinks! It smells like old people."

Katie, whose nerves and patience were both already thin, thought to herself "Well, you are an old person." Taking a deep breath, instead she replied, "I'm sorry, but it's all I have."

"I'm not surprised. I didn't think you could do any better," George gruffed back, not even looking at Katie.

Katie's anger boiled up and she felt like she had to leave George's room before she said something that might get her in trouble. Without speaking, Katie gave George's saline bag a quick glance and then darted out of the room. She planted one foot in front of the other, marching out the door where she nearly ran into Trish.

Katie spoke in an agitated whisper. "Who does he think he is, treating me like this?"

"Hey, girl, it's going to be OK" Trish consoled, not quite whispering but not speaking loudly either.

"I mean, does he think he can just roll all over me? Does he think that can just do whatever he wants and not consider how it affects me?"

"I know, honey. Men can be like that. You know, you never really know someone – even after five or six years."

"Five or six years? I just met him a couple of weeks ago. That still doesn't give him a right to be so rude to me!"

"A couple of weeks ago? I think your brain's a little too fried. Maybe you should have taken today off too."

"What are you talking about? Look it up in the chart. George Marshall has only been here for a couple of weeks."

"George Marshall?!" Trish asked, perplexed.

"Yes, *George Marshall*. That guy really gets under my skin! Who does he think he is?"

"Ohhhh," Trish exclaimed. "I thought you were talking about Kyle."

Katie shot Trish a confused look, and then sighed. "Well, I guess all men treat me like a bag of garbage."

Trish reached out and gave Katie a quick hug when she spotted Dr. Zachary Moore rounding the corner behind Katie. Whispering in Katie's ear, Trish jokingly said, "Well, here comes one man who doesn't treat you like a *bag of garbage.*"

Katie pulled away from Trish's consoling hug and turned halfway around to see Zach, who stopped to peek into a patient's room. She was thankful he wasn't looking her way. Turning back to Trish, Katie rolled her eyes and said, "Yeah, he just treats me like a bag of meat!"

Both women let out a chuckle and went their own ways. Katie felt a little lighter from the laugh and thankful that she ran into Trish when she did.

Katie spent the next few hours avoiding George. She spent some time in Evelyn Smith's room, comforting Evelyn's visiting older sister who was in surprisingly good health for someone her age. As much as Katie hated to see people hurting, she found great satisfaction in helping loved ones as they grappled with their family member's impending death.

After lunch and already visiting all of her other patients twice, Katie reasoned that she had pushed off checking on George a second time way later than she should have. She couldn't avoid it any longer and would have to go see George again soon.

She rationalized her avoidance of George, "It's not like he's been alone. They should have at least delivered his lunch. If he died or something, someone would have noticed. And besides, with the lunch delivery at least he's had someone else to belittle."

Katie felt a cross between nervousness and agitation. She felt a pit in her stomach – she genuinely did not want to talk to that old man. She also felt certain that if she took her blood pressure, it would be way higher than normal. She was fed up with his ways and not sure she could take any more of it, especially in light of the events of the last two days with Kyle.

Standing outside his door, Katie took a deep breath and confidently walked into his room. Much to her disappointment, George was awake, trying to get the last bit of jello out of its plastic cup.

"OK, Mr. Marshall. It's time to check on a few things."

"Ughhhh," George moaned, shooting Katie a nasty look and then continuing to fruitlessly dig into his near-empty jello cup.

"Oh, come on," Katie tried to sound upbeat, despite the nauseating feeling that she had inside. "It will go quickly. I just need to change a couple of bags and administer some medicine."

"Why can't you leave an old man alone," George replied without looking up. "I'm going to die anyway."

This wasn't the first time that Katie had to deal with a patient who was depressingly facing the inevitability of his last days. Katie had a natural way of grabbing a patient's hand, talking softly, and helping them feel loved and more secure in the midst of their uncertainty. On this occasion, however, Katie's natural way eluded her.

"Well, Mr. Marshall, I have a job to do – whether you like it or not. It's my job to take care of you and that's what I'm going to do."

"Take care of me, hmph!" George tossed the jello cup on the floor and flung the plastic spoon to the end of his bed.

Katie looked at George incredulously, who turned his head toward the wall. Confident that he wasn't looking at her, she rolled her eyes and picked up the spoon and jello cup.

George didn't say anything for the next few moments, in which Katie found great relief. She quickly changed his saline bag and began administering medicine through his IV. While injecting the second dose, she accidentally pinched George's arm.

"Hey! Watch it! That hurt."

"I'm sorry Mr. Marshall."

"You know, you have to be one of the worst nurses I've ever seen. Did you even go to nursing school?"

Katie, surprised by his comment and not in a position to let it slide off her back, replied "Well, yes. I did go to *nursing school*."

"I bet you didn't even go a full four years. You've probably just got some certificate or something."

"As a matter of fact, Mr. Marshall, I did go to *nursing school* for four years. I am a registered nurse… not that there's anything wrong with other types of nurses."

George, who lately had been lethargic even in his grumpiness, found a spike of energy that he hadn't had in a few days. He was reinvigorated by belittling Katie.

"Oh, I see. So you went to school for four years *and* you're a bad nurse. I bet you make an even worse wife – if a man is dumb enough to have you."

Katie, trying everything she could do to hold her tongue, blurted out, "You mean, uncompassionate, terrible, old man! How dare you speak to me like that!"

"Well, it's probably about time someone told you that you're a terrible nurse. Maybe you're still young enough to find something you'd be good at – like maybe a job where you work at home and people don't have to talk to you. All you make me want to do is die. I see that ring on your finger – I bet you make your husband want to die too."

Katie threw down the last bottle of medicine she was going to administer. Her body shook as she bent over George. She raised her finger and pointed it six inches from George's eyes. Katie yelled at the top of her lungs, "I can't stand you! I CAN'T WAIT UNTIL YOU DIE!"

Katie flung her body away from George's bed, sending his bedside cart flying against the wall and his food tray crashing to the floor. As she stomped out of the room, Brian came to see what caused the crash. Steps behind Brian, Sue made a straight line to Katie, who had collapsed against the wall just across from George's room.

"Katie! What did you do?" Sue emphatically asked with authority and judgment, like she was a third grade teacher talking to one of her eight-year-old students.

"That guy is a real jerk!" Katie hollered, not caring who heard her.

Sue, shocked by Katie's out-of-character proclamation, grabbed Katie's arm, pulled her near, and talked quietly into Katie's ear. "What has gotten into you? You can't act like this!"

Pulling her arm away from Sue's grip, Katie shot back, "Let go of me, Sue. You can't just grab me like that. George Marshall is a cranky, unloving jerk and I'm just counting down the days until he dies."

Sue gasped in horror and brought her hand to her mouth in shock. "Katie!" she spoke with a loud, whispered voice. "I think you need to go home. I don't know what has gotten into you, but you can't stay here and work like this. Gather your things and go home for the rest of today. We'll talk about this tomorrow."

Katie shook her head as she rolled her eyes. "Whatever." She went back into the break room, grabbed her purse, and headed out into the hallway. She found Trish in another patient's room and told her that she was leaving early. Trish told Katie to go get some rest at her apartment. Katie left the hospital, grateful that Trish gave her a spare key to her apartment earlier in the morning.

Katie went back to the apartment. Still dressed in her scrubs, she crashed onto the couch. She closed her eyes and hoped that she could just fall asleep and either not wake back up or wake up and learn that everything had been a crazy dream.

Instead of falling asleep, Katie surprised herself by the thoughts that she allowed herself to entertain.

"I'm done with that man," she thought, thinking about George Marshall.

"I'm done with that other man, too," she found herself thinking, this time about Kyle.

"A lot of good it does to be the 'good girl.' What a waste of my life," Katie thought while deciding that her marriage was done and probably her job was done as well.

Katie lied on the couch, not ever able to turn off her racing mind. She was so angry and she found herself thinking angry thoughts about God. Instead of reasoning her way out of her ever-worsening spiral, Katie allowed herself to go deeper and deeper into the pit created by her despair.

"What a waste of my life. All of the youth group stuff. All of the college ministry stuff. All of the 'saving myself for marriage' stuff. And what is my reward for a race well run? Crap. That's it. My reward is a big pile of crap."

Katie continued to think darker thoughts.

"Well, we'll see if I live for that stuff anymore. My marriage? Dead. My faith? Dead. My pleasing other people? Dead. It's time to live for Katie – and no one else."

Katie couldn't sleep and couldn't quiet her racing mind. She grabbed her phone and ferociously thumbed through social media. What she saw enraged her even more – a college friend holding her perfect newborn baby, a high school friend on the beach with her perfect fiancé, perfect people in bars, perfect people on trips, perfect people in perfectly posed and perfectly filtered pictures displaying their perfectly perfected perfection.

Annoyed by her phone and frustrated by life, Katie darted off the couch and dug through her suitcase. She didn't know what she was looking for – she was just looking for some clue about anything. Perhaps something to do. Perhaps somewhere to go. Perhaps someone to become.

She didn't remember packing most of the things in the suitcase and if she was thinking a little more rationally, she would have questioned why she had her favorite winter sweater, the two-piece string bikini she nervously brought to her honeymoon, and the red sundress she bought for her third wedding anniversary.

Katie paused when she found the red sundress balled up inside the suitcase. She pulled it up and looked at it, pondering the past and future directions of her life, wondering if they might align or if they had vastly different trajectories to travel.

Attempting to shake out the dress's wrinkles, she grabbed her makeup bag and the red dress and walked to the bathroom. In the bathroom she tore out the small pink bow she put in her hair this morning and left the bathroom with both the dress and her makeup transforming her into someone she was not normally. She walked back into the living room, shut her suitcase, and headed out the door.

Not entirely sure where to go, Katie thought to herself, "It's Saturday night. Certainly even in a place like Cincinnati there's something I can do on a Saturday night."

Aimlessly driving, Katie thought about a country line dancing bar that her friends went to in college. She was uncomfortable dancing in public (even for UCDM) and never went to the bar herself, but right now the thought of it invigorated her. She got excited as she thought more about the prospect of the pounding music and the high energy of the dance floor. Katie did a U-turn on the street, cut off an oncoming car, and went on her way to the bar. She felt alive – much more than any other time in the last two days – as she imagined herself making her debut on the line dancing floor. "A new Katie is born!" she thought to herself, not concerned by the fact that she didn't know many country songs and didn't know the first thing about line dancing.

It was about five o'clock and Katie was surprised by how empty the parking lot looked. Walking into the bar, she saw a huge wood dance floor in the middle of the room with tables all around it. Off in one corner was a pool table and a mechanical bull. Another corner contained the actual bar.

"Where's everybody at?" she asked the bouncer as she showed her ID and paid the small cover charge.

The bouncer laughed. "This must be your first time. It's a little early, but the place will fill up soon enough."

"OK," Katie replied, feeling stupid that she didn't even know that five o'clock wasn't a normal time to start partying. "I've got a lot to learn," she thought.

Without hardly anyone else in the bar, Katie paused after she paid the cover charge to scope out the best place for her to sit. She didn't have a plan. She wasn't necessarily sure she would dance, but she wasn't ruling it out either. Likewise, she wasn't necessarily planning to drink much, but she also wasn't ruling that out. She was there on more of a whim than with a purpose. Katie saw a table in a back corner on the opposite side of the bar. She reasoned that this particular place would be quiet and inconspicuous, so she took a seat, scanned a QR code, and looked at the menu.

Deciding she was hungry and not sure at all what to order to drink, Katie walked up to the bar and ordered chicken wings, fries, and a drink that sounded kind of fruity.

After ordering her food and drink, Katie sat back down at her table, completely out of her element. She watched a middle-aged couple decked out in their western wear, line dancing by themselves in the middle of the dance floor. She watched a group of three women sitting at the bar, also wearing varying amounts of country gear, drinking and flirting with the bartender.

Katie pulled out her phone and couldn't spend more than two minutes thumbing through Facebook and Instagram. She didn't have the motivation to care much about the posts and pictures she saw. She stuffed her phone back into her purse.

After taking fifteen minutes to nurse her fruity drink to empty, a young woman who couldn't have been just days over 21 brought Katie her food. Katie, happy to have something to do with a purpose, ate the food slowly as she watched more people trickle into the bar and more people trickle onto the dance floor.

Katie spent the next hour watching people dance, figuring out that you don't especially have to know how to line dance — you just need to know how to follow other people's leads.

Now three fruity drinks into her night and feeling less reserved, Katie decided that she and her red sundress were going to try their luck on the dance floor — cowboy hat or not.

Katie felt a little tipsy, but more like she was light on her feet rather than unbalanced. She took a last sip — really a fruitless attempt at slurping out the last bit from the bottom of the glass — and she pushed her chair back from the table as she feigned an air of confidence in her march onto the dance floor.

Slipping between two people in the back row (she figured out that newbies cut their teeth in the back row), Katie began copying the moves of the people in front of her. She kicked her feet at the right time, turned to the left and then to the right, and even let out a "Yee hah" in unison with the growing group.

Katie danced for the next two hours, only taking a break to go to the bathroom and to order another fruity drink one time when the DJ offered up a rare slow song.

Completely incognizant of the time, her sweat, or her aching legs, Katie was two verses deep into "Cotton-Eyed Joe" when someone tapped her on her shoulder.

"Well, what do we have here?" the slightly familiar voice said as Katie broke out of sync with the dancers and turned around to the voice behind her.

"Oh my gosh! Dr. Moore! What are *you* doing here?" Katie was shocked to see Zach and broke out into a huge grin.

"What am *I* doing here? I could ask you the same thing." Zach scanned Katie from her sandal-clad feet to her slightly sweaty, but dolled-up hair. "I can't say that I've seen you here before, and I think I would remember seeing this."

Uncharacteristically oblivious to his gaze, Katie asked, "*Before*? So, this is something you normally do?" Katie had to yell to be heard over the music. Without thinking, she reached out and slapped Zach on the arm, still smiling from ear to ear.

"Yep, you've found me out. I like to put on my Lucchese ostrich skin boots with my Stetson hat, and kick and turn on an occasional Saturday night."

"Well, I never would have guessed!"

"As you can see, Nurse Thurston, there's more to me than meets the eye."

"I can see that," Katie replied, still yelling. Katie laughed and snorted. She said, "Get it? I can *see* that! *More than meets the eye*!?" Katie slapped Zach on the arm again, and then she returned to dance in sync with the group.

"May I?" Zach asked, displaying a partial bow. "Or, is this your husband's spot?"

Katie turned to Zach while keeping her feet in step with the group. "My husband's not here and I can't keep you from dancing there, so go for it." Katie smiled as she danced – having a blast learning to line dance and even excited that she knew someone else in the bar.

Without saying anything, Zach danced next to Katie for the next three songs. Katie mostly concentrated on learning the moves, happy to discover that most dances repeated the moves she learned earlier in the evening.

After their third dance side-by-side, the DJ announced, "OK, country fans. Let's slow things down and take things back – way back. Here's Garth Brooks' 'The Dance.'"

As most people left the dance floor, others coupled up and began slow dancing like kids at a junior high winter dance. Zach reached over and grabbed Katie's arm. "Dance with me," he said, looking directly into her eyes.

Katie, shocked and not sure how to say no, gave in to his gentle pull and quickly found herself standing face to face with Dr. Zachary Moore, just inches apart, as he placed both of his hands a couple of inches above her hips and as her arms dangled to her side.

"Did you forget how to do it?" he asked, chuckling. Zach let go of Katie's waist and put both of her arms on his shoulders before replacing his hands, this time just an inch or so above her hips.

"There, that's not so bad is it?" Zach asked as he began slowly swaying back and forth.

Katie, still shocked and not quite processing the moment, kept her hands on his shoulders and began swaying left and right in rhythm with him.

Dancing through the first verse, Zach pulled Katie's body closer to his as the second verse began. Katie, completely out of sorts and suddenly struck with a moment of clarity, dropped her hands from Zach's shoulders and stepped back away from him.

"Hey, what's wrong? It's just a dance."

"I can't do this," Katie replied, covering her eyes with her hands and turning to the side to walk away.

Zach reached out and grabbed Katie's shoulder, "Hey, wait. It's OK. Let's talk."

"No!" Katie said, a little louder than she intended. With her loud denial, half of the people on the dance floor stopped dancing and glared at Zach as Katie hurried off the dance floor to retrieve her purse. Embarrassed and intimidated by the incorrect assumption of the crowd, Zach also hurried off the dance floor and flew immediately out the bar's door.

Katie, not even seeing Zach leave in front of her, also walked out the door and to her car. When she sat down and locked the car door, Katie began balling uncontrollably. She let out loud cries as snot ran down her face. She reached for the closest thing she could find and wiped her face with a restaurant receipt.

With a new headache and barely able to see through her teary eyes, Katie put her car in drive and left the parking lot. Her mind was racing and out of control. Katie couldn't stop crying and couldn't even comprehend where to go or how to act or what to do. For multiple reasons she was in no position to drive a car, but she didn't have the presence of mind to figure that out.

Katie headed toward Trish's apartment, but when she reached its parking lot, she kept driving instead of turning into it. Unsure of where to go, but certain that she didn't want to see anyone she knew or talk to anyone about anything, Katie drove ten more minutes past Trish's apartment when she saw an old, slightly run-down hotel. With no extra clothes, no toiletries, and just her purse and red sundress, Katie checked into the hotel. Unsure about who she was or what she was doing, Katie went to her new room in the old hotel and crashed onto the well-worn bed, unable to fall asleep, unable to look at her phone, and unable to watch TV.

Katie spent the next couple of hours that Saturday night lost in her mind, but never quite able to rationally think anything through. She was certain her marriage was over. She was certain her job was over. She knew her faith was gone – she couldn't even remember what it was like to have faith to begin with. Some time into Katie's unconsciously conscious state, Trish texted her to see where she was. Kate read the text, but didn't reply. Fifteen minutes later, Trish called Katie, but Katie didn't answer her phone. Katie remembered that she had to work tomorrow and picked up her phone to send Sue a quick text that she wouldn't be in. After hitting send, Katie turned off her phone, threw it to the side of the bed, and fell asleep.

Katie slept off and on all night Saturday, all day Sunday, again Sunday night, and into the morning on Monday. She only got out of bed to go to the bathroom and drink some water from the bathroom sink.

Her phone died soon into her midsummer hibernation. She missed two texts from her mom about how much she wished Katie and Kyle came to dinner on Sunday. She missed seven increasingly annoyed texts from Trish wondering where Katie was and if she was just going to leave her stuff at Trish's apartment. She did not, however, miss any texts from Kyle.

Katie felt dead to the world and wished that the world would just die to her.

Chapter

11

Since his exchange with Katie on Saturday afternoon, George's health quickly declined. During the night after Katie stormed out, went to the bar, and then crashed at the questionable hotel, George's breathing became more labored, his pulse weakened, and his body temperature began fluctuating wildly. While he didn't sleep well through the night, he was never quite awake either. That semi-state of consciousness continued throughout the day on Sunday when Zach, thankful that Katie wasn't at work, called Louise to let her know that he didn't expect George to be around much longer.

Louise visited George on Sunday, as did Tom, Rachael, and the girls. Louise spent most of the time crying and Tom spent most of the time bewildered at the sight of his mean, cranky dad reduced to a helpless, dying, old man.

"I love you, George," Louise said over a dozen times throughout the afternoon. She was used to not receiving a response, but George wasn't in much of a position to respond even if he could. She actually enjoyed the freedom to easily express her love to him without him saying something condescending back.

Tom thought about taking advantage of the opportunity to tell his dad how he felt about all of the years of misery that George gave him. But, despite all of the things Tom thought he wanted to say and despite all of the ways Tom crafted those words in his head, he couldn't bring himself to speak his mind to his dad. In the end, he figured it didn't matter much anyway.

Rachael, barely knowing George as a person and more knowing him as the characterization of someone she never really interacted with, alternated between squeezing her husband's hand, hugging Louise, and taking the girls to get snacks, to go to the bathroom, and to explore the hospital.

With visiting hours over and barely twenty words of conversation offered by George during the times he was partially awake, the family left George on Sunday night, with Tom assuring his mom that she would be better served getting a solid night's sleep in her own bed rather than sleeping on the couch in George's room. The group left George's room, not confident that they would see him alive again tomorrow.

Late that night, with the only sound being an occasional beep in the hallway and the only light being the faint glow of a couple of small lights in his room, George awoke from his sleep, feeling the best he had felt in the last day and a half.

Looking over to his side, he saw the little girl in a red dress sitting on the chair in the corner of the room, with her feet swinging just an inch or two above the floor.

"Hello, Mr. George. It is nice to see you."

"Well, it's nice to be seen, I suppose."

Although George could comprehend that the little girl shouldn't be in his room at whatever time of the night it was, George decided not to question her presence like he did the last time. Instead, he felt the same strange warmth of compassion from her that he felt the other night. George actually welcomed her in the room. Like the Grinch, George's heart might have been thought to be incapable of feeling much warmth at all, but strangely enough, his heart felt warmer than it had hardly ever felt in his entire life.

"Have you thought about my dog, Mr. George? You know, the one that used to be mean but just needed to be loved."

"I can't say that I have," George replied, not telling the truth. In fact, he thought about the dog and the babydoll and the little girl frequently over the last few days. He felt especially miserable when he thought about her dog though.

Unfazed by his response, the little girl asked, "How does my dog make you feel, George?"

174

Given his response, George was surprised by her question. "I don't know," George replied, losing some of his fuzzy warmth. Feeling uncomfortable and as if he were a prisoner being interrogated, George began to wish that the little girl wasn't there. "How should it make me feel?"

"I think that it should make you feel good. It should remind you that there is hope for everything, no matter how far away something is from where it needs to be."

"Well, I'm not sure there's hope for me. If you can't tell, I don't have very long left in this forsaken world."

"I believe that there is hope for everybody. If my mean, unloved dog can learn to be loved and to love again, then I think any person can do the same."

George, who was starting to get annoyed, began thinking about the little girl's words. As he contemplated his life and his choices, he vacillated between being annoyed and being comforted. Choosing annoyance, George quickly soured again and said, "Hey, are you saying that I'm a mean, unloved man? I don't think that's a very nice thing for a little girl to say."

"Is it true?" the little girl asked, staring into George's eyes and not seeming to care that he was offended.

Uncomfortable by her gaze, George turned toward the wall and stalled for time. "Is what true?"

"Both things. Are you mean? Are you unloved?"

"Well," George spoke softly and a little broken, "that's quite a question for you to ask an old man. I mean...," George paused, "I'm not perfect."

"No one is perfect, George."

The two sat in silence as George waded through the unfamiliar emotions he was experiencing and the little girl waited patiently for him to process his thoughts.

After a few moments, George broke the silence when he looked at the little girl and said, "You know, my little sister used to have a pair of shoes just like that." George raised one finger in an attempt to point down at the little girl's black and white Saddle Oxford shoes.

"Oh, these?" the little girl questioned in a high-pitched voice. She giggled and said, "These are my favorite shoes. I wear them everywhere."

"Yes, I'm quite sure," George said, mustering a little energy to elevate his upper body to see the girl's shoes more clearly. "Lilly had a pair of shoes just like those."

"Lilly is such a pretty name," the little girl replied. "Tell me about her."

George's eyes began to moisten as he turned to look toward the ceiling. He slowly closed his eyes as if he was trying to actually see Lilly clearly in his mind.

"She was only seven years old. You know, it's kind of odd. I can only remember what she looked like when she was seven. I don't remember what she looked like when she was six or five or four, or even eight. But I remember what she looked like when she was seven.

"She liked to wear dresses – all different colors. She had blue ones and pink ones and even a red one about the same color as yours. I remember her always dancing and singing. It kind of drove me crazy to tell you the truth. I suppose it would drive any nine-year-old boy crazy."

The little girl affirmed, "I do suppose you are right about that, George."

George barely realized the little girl spoke as he waded deeper and deeper into the jungle of the memory of his little sister.

"I remember one day when we were at my grandparents' farm, helping to suckle tomatoes – that's where you pick off the little shoots that grow between the big ones on the tomato plants. That makes the tomatoes healthier and the fruit stronger."

George looked at the little girl to see if she was absorbing his farming lesson. The little girl nodded.

"Anyway, Lilly got stung by a bee. Actually it was more like a hornet. I saw it, believe it or not. It was the biggest wasp or bee or hornet I ever saw.

"Lilly cried and cried. Sometimes she cried when she was scared, sometimes she cried when she was hurt, and sometimes she cried just to put on a show. But this time was different – Lilly cried pretty hard because she was both hurt and scared. And, I suppose, she put on quite a show too."

The little girl continued nodding as George talked, though he wasn't looking at her.

"Our grandparents were back at the house – grandpa had a way of putting us to work and then finding something else to do. So I went up to Lilly, put my arm around her, and said, 'It's going to be OK, Lilly. I'll take care of you. The pain will go away soon.'

"Lilly looked up at me – she had on a blue dress that day with…, I think those shoes you're wearing – and she smiled a big smile through her little tearful eyes. She said, 'Thanks, Georgie.' She always called me Georgie. And then she reached up and gave me a great big hug."

George opened his eyes and looked at the ceiling. He had two small streams staining his old, dry face.

"It sounds like your sister was lucky to have you, George. It sounds like you were a very good brother."

George squeezed his dry lips together and then licked them. Then, instead of a small stream, George started to cry out loud and larger drops dripped down the sides of his cheeks.

"There, there," the little girl consoled. "What is wrong, George? It sounds like such a good memory."

"Oh, my dear, it is a good memory. Unfortunately, the rest of my memories of Lilly are not that good."

"Oh, really? Why is that, George?"

"Well, sweetheart," George paused and wasn't even aware he was using words like *dear* and *sweetheart*. "I only remember what she looked like when she was seven years old because eight was such a terrible year for her and she didn't make it to nine."

"Oh, that is so sad," the little girl said. Her face dropped and it looked like she might cry.

"Yes, it is. We didn't know much about it at the time, but it was cancer. Who really knows now what exact kind she had, but, it took over her whole body and it took her down in a hurry."

"That must have been a very hard thing to watch."

George, no longer sobbing, but still wiping slowly forming tears from his eyes, said, "Yes it was. And I prayed and I prayed. I said, 'God, if you're there. Just take it away.' I didn't use to question if God was there, but the sicker Lilly got, the less I believed he was there. And, well, she didn't make it."

"I am so sorry, George. That is a sad story."

"It's not a story, it's the truth. My little sister died and God didn't do anything about it. I suppose I've never been the same since."

The little girl didn't have anything particularly wise to say, so she sat there as George continued reminiscing about Lilly — both the good and the bad. The little girl sat in the chair, watching George as he wiped away tears and as he opened and closed his eyes.

After ten minutes of silence, George fully opened his eyes and looked over at the chair in the corner of the room. "You're still here?" George half said and half asked.

"Yes, I am still here."

George looked at the little girl without speaking, enjoying the compassionate warmth that her gaze returned.

She spoke, "I would like to tell you a story. Is that OK with you?"

"Yes."

"One day there was a goat herder. He was a poor goat herder — his goats were the only things that he had in the whole, entire world. He didn't have a family and he barely had a place to sleep at night, but he had his goats.

"The goat herder loved his goats — not just because they were the source of his income, but because they were the most important thing in life to him. His goats needed him to lead them to food and water. His goats needed him to care for them when they were injured. And, his goats needed him to protect them.

"One day the goat herder was asleep in his uncomfortable bed in his small house when he heard the most awful bleating coming from his goat pen. He ran outside and saw a wolf inside his goat pen! The next thing he knew, the wolf hopped over the pen's fence, carrying off a lifeless goat in its mouth as it disappeared into the woods not too far from the goat pen.

"The goat herder was angry at the wolf and vowed that he would never let that happen again. The next night, the goat herder grabbed a blanket and slept outside, right next to the goat pen.

"In the middle of the night, the goat herder woke up like the night before to the most awful bleating coming from the goat pen. The goat herder sprung up off the ground, only to see a different wolf carrying off a newly lifeless goat in its mouth and also disappearing into the woods close to the pen.

"Over the next several nights, the goat herder tried many things, but he could not stop the wolves. He slept inside the pen and outside the pen. He even stayed up all night, only to be overwhelmed when a pack of four wolves worked together to take three goats in just one night.

"The goat herder was very angry. The only thing he loved in the world was being ripped away from him, one by one. The next night, the goat herder could hardly fall asleep as he thought about the wolves. He obsessed about the wolves. His rage burned inside him. 'If only I was as strong as a wolf,' he said out loud, 'then I could protect my goats.' The goat herder wished so badly that he could not only become a strong wolf, but that he could become the strongest wolf in the entire world. Then, perhaps, he could protect his goats and no more wolves would kill his precious goats.

"That night, as the goat herder tossed and turned, trying to get even a little sleep on the hard ground beside the goat pen, something unexplainable and amazing happened. The goat herder woke up, like most other nights, to the sound of awful bleating. But as he woke up, the goat herder realized that he too was now a wolf! He was a big and strong wolf! He sprung high into the air as he leapt over the fence. He growled as he snapped at the lone wolf who was trying to snatch away one of his few remaining precious goats. And, you know what? The new, great wolf was successful. He got one good bite on that other wolf's leg and the other wolf yelped as it leapt back over the fence without a goat in its mouth.

"The great wolf was very happy. He howled as loudly as his new voice would allow. He leapt over the fence, away from his goats, and ran and ran and ran. He enjoyed the rush of the wind on his face and the power of his legs as he jumped and ran and skipped across the woods and through the fields.

"The great wolf was the biggest wolf in all of the woods. He decided that his new purpose was to exercise his superior strength over all the other wolves. He found each wolf in the woods, one by one, and he killed those wolves. As he sunk his big, sharp teeth into each one, he imagined that wolf as it might have sunk its own teeth into one of his little goats. When he got a wolf in his mouth, he violently shook it to its death. The more wolves he killed, the more violent he got and he became angrier and angrier at those wolves that had taken away so many of his precious little goats.

"Soon, after a couple of weeks, all of the wolves in his woods were dead, and the great wolf felt empty. He enjoyed exacting his justice on those wolves and grew quite upset that there were no more wolves on which to dish out his revenge.

"One day, very mad that he had no more wolves to punish and not quite sure what the purpose was in being a great wolf if he could no longer punish the wolves who hurt his goats, the great wolf went away on a long journey. He passed over streams and hills and valleys. He entered new woods and new fields. He saw new villages and new people.

"On his journey, the great wolf came to a different goat pen. It was one he had never seen before. It was small and not very well kept. Inside it were about a dozen goats.

"He carefully watched the goats in that goat pen from the cover of some nearby bushes. He studied their movements and interactions. He watched them stretch their necks through the fence and eat the weeds that grew nearby. And much to his surprise, he watched them fight with each other.

"The great wolf was confused and upset by the goats' fighting. They would butt heads against each other and push each other around. One goat in particular was very mean to the other goats, even stepping on the smallest goats after it had pushed one to the ground.

"The great wolf grew angrier and angrier. He was mad that the mean goat bullied the other goats. And, as he grew angrier and angrier, his desire to exact punishment on that goat grew stronger and stronger.

"One night, the great wolf could stand it no longer. He burst out from the bushes where he was hiding and he growled as he leapt over the fence and snatched up that mean goat into his jaws. He sunk his teeth deeply into its neck and shook the goat violently back and forth as it let out the most awful bleat. As its bleating fell to silence, the great wolf saw a man run out of a nearby house with a flashlight, yelling at him to leave the goat pen. With the newly dead goat still in his mouth, the great wolf leapt back over the pen, into the bushes, and then into the woods just a little farther away.

"Over the next few nights, the great wolf continued to watch the goats in the new pen and every night the great wolf grew angry when the goats fought with each other. Each night the great wolf could stand it no longer and he would burst from the bushes to capture and kill the most offending goat.

"After five nights passed with five goats dead, the wolf sat in the bushes on the sixth night, watching the goats fight yet again and growing angrier and angrier. Like each other night, when he could stand it no longer and his rage began to boil over, the great wolf burst out of the bushes and leapt over the goat pen to snatch up that night's most offending goat.

"Only this time, as he landed on the ground and turned toward the goat, the great wolf saw the goat herder, cowering in fear, but sitting in front of the little goat that the great wolf was about to take. The poor goat herder held a small stick in his hand, ready to defend his last, precious goats. The great wolf froze in place, just a couple of feet from the goat herder and the goat. He saw the tears in the goat herder's eyes as the goat herder protected one of the last few goats that he had remaining.

"The great wolf could not attack the man and could not attack the goat. The great wolf was shaken by what he saw — the power and effects of his own anger, his own justice, and his own righteousness.

"The great wolf turned around and leapt back over the pen and ran into the woods. He ran back across streams and hills and valleys and villages. He ran all the way back to the woods beside the pen where he raised his own goats. As he reached his pen, the great wolf slowly walked out of the woods and walked up to his pen. The pen was empty — there were no more goats. He did not know where they were or what happened to them, but he knew that no one had been there to lead them to food and water, no one had been there to care for them when they were hurt, and no one had been there to protect them.

"Sad, the great wolf went into the pen, curled up in its corner, and cried as he fell asleep, weary from his long journey and greatly missing his little goats.

"The next morning, the great wolf woke up and saw that he was no longer a great wolf, but was retransformed back into the goat herder that he used to be. Only now, he looked around at his once full pen and saw that he had no goats left to herd."

The little girl in a red dress stopped talking and looked at George with her compassionate, loving eyes.

George sat in silence, licking his lips and blinking his moist eyes.

After a moment of silence, George asked softly, "What happened to the goat herder?"

"I do not know, George, I told you the only part of his story that I know. What do you think happened to the goat herder?"

George paused, not wanting to convict his own life with his answer. "I suppose…," he paused again, "I suppose that he died lonely and without goats."

"Perhaps," the little girl replied. "Or, maybe he decided to raise new goats."

"Yeah, I suppose," George replied, barely audibly.

George thought about the story for a minute while the little girl sat quietly. He thought about the possibilities of the rest of the goat herder's life. Although he wasn't quite sure what the story meant for the rest of his short life, George appreciated it. "Thank you for that story. It was a very nice story."

"You are quite welcome, George. It is one of my favorite stories when I imagine all the good things that the goat herder might have become after his experience as the great wolf."

George nodded his head as he looked at the little girl. She smiled at George. Once again, he felt great warmth from her smile.

The little girl used her little arms to push herself off the chair. Her feet landed on the ground and the little girl stood in front of the chair.

"I think it is time for me to go now. I hope you have a good night, George."

"Yes, that seems like the right thing to do. I'm getting pretty sleepy."

"Would it be OK to see you one more time, George?"

"Yes, I would like that. I would like to see you as many times as you can."

"OK, George, I will see you again. Good night."

"Good night."

George leaned his head back on his pillow and didn't even watch the little girl leave the room. George, who wasn't used to crying, was emotionally exhausted from his night of tears. He lied in bed with his eyes closed and his mind less and less able to put together complete thoughts.

Although he seemed to be out of tears to cry, George 's cheeks still managed to absorb a drip or two as he eventually fell into a deep sleep. Subconsciously, George was between a place of peace and a place of turmoil, both feeling satisfied with his conversation with the little girl in a red dress and also feeling incomplete, like something had been left unsaid and like there was still business left to finish.

Chapter

12

. . . .

Monday morning Katie woke up with a stiff neck and sore body, still wearing the same red dress from two nights ago. She finally felt well-rested, though she was hungry and had a headache.

Katie wasn't ready to take a full account of her actions and definitely not ready to sort out her feelings, but she figured that she couldn't live the rest of her life in a hotel room. While her body was far from 100%, Katie's rest provided her brain the chance to reset. She knew that the right thing to do would be to reach out to Kyle. She reached for her phone to give Kyle a call. She wasn't exactly sure what she was going to say and she wasn't sure what she wanted to hear him say, but she figured that it was time that they talked. She powered on her phone – its battery was only at 12%. She was grateful that she had a charger in her car.

As his phone buzzed in his pocket, Kyle, who had been at work already for a few hours, pulled it out and saw Katie's face and number on his screen. Although he wasn't allowed to talk on the phone in the middle of his shift, he could have paused what he was doing, stepped off the floor, walked into the hallway, and taken the call.

It was a bit of a miracle that Kyle was at work on Monday. Friday, after Katie left with a full suitcase and after Kyle tried to text Tony on his dying phone, Kyle fell back asleep and woke up early Saturday morning. The effects of his high and subsequent crash had worn off and Kyle felt well-rested from all of his sleep. His back was stiff from lying in bed so long, but it wasn't in pain.

That Saturday morning, Kyle vacillated between shame and determination. He couldn't believe what his life had come to and that his wife actually packed a bag and walked out. He had know idea where she was, and every time he thought about texting her to make sure she was OK, he convinced himself that she was better off without him and that he didn't deserve another chance.

On top of it all, Kyle couldn't believe that he actually shot up herion. In the months of his pain pill use, Kyle justified that he wasn't a bad person. At best, he was a person who was just in a lot of pain. At worst, he was another victim of the opioid crisis. Now, however, he couldn't believe that he allowed himself to not only use heroin once, but also attempt to use it again. As Kyle replayed the events of the last few days, he didn't recognize himself, but he feared that this unrecognizable person might be who he really is.

On the other hand, Kyle's shame and self-pity were accompanied by a growing desire to fix the problem. He wasn't necessarily sure how he could fix his marriage – he realized that fixing it would require participation from Katie as well. However, he had a certain clarity about the issues that he could control, primarily the issue of his use and the issue of not seriously jumping into recovery. Yes, he wanted to fix his marriage, but he figured that he would start on himself first.

So on Saturday, while Katie was hollering at George and learning to line dance, Kyle went to the family meeting by himself, where he barely talked to Ralph. Later in the day Kyle carefully went through the entire house, making sure that he and Katie had in fact thrown away all of his pills. On Sunday, while Katie was passed out at the run-down hotel, Kyle visited a large church about a half hour away. He didn't want to attend his regular church without Katie and he didn't want to go somewhere people might know him, but nevertheless, he felt like he needed to go to church.

He spent Sunday afternoon doing things to feel productive: he did laundry, he read, and he changed the oil in his truck. He was content being alone these two days – it gave him the silence he needed to think and he kind of felt like it was his deserving punishment. He even wondered if his staying alone for the rest of his life would be the best thing for Katie. In fact, other than a few obligatory greetings to people he recognized at the Saturday family meeting and people he didn't know at the Sunday church service, Kyle barely talked to anyone both days. By the end of the day, however, Kyle was getting lonely.

As he lied in bed Sunday night, Kyle new he needed to go to work on Monday and own up to his two missed days last week. Trying to fall asleep, he noticed how quiet the house was. It felt more like a jail cell than a home. Kyle turned over, half expecting to see Katie lying beside him. Disappointed, Kyle fell asleep convincing himself that he didn't deserve anything better. As he drifted off to sleep, he even tried to imagine other ways that he should find to further punish himself.

Now in an awkward Monday morning at work shortly after Kyle witnessed the look of disappointment in his manager's eyes, Kyle froze as he felt his phone buzz and saw his wife's name on its screen. Already struggling with an overwhelming weight of guilt, Kyle didn't feel worthy enough to answer the phone. He didn't want to hear Katie lecture him or tell him what a failure he was. He didn't feel like he had the emotional energy to answer her questions and accusations.

"She's better off without me," Kyle thought as his eyes glossed over and his phone continued to buzz. Kyle stared at the phone until it stopped. When it did, he let out an audible sob, excused himself from the floor, and went to the bathroom.

Katie was both disappointed and relieved when Kyle didn't answer the phone. "I'll try again later," she reasoned. "Maybe he is at work."

Katie thought more about the prospect of her husband going into work today. On the one hand, today was Monday and that's where Kyle should be. On the other hand, Katie didn't know if Kyle would be at work, would be shooting up, or would just be passed out at home.

Thinking about it some more, Katie decided that she needed to take a chance and hope that Kyle was at work, or at least not at home, so that she could swing by the house to get a few things. Her suitcase of weirdly assorted clothes and shoes were still at Trish's apartment, along with her toiletries. Being AWOL the last two days, Katie was too embarrassed to go back to Trish's apartment to get her stuff. She figured she would put off dealing with that issue.

Katie was scheduled to go into work tomorrow, so she planned to drive home this morning to get a pair of scrubs and piece together whatever toiletries she could find. The rest she could get from a store if she needed to. As she walked out of the hotel to her car, she was overwhelmed by the scent of freshly cut grass, the brightness of the sun, and the crustiness of her clothes.

Katie made the 20-minute drive in 25 minutes, not really in a hurry to see if Kyle was home or not. As she rounded the corner beside her house, she was relieved and a little distressed to see her driveway was empty.

"I hope he's OK," she thought as she put her car in park and walked up to the house.

Katie felt odd walking into her own house. It felt like she hadn't been there in a long time. She noticed her house's smell – something she was only aware of when she and Kyle went away on vacation. The house felt empty to her, devoid of the love and warmth that she usually felt when she walked through the front door after a long day of work or an evening out with her husband. It felt like an odd collection of rooms and furniture. Even the pictures on the walls looked foreign.

Katie scanned the open-concept living room. Aside from not feeling normal, everything in the house looked normal. Katie didn't know what she expected to see – maybe things torn apart as Kyle looked for drugs, maybe syringes and pill bottles lying around, or maybe just dishes piled up in the sink and fast food bags left on the table.

Katie was surprised when she walked into her bedroom and saw that their bed was made. Bed making was always more Kyle's strength than hers, but she didn't suspect that Kyle was in a bed-making state of mind.

Katie walked into the bathroom and found an old toothbrush and trial-sized toothpaste in the back of the drawer. She realized that she hadn't brushed her teeth since Saturday morning. As she brushed her teeth, she looked over at the shower where everything fell apart a few nights ago. She felt emotional though confused, because she didn't feel particularly sad, mad, or upset.

Katie determined she was not going to be ruled by her last experience in that shower, so she decided to take a long, hot shower. The longer she stayed in the shower, the less emotional it was to be in it. Afterward, she put on clean clothes, packed up what toiletries she could find, grabbed some pajamas and a set of scrubs, and headed for the door.

As she started walking out the front door, Kyle's backpack on the coffee table caught Katie's eye. She froze and turned around to look at it. She stood in the front doorway, halfway inside the house and halfway outside the house with her hand still on the doorknob.

"Maybe I should take a quick look," Katie thought. Before her conscience could make a counterargument, Katie shut the front door and grabbed his bag. Feeling like a detective about to comb through evidence, Katie gave a quick glance around the room to look for a pair of rubber gloves that she knew they didn't have.

Shaking her head, Katie returned her attention to the bag. She unzipped each zipper one by one and looked into the dark holes. She didn't know what she might find or what she hoped to find, but Katie's heart began to race.

Katie grabbed a pen off the table and began moving things around inside the bag while holding it wide open – just like she saw security officers do at Kings Island. She couldn't see well, so she grabbed her phone and used its flashlight to peer into the bag.

Katie searched the two main compartments, the tiny cell phone compartment on the top of the bag, and the other small compartment inside the front. She couldn't find anything. Frustrated by her failure and not convinced she could adequately see everything inside the bag, Katie flipped the bag upside down and shook it until everything fell out onto the floor. Throwing the pen back onto the table, Katie spread out all of the stuff that fell out of the bag – hand sanitizer, napkins, a couple of screwdrivers, a pair of sunglasses, mints, coins… but nothing that looked like drugs or anything a druggy might need.

Half relieved and half irritated, Katie tossed the bag down on the floor on top of its pile of contents and headed out the door.

Once again realizing she was hungry, Katie grabbed some fast food on her way back to the hotel and ate it on her hotel room bed, deciding to pass the day binge watching shows on her phone and wondering if Kyle would call her back. At one point in the afternoon Katie remembered that Trish tried to call her on Saturday night. Katie thought about calling her – or at least texting her – but didn't have the emotional energy to call or text her back, instead putting off that conversation for now. She also remembered her mom had texted her twice yesterday, but definitely didn't want any part of that conversation today.

Later that evening, Katie was starting to fall asleep. She took one last look at her phone, thinking that perhaps she had somehow missed a text or call from Kyle. Not seeing anything, she turned off the lamp beside the bed and went to sleep.

Later that night, around 11:30, Kyle arrived home from working a double shift. Although his body was tired, his mind kept thinking about his missed call from Katie. He knew he should call her – but after he decided not to answer her call and then not to call her back on his lunch break, it just became easier and easier to put it off. He figured he had already passed some reasonable time limit to call her back, so waiting longer couldn't make things much worse.

Walking into the living room, Kyle flipped on the light switch and saw his bag lying on the floor with all of its contents emptied out. Kyle immediately knew it was Katie. He stood there numb, not knowing if he should feel angry or ashamed. Kyle chose not to feel either, walked past the bag, and went into the bedroom.

As Kyle showered to get ready to go to bed, he tried to remember details of his conversations with Katie on Thursday night and Friday, but couldn't really put it together. He badly wanted to replay those conversations. What did he say? What did she say? Truthfully, it was all such a blur and his memory of it all was based on small snippets of conversations and brief images, like Katie sitting on her suitcase or Kyle running around the house only wearing his towel.

Like so many other times in the past two months, Kyle's lonely shower turned into a deep dive into his personal shame. And, also like so many other times in the past two months, his deep shame led to a mental replay of the day Katie first found out he was abusing pain killers. It was an embarrassing, tough evening.

"Kyle, can you come here?" Katie called out from the kitchen to Kyle who was watching TV in the living room.

Kyle walked into the kitchen and replied, "Hey, what's up?"

"What the heck is this?" she asked, holding a plastic bag with twenty pills in it.

"What do you mean? I don't know what they are." Kyle looked down at the floor when he talked.

"What do you mean, you *don't know what they are*? They look like pain killers — just a different brand than the ones you take."

"I don't know, Katie," Kyle nervously said as he avoided eye contact, stuck his hands in his pocket, and turned to walk out of the kitchen.

"Hold on!" Katie exclaimed. "We're not done."

Kyle stopped in his tracks, took a deep breath, and turned around. "What?"

"Kyle, these are pain pills. I found them in the old sugar bowl on the top shelf in that cabinet." Katie half-hollered as she pointed to the cabinet beside the refrigerator. "I know they're pain pills, I know they weren't there before, and I know they aren't your normal pain pills." Katie paused. "I didn't put them there and they didn't get there by themselves. Now, please tell me, why were they there?"

Kyle began to cry uncontrollably which shocked Katie.

"I'm. So. Sorry. Katie." Kyle said each word between a massive inhale of snot.

Katie's demeanor went from prosecutorial to motherly. She wanted to reach for her husband, but also felt oddly afraid to touch him.

"It's OK, honey," she consoled with a softer tone, arms lifted partway to embrace him, but not high enough to invite him in. "Tell me, why are you so sorry?"

Kyle cried loudly for a few seconds, not able to get any words out.

Pushing her arms to do something her instincts forbade, Katie reached out and hugged Kyle, running her fingers through his hair and pulling his head down onto her shoulder.

"Come on, Kyle. Tell me what's going on," Katie whispered.

Katie and Kyle walked over to the kitchen table where Kyle explained that he had been buying extra pills and taking too many every day. He explained that he started doing it because his back hurt worse than he let on. However, he didn't share that lately he wasn't taking the pills for his back – but rather he was taking them because he felt like he had to take extra pills, like he couldn't *not* take them.

Holding Kyle's hand and sitting across from him at the table, Katie's nurse mode kicked in. "Kyle, this is a big deal, but it's going to be OK."

"I don't know if I can stop, Katie."

Katie, not really understanding the hold that addiction had taken onto Kyle's life, tried to encourage him. "Of course you can stop, honey. I'll help you do it."

"There's more."

"More? More what? More pills? More to your story?"

"Pills."

"OK, show me."

For the next few minutes, Kyle led Katie around the house, removing bag after bag of pain pills. Kyle showed Katie bags of pills that were hidden under their bedroom mattress, behind books on the bookshelf, underneath clothes Kyle never wore, in his truck, in her car, and even in a pair of old tennis shoes.

Bewildered, Katie asked, "Oh my gosh, Kyle. This is crazy. Is this all of it?"

"Yes."

"I can't even imagine how much all of this cost! How much was it?"

"I don't know, Katie."

Partly frustrated and partly shocked, Katie grabbed Kyle's collection of pills and emptied them onto the dining room table. It looked like they were kids getting ready to sort their Halloween candy. Katie scooped them all into a bag, abruptly got up, and carried them to the bathroom. She didn't say a word as she made her march. Kyle chased behind her.

"Hey, what are you doing?!" Kyle yelled out of shock.

"Getting rid of them."

"But what about my back? I'll still need some for my back."

"You can take Tylenol."

With Kyle a step or two behind, Katie reached the toilet where she dumped all of the pills. Kyle stepped up beside her and the two of them looked at the pills covering the bottom of the toilet.

Kyle took a deep breath, and said, "I don't think I can do it."

Katie, torn between discipline and compassion, grabbed ahold of Kyle's hand, moved it to the toilet lever, and pushed down on his hand to flush the toilet. Losing her motherly demeanor, Katie shot Kyle a disappointed look and walked back into the kitchen.

Kyle cried in the shower as he replayed Katie's disappointed look. The shower water started to turn cold as Kyle snapped out of his daydream-like remembrance of that fateful night. Kyle reached down and turned off the water. He dried off and went to bed, thinking about his failures and Katie's right to give up on him.

Chapter

13

. . . .

The next morning Katie arrived to work ten minutes early. She was thankful that Sue wasn't working today, but she knew that she was going to have to eventually sit down with Sue and receive whatever chastisement Sue doled out as a result of her outburst with George.

Katie had only been to work about five minutes when Trish walked in.

"What the heck?!" Trish asked/yelled at Katie in the hallway, apparently not caring about who might hear. "Where have you been?"

"I'm so sorry, Trish. I guess I had a meltdown."

"Meltdown? I've been worried sick. You left work early and then you left all of your stuff at my house. You wouldn't return my texts or calls. You called off work on Sunday. I mean, what the heck?"

Brian walked by, slowed down and looked at the women. Trish stared at Katie while Katie stared at Brian. Realizing he wasn't going to be satisfied, Brian walked by.

Katie whispered, "I don't know, Trish. I know it wasn't right. I'm sorry."

Not caring to keep it hushed, Trish continued her rant out loud. "I'm not sure that's good enough, Katie. I mean… where did you even go? You didn't go back home to Kyle did you?"

"No, Trish."

"Thank goodness! So where did you go?"

"I went to a hotel."

"A hotel?!" Trish nearly yelled that. "Why would you pay for a hotel *and* not return my texts or calls? I mean, I don't get it, Katie." Trish's face turned the color of the apple she was eating for breakfast. Katie could hardly make eye contact with Trish, and badly wanted to leave the conversation.

"It's a long story, Trish." Katie paused. "Actually, not long, just really weird and embarrassing. I promise I'll tell you later and I'm sorry. I'm so sorry. Thank you so much for everything you've been doing for me. I'm just confused and a bit of a mess right now."

Trish, still hurt and not ready to accept Katie's apology, snapped back, "Well the princess now knows what it's like to be a mess. Sheesh, you don't even know what real messes are." Trish abruptly turned around and walked away.

Katie hung her head. She couldn't believe that she ghosted Trish the last couple of days – it was so unlike her. Remembering she was at work and had a job to do, Katie walked over to the nurses station and looked at the list of her patients for today. Right at the top, she saw George Marshall's name. Katie sighed and rolled her eyes. She felt bad about the way she snapped at him on Saturday, but she also didn't feel like she could take more of his anger and mean comments today.

The more she thought about it, the bolder she got in her determination to go into his room, put her head down, do her job, and not let him bully her. Yes, she had crossed the line on Saturday, but in all truth, she felt that he deserved it.

Instead of spying around the corner and then gingerly walking into his room, Katie purposefully marched into George's room where she barely looked at him and walked straight to his bedside and the computer next to it. Katie pulled the keyboard up to her stomach, logged in, and began to type. She typed for a full thirty seconds before she even bothered to look at George, who much to her surprise, was asleep.

Katie stopped typing and stared at him, trying to imagine how George's family could stand to live with him all these years. His face looked calm and peaceful as he slept. Katie was surprised. She expected him to look annoyed and angry all the time.

Katie returned to typing in George's chart when she was startled by George's voice. "Hello," he said with a soft voice.

Katie didn't turn her head, but suspiciously looked at George out the side of her eyes.

"Hello," she offered back curtly.

Katie allowed her side gaze to linger for an extra second. George wasn't looking at her and she honestly couldn't tell if he was really awake or just talking in his sleep. Katie returned to typing in his chart.

"I don't think I have much time left."

Katie, again startled that George talked and also startled by the absence of harshness in his voice, stopped typing and turned to face George.

"Well, you never know," Katie said, trying to be polite. "You just might outlive us all."

"I know that won't happen," George replied matter-of-factly, taking one hand and rubbing his eyes.

Katie didn't know how to respond and didn't really feel like responding, so she went back to his chart where she finished up.

As she examined his bags, George spoke again, this time with a little more life and a little less sleep.

"I'm sorry."

Katie was unsure what George meant. Was he sorry that he was dying? Was he sorry that he was mean to her? Was he sorry that he was still alive? Katie wasn't sure what George was sorry for and couldn't even think of a polite way to respond. All she could offer back, was "Yeah?"

"Yeah, I'm sorry. I'm sorry for saying the things I said the other day."

Katie couldn't believe that the cranky old man who she had come to avoid these last two weeks was actually apologizing. She knew that she should happily accept it, but she didn't want to. She didn't think that he should be able to treat her like that and make the entire palliative care unit miserable for the last two weeks and then simply have it wiped out with two quick words.

Instead of accepting his apology or letting it go, Katie felt the overwhelming urge to let George know that sorry wasn't enough. She stood there quietly, acting like she was working on his bags while she tried to figure out what to say and quickly sort through her emotions.

Finally, in a burst that came out a little more aggressively than she intended, Katie said, "You know, sometimes sorry just isn't enough."

George, not used to the position of apologizing, certainly didn't expect her to respond so coldly. He didn't say anything.

Katie, annoyed that he apologized and then annoyed that he didn't respond to her condemnation, decided to give George a little more. She calmed herself and spoke without anger or much emotion at all. "In fact, you can't just take advantage of people and then treat them like they're not important. You can't call people names and you can't be ungrateful when people try to help you."

"I know."

Katie, not satisfied that George really knew, felt her heartbeat pound in her neck and decided that she needed to explain it further. "I don't think you do know," now speaking with a little more volume and waving her hands as she lectured. "I mean, you come in here an absolute mess. You haven't taken care of yourself and you treat your family like crap. You aren't happy that you're going to die and you don't seem happy to live either. Then, we try to do everything we can to make things as easy as possible for you, and you belittle us, and are mad at us, and make us feel like we are insignificant and stupid."

George listened in silence. He closed his eyes and tears sept from underneath his eyelids.

"In fact," Katie continued without really looking at him. Now she waved her arms and paced around the room, almost loud enough to attract attention. "You can't just let people trust you and feel safe with you and give you everything they have and treat them like this. You can't be your own person and fight your demons by yourself and shut me out of your life!"

George, not taking issue with accepting his punishment, opened his eyes and looked at Katie with a confused look. "Shut me out of your life?" he quoted back.

Katie, now with a red face and breathing heavily, paused and looked at George.

"Never mind," she said.

"No, what do you mean?" George insisted, but without being mean or attacking.

"It's not what I meant. I didn't mean to say it to you." Katie looked away from George and logged out of the computer.

"OK," George acquiesced, "but I accept the rest of it. I haven't been a very good person."

Katie, surprised by his admission and now a little embarrassed about her outburst, asked in a much calmer manner, "Why haven't you been a good person? Why are you so mean?"

"I don't know," George said. "It's just how I've always been. I don't feel good about it and I know it hurts people. Goodness, I know I've hurt my wife so much. I can't understand how she's stood to be around me all these years."

"If you know it, then why don't you just stop? Why do you keep doing it?"

"I don't know," George paused. "It's like it's just part of who I am – something I can't control and something I stopped fighting years ago."

"That doesn't seem good enough," Katie said. "You can't stop fighting. When you stop fighting is when you lose."

"Yes, you're right. I suppose I lost a long time ago." George reached up and grabbed Katie's arm. He lifted his head slightly and stared into her eyes. "Don't stop fighting – ever. Don't give up."

Katie was really uncomfortable with George's touch and George's gaze. She froze a second, before moving her arm a little which made him let go. George said, "I suppose I've run out of time to fight." He laid his head back on his pillow and closed his eyes.

Katie didn't have anything left to do in George's room, but she didn't feel like leaving. She grabbed a stool that was against the wall, drug it over beside the bed, and sat on it beside George.

"You don't have to quit now, just because you don't know how many days you have left. You can decide to fight it and change it – even right now."

"Maybe you're right."

Katie sat quietly while George lied on his bed quietly. The both thought about their conversation and the issues of their own lives. Finally George spoke up.

"So, what did you mean by 'shut me out of your life?'"

"Oh, it's nothing. I didn't mean to say it."

"But I think you did. Who is shutting you out of their life?"

Katie felt like she was in a weird, parallel dimension. Here was the ungrateful, irritable, angry George Marshall, asking her to reveal the most gut-wrenching thing her life has ever gone through. She didn't feel like sharing her story with George and she wasn't too interested in whatever unlikely sage advice he could offer in return.

"I don't need to trouble you with it. Seriously, it's nothing. Besides, it seems over now. There doesn't seem to be anything I can do"

"It's obviously not *nothing* and I think someone wise just said 'when you stop fighting is when you lose.'"

Katie, not expecting to receive counsel from the cranky, old man or to have her own words used against her, sat speechless, unsure how to respond. After a moment, she spoke.

"It's my husband. He's been shutting me out. I'm not sure it's worth it anymore."

"Oh, I see. He must be a little bit like me."

Katie snapped back, "He's nothing like you!" She paused for a moment. "I'm sorry. I didn't mean it like that. What I mean is that he is a good man and he has always treated me well. It's just that he's going through something, and he's shutting me out."

"Oh…," George replied. "Well, I can tell you that I'm glad Louise never gave up on me."

"Yeah, I bet."

"This reminds me of a story I heard," George said. "It's an odd story about a man who became a wolf because he wanted to fight off the other wolves and protect his goats. Except that he turned into the thing he wanted to fight – a mean old wolf that killed other people's goats. In the end, he realized that he spent his entire life destroying everything and ending up with nothing."

"Hmmm," Katie said, not really processing the story, but rather thinking about how odd it was that George was sharing some type of parable with her. She never would have guessed that he had this kind of emotional depth. Half thinking about what he said and really just trying to continue the conversation, Katie said "I guess there's some truth in there about letting the wrong things consume us or something."

"Yeah, I guess there is," George said. "Though it's funny, she never really told me what the story was about. I guess it's a matter of personal interpretation."

"Oh yeah, who is *she*? Your wife? Did your wife tell you this life-changing story."

"Ha!" George chuckled. "Louise is good for a lot of things, but stories that illustrate the deeper meanings of life is not in her wheelhouse. Actually, a little girl told me the story."

"Oh, that's nice. Is she your granddaughter?"

"No, I can't really say who she is. I figure she must be someone's granddaughter who's in the hospital. She stops by and visits me sometimes."

"Well, that sounds sweet. We have all kinds of people – old and young – who visit their loved ones in our unit. It seems nice that she would stop in and spend time with you."

"Yeah, she reminds me a lot of my younger sister. She died when we were kids." George paused. "I mean, I know she's not my younger sister, but she wears the same kind of shoes my sister wore."

"Oh, really? Those must be special shoes to still be in style from so long ago."

"I suppose so. She's such a sweet little girl and she always looks so neat and pretty. Those black and white shoes and that pretty red dress."

Katie's brain caught up to her ears and her face slowly turned white. Katie suddenly lost all sense of feeling in her body and felt like she was about to fall off the stool. Seemingly unable to either fall or move, Katie asked, "Little red dress? Is that what you said?"

"Yes, she is such a sweet little girl. If you see her, tell her I said so."

Katie, confused and feeling out of her body, excused herself and left George's room. Not entirely confident in her legs' abilities, she grabbed onto his bedrail and stood up. George was a little offended that she so quickly left. As she walked out of the room, Katie thought, "A little girl? In a red dress? It can't be! Can it?"

Katie, dazed and not really aware of her surroundings, nearly ran directly into Trish in the hallway.

"Hey, watch it!" Trish said, still upset but less antagonistic now that she had the chance to speak her mind.

"Oh, sorry Trish," Katie replied, speaking softly and a little dismissively.

Trish, not too pleased that Katie was dismissive and not groveling like earlier, asked, "Hey, what's up? You about knocked me down!"

Katie blankly looked at Trish and then looked back toward George's room.

Trish followed her gaze and softly asked, "Did something happen with George again?"

Katie looked at Trish. "No, nothing happened.... Well, yes, something did happen.... But nothing like that. He was actually pretty nice."

"Nice? Now that is odd. That would take any of us by surprise."

Katie didn't care about Trish's attempt at lightening the tension. Intently focused on George's shocking revelation, Katie asked, "Trish, do you remember that lady from a few weeks ago?"

"Katie, you've got to be a little more specific than that. We've had a few ladies here in the last few weeks."

"Oh yeah, sorry. Uhm… Lucille. Lucille was her name."

"Oh, for sure! Such a sweet old lady. I wish that lady could have been my grandma."

Katie remembered Lucille's sweet demeanor, broke from her stupor, and smiled. "Yeah, I think we would all love to have grandmas like that."

"So, what about her?"

Katie's face turned serious again. "OK. Now, you're going to think I'm nuts and you kind of made fun of me a few weeks ago, but do you remember when I said that Lucille said she saw a little girl in a red dress?"

"Oh, come on, Katie. Yes, I remember it and I'm also mad that you and Sue weren't sharing with me whatever edibles you were taking that day."

"Ha. Ha," Katie said snottily. "No, I'm serious." Katie gave Trish a disapproving look and then continued. "Anyway, George, who is acting totally different and weird, was telling me that he's been visited by a little girl... in a red dress!"

"What?" Trish asked. 10% unsure about what to think and 90% sure that her friend needed more days off work.

"I'm serious, Trish. This morning he was all apologetic and nice and stuff. He's acting so differently – unlike any way he's been the entire time he's been here. And finally, after we had our little heart-to-heart (which is the last thing I thought would happen today), he told me that a little girl in a red dress has been visiting him and he even shared some weird, life-changing story she told him. He thought maybe she was another patient's granddaughter or something."

"That's weird, Katie. I don't know. There are all kinds of kids in and out of here. I'm sure sometimes there are girls with red dresses."

"Like, I get that, Trish. But he was so different this morning after he said he talked to her, and the story he said she told him was really deep and personal. It really applied to his life. I think that story changed him."

"Hey, ghosts, angels, demons, aliens,… I don't care. If it turns George Marshall into a nicer guy, then I'll take it." Trish really didn't give much thought to spiritual things and didn't plan to start thinking about them now.

"I know it sounds crazy, Trish."

"Yeah, it really does, Katie. But, who am I to judge. It's not like I've got it all figured out or anything."

"Yeah, me too. But there's one more thing. It's like the story that she told him — it's like it applied to me and Kyle too. It was just so weird."

"OK, Katie. Now I know you're going crazy. You're reading into things way too much and jumping to some pretty crazy conclusions."

"Yeah, maybe, Trish. It's just got me kind of weirded out."

Trish, not able to figure out this phenomenon and not really caring to figure it out either, convinced Katie to check out of her hotel later this evening and come back to her apartment for the night. Katie agreed that it would be best to be with people rather than by herself.

Throughout the rest of the day, Katie thought about her conversation with George. She went into his room several other times, but he slept the entire day, even with Louise by his side. Thinking about her marriage, her encounter with George this morning, and the uncertain mess her life had become, Katie decided to finally shoot a text to Margie, her old youth group leader. Margie responded right away, and soon Katie had dinner plans after work.

Chapter

14

. . . .

That evening when he got off work, Kyle, who was still too nervous and ashamed to talk to his wife, had coffee with Ralph. When Kyle saw Ralph Saturday morning at the family meeting, he kept the conversation as brief and as general as he could. He didn't want to tell Ralph anything that had happened, but Ralph could tell that things weren't right. Ralph pressed Kyle a little on Saturday, but Kyle wouldn't budge. So, Ralph kept bugging Kyle through texts on Sunday and Monday, until finally during work on

Tuesday, Kyle sent Ralph a text and asked if they could meet.

Ralph and Kyle usually met at a Starbucks halfway between their houses, but Ralph suggested that this time they meet in the lobby of the recovery center where they go for the family meeting. Ralph could tell that Kyle had some pretty heavy stuff to share and Ralph figured that not only a change of location might help Kyle feel more free to share, but also that sharing in a location where everyone else is talking about recovery might make Kyle more comfortable.

After shaking hands and getting their not-quite-Starbucks coffee from the recovery center cafe, Ralph and Kyle found a table in the corner where Kyle opened up about everything from the last few weeks. Kyle didn't hold anything back. He shared that his back was hurting again. He shared that at first he only wanted to take care of the new pain, but that it became more about wanting to get a hit. He shared about his fateful Thursday shoot up. And, he shared about his fights with Katie and their inability to connect with each other these last few days.

"So, anyway, I really screwed up, Ralph. Katie's so mad and I don't blame her. I feel like I really need to do everything I can to fix my marriage, but everything else in my life feels so out of control that I just feel paralyzed. How can I fix one thing when I'm just a broken mess to begin with? And, why should I feel like I deserve the chance to fix my marriage?"

"Thanks for sharing, brother. That was a really tough thing for you to tell me. I've been there – taking a drug I never thought I'd ever stoop to, taking my marriage to the edge of a cliff and pushing it off, and risking my job all because of my addiction. I get it."

"I feel so bad, Ralph." Kyle had cried through most of his story. At this point his posture was slouched over and he barely looked up at Ralph when either of them talked. "Here you go." Kyle pulled his 30-day chip from his pocket and tossed it on the table over toward Ralph. "I don't deserve this."

"That's not how it works," Ralph said as he took an ink pen and slid the chip back in front of Kyle. "Even when we mess up, the old chips remind us that we were strong enough to do it before, so we can be strong enough to do it again."

Kyle reluctantly picked up the chip. He flipped it over a few times in his hand, looking at it as if it had something insightful to tell him. After a few flips, he put it back in his pocket.

"So, what do I do? How do I get Katie back when I don't even know how I'm going to stay clean. I mean, I know my back will hurt again. I don't know how I can hold down a job when my back hurts and all I can think about is trying to use something to relieve the pain and dull out the emotions."

"Well, my friend, you went to work today, didn't you?"

"Yeah, it wasn't easy, but I did it."

"And, you went to work yesterday, didn't you?"

"Yeah. Again, it wasn't easy. I really just wanted to stay in bed and never get up."

"And, you went to that family meeting on Saturday – without any *family* – didn't you?"

"Yeah…. Hey, what's your point?"

"One day at a time, brother." Ralph smiled broadly as he spoke. He laughed a little and continued. "I know it sounds cliche and everybody says it, but that's really what it takes. You didn't go to work yesterday thinking about how you had to make it to work two days in a row. You went to work yesterday, fought your battles yesterday, and guess what?" Ralph paused, but Kyle didn't take the bait. Ralph answered his own question. "You made it through the day. Then, you went to work today, fought your battles today, and believe it or not, you've almost made it all the way through today, too!"

"I don't know, Ralph. That makes it all sound too simple. But I don't think it's that simple."

"Dang right, it's not that simple. But it also doesn't have to be that complicated, either. Don't confuse complicated with hard." Ralph's face turned serious and leaned in as he said, "Is it hard? Heck yeah, it's hard. But that doesn't mean it's complicated. You just take today's troubles and deal with them today. Don't worry about how many days in a row you can make it or what Katie's thinking this very moment. Just breathe in and breathe out and focus on the breaths that it takes to make one more minute count in your blessed life."

Kyle exhaled, letting Ralph's words sink in. "I suppose that I do overcomplicate things sometimes. But taking things one day at a time doesn't solve all of my problems."

"And you know what, you're not going to *solve* all of your problems. That's not how life works. You'll have problems and you'll need to try your best to fix them. But, some problems can't be fixed and you're never going to be problem free."

"Yeah, I get that. I mean, I know life isn't perfect and won't ever be perfect." Kyle paused, thinking about everything. "So, *one day at a time* is a real thing, huh?"

"Absolutely, just take whatever today throws at you and deal with it. Don't worry about how you're going to do the same thing tomorrow. Don't worry about how well you did yesterday. Just face *today* with all of its joys and sorrows. Face today with all of its temptations and victories. Face today – and only today!"

Kyle and Ralph sat silently as Kyle processed the things that Ralph told him. After a moment, Kyle spoke up.

"Thanks, Ralph. That sounds too easy, but I guess I know that it's really hard. That's how I need to live." He paused for a second. Then he sat up straight and looked Ralph in the eye. "That's how I'm going to try to live." Kyle paused again. "That sounds like the only way I really *can* live."

"That's the spirit, brother!" Ralph said as he slapped the table in front of him. "You're problems won't be magically solved and it's hard as heck, but don't take onto yourself more junk that what the current day gives."

The two guys chatted for a while, catching up on family and sports. Kyle left the recovery center and drove home, reinvigorated and with the best attitude he'd had since his first NA meeting a couple of months ago. Kyle left the recovery center knowing that he belonged there — knowing that his addiction was real and that he was like so many of the other people there too. And, on top of it all, Kyle was OK with that. He was OK with admitting his powerlessness over his addiction. He was OK admitting that it was hard. He was OK admitting that he needed help and support. He knew that life wouldn't be as easy as the natural high he felt tonight from his talk with Ralph, but he celebrated today's victory with joy and relief as he drove home.

Kyle turned around the corner and saw his house. He was disappointed that Katie's car wasn't in the driveway. He had no reason to expect that she would be there. She hadn't been home the last few days and he didn't even answer her phone call yesterday. He just figured that for some magical reason, since he was making the right decisions and since he had this newfound mantra of one day at a time, then she would be waiting at home for him with open arms, ready to reconcile their marriage and move forward together.

"One day at a time," Kyle said out loud, pep talking himself, disappointed that Katie wasn't home. Before he got out of the truck, he decided that he would call Katie and try to talk to her. He was in a better place now. He felt like he could answer her questions now. Certainly she would answer. After all, she just tried to call him yesterday. Now he was ready to talk. Now they could start to work on this together.

Still sitting in his truck in their driveway, Kyle pressed her name on his phone and nervously held it to his ear.

One ring.

"This is it," he thought. "We are going to start fixing this."

Two rings.

"I bet she's ready to come home. I don't even know where she's been sleeping at night."

Three rings.

"Come on, Katie. Pick it up. I'm ready now. Ask me anything you want."

Four rings. Kyle's mind went blank.

Five rings and then voicemail.

Kyle hung up the phone, walked out of his car, and went inside his lonely house.

"One day at a time," he thought to himself, hooking his keys on the hook on the wall.

Kyle went through the bedroom and into the bathroom to take a shower. He flinched as he noticed that his back was starting to hurt a little bit. He took a couple of Tylenol, but was determined that Tylenol was going to be all he took – pain or no pain.

"One day at a time," he said out loud, as he grimaced a little bit when he took off his shirt.

Kyle took his shower and then got ready for bed. He checked his phone every couple of minutes, hoping that Katie had called or texted and that somehow he simply missed it.

Finally, a little later than normal and losing hope that today's one day at a time would be *the day that he fixed things with Katie*, Kyle went to bed. He took one last look at his phone and opened up every app he had, making sure that he didn't miss a message, a text, a snap, a poke, or anything from Katie. Seeing nothing, Kyle reminded himself once again, "One day at a time," and then he went to sleep.

Earlier that evening, Katie didn't even know her phone was ringing when Kyle called her. She had her phone on silent and for some reason it wasn't connected to her watch. Even if she had felt her watch buzz or her phone vibrate, she might not have answered it. She was so engrossed in her conversation with Margie, inwardly fighting back and forth – wanting to accept Margie's wisdom and advice, and at the same time wanting to reject it.

"Everything seems upside down, Margie. It's so crazy. I've never felt like this before in my life."

"Hey there, Katie. It's going to be OK. So it sounds like there's a lot going on right now. Your marriage. Your faith. Is that it?"

Katie had shared just about everything with Margie. She shared her and Kyle's entire story – the injury, their failed pain plan, the pills, the heroin, and now the separation. She couldn't bring herself to share about the night at the line dancing bar, her encounter with Zach, or even her two-night crash at the hotel. She was embarrassed to shed too much light on her darkness and in the process drown out the seeming-fake light of her good-girl past. Katie did, however, share about her struggles with her faith. Inexplicably, Katie didn't have a problem telling Margie about how she struggled believing in God, and how that she hadn't been to church in a long time.

Katie replied to Margie's assessment. "Yes, mostly – my marriage and my faith. I mean..., those are the big things." Margie did a great job listening to Katie over the last fifteen minutes without offering any advice. She wanted to make sure that she had a firm grasp on where Katie was. Katie continued, "But then there's also this little girl, and I can't make sense of it."

"Little girl? What in the world are you talking about? You've told me all about Kyle and his addictions. You've told me about how you haven't been going to church and you're not sure what to believe. Now, what's this about a little girl?"

Katie could see the confused look on Margie's face. Katie regretted saying anything about it, embarrassed by the seeming absurdity of it all.

"OK, so I've had two patients in the last month.... You know that I work with patients who are about to die, right?"

"Yeah, I think I remember seeing that on Facebook. What's it called again?"

"Palliative care."

"Oh, that's right."

"Anyway..., so a couple of weeks ago this sweet old lady in our unit was talking to a little girl who wasn't really in the room. She talked to this non-existent little girl in the moments right before she passed away. I watched her do it – it was kind of eerie and kind of sweet at the same time. It shook me up a bit, but I've seen other patients think that there was something or someone in the room with them before they passed. It sounds really weird, but it's kind of common. It's generally unexplainable, but yet a sweet, intimate moment."

"That *is* weird. So, you've actually seen that before? I've heard stories, but I've never experienced it."

"Yeah it's weird, but it happens all the time — not like with every patient or even every day. But, it does happen a lot."

"That is so fascinating."

"Yeah. Anyway," Katie continued talking in a fast pace and with her hands. When she shared her struggles about Kyle just a few minutes ago, she spoke softly and slowly, often looking off to Margie's side and shuffling her feet. Now she felt invigorated. "I was talking to another nurse about it and I mentioned how weird it felt while I was watching it. It just felt different than the other times I've seen it. I couldn't see anyone, but — I know I keep saying it — but it was just so weird. So, I was telling another nurse about it and I mentioned that the dying woman said she was talking to a little girl who was wearing a red dress." Katie leaned in and whispered to Margie. "That nurse froze in her tracks and told me that several years ago several other patients saw a little girl in a red dress right before they passed away."

Margie shot Katie a look of unbelief. "That isn't just kind of weird — that's really weird!"

"Well, it gets weirder. This other patient I've had since that lady died a couple of weeks ago has been the absolute worst patient I've ever had in my whole life. He's been mean and cranky to everyone. And, he's said some really mean things specifically to me. I actually lost my cool with him once, but we're over that now."

"OK…," Margie wasn't convinced that Katie was really over it.

"So, George and I…. Oops, I'm not supposed to tell you his name. Anyway, *Fred* and I were having a forgive-each-other, heart-to-heart talk when he said that he had been talking to a girl in a red dress too."

"Oh my, that is so crazy." Margie said, dumbfounded. Katie paused, expecting more out of Margie. Margie offered, "Well, I guess this might help with your broken faith."

"I know, right?" Katie smiled and grabbed Margie's arm, excited to share her story and forgetting about all of her doubts. "Anyway, there's more. It's like she's been talking to me through George, … er, Fred. I don't mean like she's talking to me while I'm in the room or we're having a weird seance or anything, but it's like some of the things that she's been helping him with have been helping me too. It's like the advice she's been giving him applies to my life too."

"That's really cool, Katie. And, we shouldn't be surprised, should we? I mean, we know that God works in mysterious ways."

"Yeah, I know…" Katie paused and her smile faded away. The enthusiasm she had in sharing her unique and otherworldly story hadn't transferred to a decision to actually believe anything. "These last few weeks – really these last few months – I've felt like my faith has just been so messed up." Katie thought for a second and Margie stayed silent, letting her think. "But, this has been a cool moment to rethink about my faith and realize that maybe things aren't quite so out of whack." Katie paused again. "I don't know, honestly."

"Well, Katie, in my experience, faith is like an ocean tide. Sometimes it's high and sometimes it's low. Sometimes it's mighty and strong, while other times it doesn't seem to even exist. But, give it time and it will come back – just as strong as before."

"Yeah, I suppose that makes a lot of sense. You always have a way of making sense, Margie. I guess I just haven't had too many times when the tide has been low."

"Well, don't give me too much credit. I struggle like everyone else. I certainly have had my own set of problems too."

The ladies paused for a moment. Katie wasn't sure if she was supposed to ask Margie what she meant about her own problems, but before she could decide to ask, Margie spoke again.

"So, what do you think all of this means for you with Kyle? I mean, maybe your faith is being rekindled by this little girl, and I believe that God is clearly working in your life. You can't separate Kyle from all of that, can you?"

"No.... I mean, I don't know.... I mean, no." Katie paused. "No, I know I can't separate it all from Kyle, but that doesn't mean I don't want to. Honestly I'm not really sure what I'm supposed to do."

"Well he is your husband and you took some pretty serious vows. I even remember the day – I was there, you know. I'll never forget – there's pink everywhere. Your bridesmaids' dresses were pink and of course, your flowers were pink." Margie gave Katie a perplexed look. "By the way, it's kind of odd to see you not wearing pink. That red hair tie wrapped in your hair just doesn't quite look like you."

"Well, pink hasn't been my thing lately. And, yeah, I know we took some pretty serious vows."

"And you already know life isn't easy. You knew when you signed up for this marriage thing that there would be snags along the way. Kyle is a good guy, and addiction is a really hard thing. Certainly you learned something about addiction in college?"

"Yeah, I did. It's just easier to read about it in a book than to experience it in real life. I mean, real life has consequences, doesn't it? Or, at least, shouldn't it?"

"Consequences? I suppose, but I'm not in the business of being the person to dole those out. And, absolutely, it's easier to read about something in a book than to live it in real life, but who wants to live in a book, anyway?"

"True, very true."

"You know, Katie, you had a really solid faith in the youth group. And, as far as I could tell, you had a really solid faith in college. But, the truth is, it's different to have a solid faith in the bubble of a youth group and even in the bubble of a college when you surround yourself with other Christians and you attend Christian clubs and events. And, if Facebook doesn't lie," Margie winked," I would guess that you've had a pretty solid faith as an adult."

Katie blushed.

Margie continued, "It's true that there are some high school, poster-child Christians who don't do so well in college and beyond, but you're like the poster-child of poster children – a solid faith in high school that became a solid faith in college that even became a solid faith in adulthood."

Kate squirmed a little, uncomfortable that someone else was labeling her faith as solid when she knew that it was anything but solid.

Margie kept talking, bubbling out with the advice she had kept in for so long this evening. "But, and this is the big but, now your faith is challenged for real for the first time ever in your life, and I think you are finally grappling with the idea of making your faith your own. It's not going to be the faith of the kid way back in the youth group. It's not going to be the faith of the kid in college. It's not even going to be the faith of the honeymooning woman who had a fairytale marriage. It's going to be a tough, adult, messy faith. That's what you're working toward. And, by the way, that's real life."

Katie felt like crying. Emotionally spent and unable to produce tears, she replied, "I just don't know if I can do that. I know there's something about it all – Kyle, George, that little girl..., and I can't explain it. I just don't know, though, if I want to keep on believing. I don't know if I want to keep on trying. I don't know if I can trust him anymore."

"Trust who? Kyle? God?"

"Either."

Despite their conversation that lasted over two hours and encompassing marriage, having children, working jobs, and even memories from their old youth group, Katie still wasn't quite sure how to move forward. She was really hurt by Kyle and couldn't find the faith to believe that he would really change and that any changes he could make would last forever.

The ladies exchanged hugs and promises to keep in touch rather than just stalk each other on Facebook. It was pretty late and Katie saw she had a missed call from Kyle, but that he left no voicemail. Although she wanted to call him back, she didn't feel like after her conversation with Margie she had the right things to say anymore. She couldn't imagine having the energy to properly talk to Kyle tonight. She also was not ready to go home to Kyle and she knew Trish was already expecting her to come to the apartment, so Katie drove over to Trish's apartment for the night and decided not to return Kyle's phone call.

Although she couldn't see the path to take, Katie had a weird feeling that things in her stalled life were starting to move forward. It scared her a little bit because she wasn't sure if moving forward meant with Kyle or without Kyle. She got to Trish's house twenty minutes later, and after forcing herself to hang out with Trish for a little bit, Katie went to bed on Trish's increasingly familiar couch, knowing that she had another early morning tomorrow at the hospital.

Chapter

15

. . . .

"What color do you dream in?" asked the little girl who was wearing a red dress.

George turned his head toward the girl who was sitting in the corner of the room. George's eyes lit up as he actually let out an audible laugh – something George did very rarely in his life. In fact, George's laugh sounded foreign to himself, as if a third person was in the room laughing instead of him. Smiling because he was happy to see the little girl, George heard what she asked, but wanted to buy a little time to think about it. "What did you say, child?"

"What color do you dream in?" the little girl asked again, not the least bit annoyed that she had to repeat herself.

Although George reacted harshly the first time the little girl asked the question a few nights ago, tonight he didn't belittle the girl or her question, but rather he thought about it for a moment.

"Believe it or not, I've given this question some thought the last few days. And unfortunately, my answer is the same. I dream in red." He paused. "I've tried to dream in other colors these last couple of nights – sometimes in the daytime too. But red is the only color my dreams seem to be able to produce."

"You know, George, dream colors come from within us – deep within us. They come from a place that we know is there, but we are not quite sure how to find it. Your red dreams come from that deep place. Tell me, what do you see when you dream in red?"

"Sometimes I see my sister, Lilly, when I dream. I see her lying on that hospital bed – the bed that she never got back up from.

"Sometimes I see my wife, Louise. Sometimes I dream about how mad I get at her and other times I dream about all of the hurt that I've caused her over the years.

"Sometimes I dream about Tom, or my old job, or my parents.

"Sometimes I dream about nothing in particular at all. I'm just washed over in a seething anger, and all I can see is nothing but red."

"Those sound like very difficult dreams," replied the little girl.

George didn't immediately respond, caught up in his own world – a world of painful memories and critical appraisals. George stared off to the ceiling, unhappy with the contents of his dreams.

Unfazed by the little girl's sympathy with the difficulty of his dreams, George said, "I wish I could do those dreams over. I wish I didn't live my entire life so mad all the time. I wish I would have given Louise the life she deserved. I wish I would have supported and shown Tom love. I even wish I would have been nicer to Rachael – though she never would have been good enough for my Tommy."

"It sounds like you are blessed with people in your life who love you, despite the painfulness of your dreams," the little girl responded, sensing George's frustration and genuine remorse for the life he lived.

"They do love me. And, they're good people too. Unfortunately I wasn't just a terrible person with them in my dreams, I was a terrible person with them in my awakes too. Those were dreams that I lived…, and dreams I made other people live too."

George continued looking at the ceiling, lost in his own world of memories. Over the next several moments, his face provided a window into the emotions that his memories supplied. The little girl watched as George's face contorted into various disapproving shapes and as the small tears that his eyes could muster slowly fell down onto his dry, wrinkled cheeks.

A moment later, George snapped out of his catatonic state and turned his head back to the girl. George studied the little girl. Although he had seen her a couple of times now, he was still surprised by the warmth and joy he felt when he looked at her. She was a pretty little girl — her long blond hair was unbraided and neatly brushed.

Studying the little girl's hair reminded George about Lilly's hair. He hadn't seen Lilly's hair in his memories for many years. Lilly's hair was different than the little girl's hair — George could see it clearly in his mind now. Lilly's hair was always tied into two braids that rolled down her back. George smiled as he remembered Lilly's hair for the first time in decades. He could picture her two braids bouncing up and down as she ran around their yard. He could picture his mother brushing Lilly's hair after her bath and putting her hair up into those two braids. He could picture Lilly putting her doll's hair into two braids to perfectly match her own.

George continued studying the little girl. She wore a crisp, short-sleeve red dress that extended just past her knees. The little girl's feet swayed back and forth just an inch or two off the floor as she sat in the big chair in the corner of the room. George looked the closest at the little girl's shoes — black and white Saddle Oxford shoes, just like the ones Lilly used to wear.

George appreciated the visits he had with the little girl. Despite his unpleasant memories of an unfulfilled life, these last couple of weeks had been quite the journey for George. He had a lot of time to think and a lot of time to remember. George did not like thinking about his life so intently. He was disappointed in the man he was and he regretted how he lived his life. However, during this last day or two his thoughts were begrudgingly leaning more forward than backward. Like an alarm clock awakening a weary worker for an upcoming day of drudgery, the fear of the uncertainty of what might come even felt worse than focusing on the disappointing thoughts of what used to be.

George stared at the little girl, and for no reason that seems logical to share with a little girl, George confessed, "I'm afraid of what's to come."

"Not knowing what is to come can be exciting," replied the little girl, unfazed by George's transparency. "Like the moment before you unwrap a present – that is a most exciting time."

"I don't know if this is a gift that I want to unwrap." George paused for a second, looked up at the ceiling, and continued. "I mean, I know that we all have to do it. I understand that it's just part of life. But that doesn't mean I have to *want* to do it, does it?"

"You do not have to *want* to do it," replied the little girl, speaking matter of factly, yet warmly. "But, you do not have to fear it either."

George didn't respond. He continued looking up at the ceiling, deep in thought, trying to process his fears and uncertainties.

"I don't know what's to come. I haven't had a faith like Louise's faith. I used to go to church, but that was as a little boy. I stopped believing in God when Lilly died. I don't know if God stopped believing in me, too – and that's a little scary."

"When I am scared," said the little girl, "I just fold my hands like I am praying and close my eyes." The little girl demonstrated for George. "I just kind of drift away – I do not have to be in the scary place anymore. I can be somewhere nice, like in a field with pretty flowers or on the floor playing with a puppy."

"Like the puppy you took home from the animal shelter?" chimed in George.

"Yes, like the puppy I brought home from the animal shelter," the little girl said as she giggled.

George looked back at the little girl and the little girl smiled at George. It was a warm smile and it made George feel lucky to have the company of such a sweet, innocent creature with him on this dark, scary Tuesday night.

George wanted to see the little girl better, and he moved his hand to a button on his bedrail. George raised the head of his bead so that he could see the little girl more easily.

"There, that's better," George said. "Now I can see you nice and clear."

Despite his ability to see the little girl better, George closed his eyes. He desperately wanted to dream in the little girl's favorite dream color, white. George tried to think of white things – paper, snow, a magician's white rabbit, Louise's fine China – but he struggled holding onto those pictures as they were replaced with various hues of red.

George coughed and clutched his chest. "I think I'm going to rest some now. You can stay if you like."

"That is fine with me. I will just sit here in this chair while you rest."

George drifted asleep, though subconsciously his brain kept working through the memories of his life and pondering the short amount of time that he had left to try to live his life any differently.

Katie woke up on the familiar couch, strangely refreshed and ready to attack the day. She had a lot going on today. She would see Sue at work today for the first time since Saturday's outburst, she would undoubtedly come across Zach, and she knew that one way or another she and Kyle needed to talk this evening after work. Despite feeling rested and motivated to go about her day, Katie was strangely without a plan or without an inkling of how any of her conversations would go.

Katie tried to think about her first awkward task, her upcoming conversation with Sue. Normally she would be apprehensive about working through such a conflict, but today she seemed indifferent. It's not that she didn't care, but rather Katie had confidence that she could handle the consequences, no matter how heavy or light. And, on cue, Katie happened to park beside and even walk into work with Sue.

"Good morning, Sue," Katie said a little sheepishly as she caught up to Sue who was already five steps ahead of her.

"Good morning," Sue replied, unusually warm. Not previously thinking about Saturday's outburst, Sue suddenly remembered what happened and reevaluated her greeting, determining that this shouldn't be just another normal morning greeting. Katie could faintly see the half smile on Sue's face turn sour.

"So, are you feeling like wishing any patients dead today?" Sue asked, not joking.

"No, Sue. Not today." Katie chuckled, making an attempt to be funny, but she knew that her audience probably wouldn't see it that way.

"Well, I sure hope not. You're lucky that Mr. Marshall's family hasn't said anything,… yet. You could get us all in real trouble."

"Yeah, I'm sorry about that, Sue. I've just been having a really tough time. I mean, I know it's not an excuse…. Don't worry, it won't happen again."

"You're darn right it won't happen again. If it does, then you might not have the chance to let it happen a third time." Sue enjoyed flexing whatever power she perceived herself to have.

Katie walked in silence and didn't reply. It's not that Sue had the power to fire her, but Katie knew that outbursts like hers weren't good for any nurse, let alone a palliative care nurse.

When they made it to the elevator, Sue spoke again.

"You're going to have to apologize, you know."

"Yeah, we already made up. I talked to him yesterday." Katie didn't feel like mentioning George's encounter with the little girl in a red dress.

"Well, you can talk to him again today. I'm not putting him on your load – I'm not that dumb. But you still need to talk to him again, just to make sure he's OK."

"Believe it or not, Sue. I was actually planning to do that already."

Nearing their floor on their shared elevator, Sue shot Katie a half-annoyed look. Sue was hoping she was punishing Katie by making her talk to George. Sue exhaled and didn't respond.

As the elevator dinged and the ladies walked onto the floor, Sue grabbed Katie's arm and stopped her.

Katie was a little surprised that Sue grabbed her arm and even more surprised when she turned to look at Sue who had an actual look of compassion mixed with a touch of seriousness on her face.

"By the way," Sue spoke in a hushed tone. "I've heard some of the things that's been going on with you and Kyle. Billy and I went through some of the same things years ago. Billy used to be on the bottle, but he's been sober for twenty years. If you need to talk, let me know."

Sue let go of Katie's arm and kept walking while Katie stood still, blocking the door to the elevator. Katie was shocked equally by Sue's display of a heart and also by Sue's admission that her own husband was in long term recovery.

A moment later, Katie started her morning shift and actually traded Trish patients so that she could have George. Trish thought Katie was crazy when Katie refused Trish's offer to buy her lunch, but Trish wasn't going to say anything to risk Katie changing her mind. Trish was happy to not have to deal with cranky George – or even worse, ghost hunter George.

Katie walked into George's room soon after she arrived at work and was disappointed to find him asleep. She did the necessary work on his chart and reviewed his care plan for the day. After she was done, instead of leaving the room, Katie pulled up the stool from beside the wall and watched George sleep. She wondered what was going on in his dreams as he slept. She wondered if he was a changed man or if their encounter yesterday was nothing more than the incomprehensible talkings of someone so near his last days of life.

As Katie sat there, she thought about her own life. She didn't want to live a life of regrets like George had lived. But, what did that mean? Katie couldn't decide if staying with Kyle would lead to that life of regrets – a life full of suspicion and deceit, a life full of disappointment and broken promises. On the other hand, Katie wondered if a life of regrets would instead come from the incorrect decision to leave Kyle. She feared that maybe the cost of such an action would set her life on a course not too dissimilar from George's life – a course of bitterness and loneliness, a course of shutting out other people from her life.

Katie sat there for a few minutes, hoping that George would wake up. While trying to make the decision to get up and leave, Katie realized that the head of George's bed was raised. She reached over to lower it and then froze. Katie had a flashback to lowering Lucille's bed right before she died. Katie decided to leave the bed in place and turned around to look at the chair in the corner of the room. It was empty.

Katie looked back at George, hoping that he was waking up. He was not, so she got up from her stool, gently placed it back beside the wall, and left his room to visit her other patients.

Some time later that morning with Katie out of his room, George woke up from his sleep. He felt out of sorts and wasn't quite sure where he was or what was going on. He cracked open his eyes and saw a breakfast tray sitting beside his bed. Slowly remembering where he was, he looked past the breakfast tray to see if the little girl was still in the corner of the room.

"Are you still there, child?" George asked as he looked over at the girl from his raised bed.

"I am still here," she called out, able to see that George was looking for her.

"Thank you for staying. I had some more dreams," George said. "And, I tried as hard as I could, but those dreams were still red."

"That is OK. It is very nice that you are trying."

"I suppose," George replied. Then, even though he knew the answer, George asked, "What color did you say you dream in, again?"

"I dream in lots of colors, but white is my favorite color to dream in. I really like white because it is so clean and pure."

"It seems like white would be a very nice color to dream in."

"Oh, it is such a wonderful color. Many people don't choose white as their favorite color, but to me, white represents peace. I think of white as something being made clean. I think of white as restoring hope. I think of white as finding a purpose."

"I don't think I could ever dream in white. Those things sound so nice, but they sound so foreign and far away from me. And, besides, I don't think I have the time left to figure out how to get there."

"That is OK," the little girl replied. "Maybe you do not have to see white in your dreams. Maybe your dreams can be a mix of where you've been and where you'd like to be. Maybe it would be enough for your dreams to be a mix of both red and white."

"I think I would like that," George proclaimed. George had been very emotional during the last few days, crying some of the only times of his adult life and feeling things like remorse and empathy some of the only times of his adult life.

But now, visiting with this little girl on this late Wednesday morning after yet another set of dreams painted all in red, George experienced mixtures of emotions that he had never experienced together before. He was sad, yet hopeful. He was disappointed in himself, yet repentant.

"I'm so sorry for my life," George said.

"I know you are. It is OK to be sorry, but you do not have to stay there."

"I don't think I have enough time left to go anywhere else."

"If you have enough time to say you are sorry, then that is all the time that you need."

George closed his eyes, thinking about the little girl's words, and then he fell asleep.

Chapter

16

. . . .

Midmorning, Katie took a walk by herself to the hospital cafeteria to grab a snack. Turning a corner in the hallway, she literally ran into Dr. Zachary Moore.

"Hey, watch out!" Zach called out before he realized who ran into him.

"Excuse me," Katie replied, averting her eyes while moving around Zach, hoping to walk by unnoticed.

Katie didn't get two steps away from Zach before he called out, "Hey, wait a second."

Katie rolled her eyes, turned around to face Zach, and raised her eyebrows while placing her hands on her hips. Katie asked in an annoyed tone, "What?"

"I'm sorry. I didn't know it was you."

"It shouldn't matter who it is. A decent person doesn't tell someone to 'Watch out' when he runs into them."

Without missing a beat, Zach shot back, "Yeah? Well, first of all, you ran into me. And, second of all, a *decent person* doesn't dance with someone who isn't her husband."

Katie was mortified, all at once feeling that Zach was going to use their unfortunate moment as leverage over her – making her live forever in fear of people finding out what happened.

Katie paused in her shock, collected herself, and then said somewhat defiantly, "Yeah, you're right. But you kind of took advantage of me."

Zach got immediately defensive, "Hey, wait a minute! I didn't do anything wrong!" A scared look washed over Zach's face and he whispered. "You can't say that to anyone!" Zach paused. "You haven't said that to anyone, have you? That I... *took advantage of you*? You know that's not the way it happened."

Katie exhaled loudly and let down her defenses. "No, I haven't said that. And, I didn't mean it like that. I just had a really bad day on Saturday and I drank more that evening than I've drunk in the entire last year. You shouldn't ask a married woman to dance."

Ignoring the advice, Zach replied, "Whew! I just don't need someone going around saying I'm trying to use my power to manipulate women or something."

Katie rolled her eyes and said, "Yeah, well that didn't *exactly* happen, but just so you know – I'm not interested. I'm married and that's that."

"OK, OK, I'll back off." Zach looked away from Katie and looked at his reflection in the glass of an empty patient room beside them. He touched his hair, fixing something he thought was out of place. In a weird, creepy way, Zach turned back to Katie, winked, and said, "Catch you later." She stood still while he turned around and continued walking down the hall. Katie rolled her eyes again and continued on to the cafeteria to get a snack.

While Katie was away from the floor, George woke up again, though this time he didn't open his eyes. The little girl could tell he was awake.

"I'm afraid," George said with small tears starting to run down his face.

"You will be fine, George. Very soon, you will be fine," the little girl spoke, reassuring George and speaking with a maturity and authority that most little girls did not possess.

Without opening his eyes, George smiled.

"Do you like to read, George?" the little girl asked.

George, feeling weak and tired, barely opened his eyes as he talked. "Yes…, some. I read the newspaper just about every day. And I like old western books. I always was a sucker for anything out west." George paused. "I don't suppose I've got much reading left in me, though."

The little girl asked, "Do you know what my favorite part of a book is?"

"What?"

"The end of the book. Now, do not misunderstand. I am sad when a really good story is over, but I especially like the end of the book. Do you know why, George?"

"No, I suppose I don't."

"I like the end of a book because that is where we get to see the final result. That is where we get to see our hero be heroic. That is where we get to see the happily ever after. That is where we get to see that, despite all of the scary and bad things that happened to someone in a story – or even all of the scary and bad things that someone did in a story, they can make it all right at the end."

"Yes, I suppose that is a lovely part of a book."

"You have written many chapters in your book, George."

George thought for a moment. "Yes, and I suppose that I'm just about finished writing them, too."

"You still have control over how it ends. You still get to be the hero. You still get to have your happily ever after."

George's eyes moistened with only the tiniest amount of tears they could muster. George thought about his life – his wife and his son, his job, and even his neighbors. George thought about his own parents and his little sister. George thought about the cars he owned and the projects he did around the house after Louise nagged him enough.

The little girl watched George intently as he reminisced. She could see the warmth in his face as he thought about his happy memories. She could see a pleasant expression barely creep across George's face. She said, "It looks like you are having dreams that are white."

George didn't respond. The longer he thought about the good things, the more the bad things slowly crept in and overtook the good memories. Eventually, George could only remember bad memories. George thought more about his anger and bitterness. He thought about how he acted impossibly with his wife and was unloving to his son. He thought about how he hated the hot days at his job and how that he would sometimes act like he wasn't home when he saw a neighbor out walking a dog. He thought about his parents – his own father's cruelty (on the days that his father bothered to be around). And, most painfully of all, he thought about his sister and the unfortunately short life that she was sentenced to live.

The longer George read through the chapters of his life, the more tense his face became. He was filled with regret and sadness.

The little girl, watching George's transition from peace to angst, spoke again. "Are you OK, George?"

George started licking his lips and moving his lips, but he didn't talk.

"Are your dreams red again, George?"

George still didn't speak. His eyes were closed, but they began to release small tears.

"I can't change it," George finally said.

"You do not have to change it. You are right, you cannot change it. Take the good and the bad – the white dreams and the red dreams – and let them flow together. Finish your story well, George."

"I want to finish well. I want to believe I can. I'm so sorry for who I've been."

"You are finishing well, George."

"How do I know I am? I've been so bad."

"Wanting to finish well is evidence that you are finishing well, George."

"I want to believe."

"You have already believed, George. You just have to let that belief out of the prison that you locked it in so many years ago."

"I want to believe," George repeated with his eyes still closed.

The little girl watched George as he fought within himself.

His face relaxed a little as he whispered again, "I want to believe."

The little girl in a red dress, sitting in a big chair in the corner of the room, watched George drift off to sleep as he barely whispered one more time, "I want to believe."

Katie carried her snack back to the palliative care unit to eat in the break room. Shortly after she sat down to eat, Sue came into the room and sat across from her.

"I don't really know the details, but I hear you've been having a rough go of it," Sue said.

"That's putting it mildly."

"Well, you don't need to tell me all of your business, but let me tell you a little bit of mine."

Sue settled into her seat and Katie leaned forward, not believing that Sue was about to open up.

Sue said, "A long time ago – before we had kids – Billy was just getting worse and worse with his drinking. I know people don't expect it from me now, but we both used to be quite the partiers. We were always looking for a good time and we measured how good our time was by how little of it we remembered the next morning."

Katie listened to Sue in shock, unable to picture Perfect Sue trashed and passed out.

"Anyway, I could handle it better than Billy – I just knew when to stop. He wasn't terrible, but he couldn't go a day without drinking. And, sometimes he would drink too much and get kind of mean with me.

"Well, I found religion and Billy didn't. I stopped drinking and Billy didn't. Finally, I was so fed up with it, I told Billy that I wasn't starting a family with him like this and that I had a lot of good years left to live – I wasn't going to waste them on him. I quite my first job at this hospital, packed up my bags, and left town. I actually moved to Florida for six months – lived with an aunt down there."

Katie wanted to offer an obligatory *uh huh* or *yeah*, but she couldn't speak. Mostly she was shocked by Sue's admission to being a drunk, but she was also shocked by the mere fact that she and Sue were having a heart-to-heart talk.

"Now, I don't need to know any of your business, but does any of this sound familiar?"

Katie, realizing that now she had to talk, offered back, "Yeah, it actually kind of does."

"Well, let me tell you that I was serious. We were through. And eventually Billy found God too and we got back together. So, you can say it all worked out, but I made one big mistake."

Katie was curious – not because she was ready to apply Sue's great truth to her own life, but curious in the same way that someone can't wait to find out what happens the next day on a soap opera. Despite the seriousness of the conversation and all of the difficulty her life was currently embroiled in, Katie leaned forward as she anticipated hearing Sue's first ever admission to making a mistake.

Sue looked at Katie, waiting for a cue to go on.

Katie, realizing her role, said, "And what was that mistake?"

"I just about killed the man, Katie." Sue paused and Katie looked on, wide-eyed. "I don't mean that I about took a gun and shot him, but my leaving those six months just about drove him to his grave. He got into a really dark place and I almost lost him. Now, I don't know your situation and I'd never tell you to go live with someone who is abusive or who risks your safety, but I will tell you my story. And my story is that I gave up on Billy too soon. I didn't do my job of being his wife. I almost lost him – thank God that I didn't – and now I don't know what I'd do without him. He's my husband – the man I married – the man I wanted be with my entire life – and I almost lost it all."

Katie, now less enthralled with Sue's sudden humanity and more convicted by Sue's words, was overcome with emotion. Katie didn't cry and she didn't speak. She just looked straight ahead as her eyes glossed over and her feelings went numb.

Katie didn't know what to say about Billy. She didn't know what to say about Kyle. After a moment of silence, Katie spoke, "Yesterday George said that he saw the little girl – the one in a red dress."

Sue's eyes opened wide. She didn't expect their conversation to go in this direction and was actually a little annoyed that Katie didn't offer some profession of her debt of gratitude or a newfound revelation of purpose. Nevertheless, Sue was surprised to hear about the little girl and replied, "Really? He told you that?"

"Yeah, he said something about how that she has been visiting him and talking with him."

"That is really unbelievable. And, to think – two of *your* patients now in the last month."

Sue looked at Katie with convictingly big eyes.

Katie was uncomfortable and broke eye contact with Sue. Katie said, "I know – it's weird. I don't know what to think. Could it mean something?"

Sue paused as she looked off in space for a moment. "I don't know, Katie. Weirder things have happened. Maybe it does mean something."

Sue reached over and grabbed both of Katie's hands, gave them a squeeze, and then left the break room, mumbling something about the little girl under her breath. Katie watched Sue leave the room, and sitting at the table by herself, Katie's emotions were once again flooded beyond her ability to think or process.

Chapter

17

. . . .

George slept in long spurts most of the day. Katie came into his room several times, curious to see if his softness from yesterday was a fluke, and also curious to see if she could get a glimpse of the mysterious little girl in one of her equally mysterious interactions with George.

After lunch, Louise and Tom came to visit George one of the times Katie was in his room, needlessly inspecting George's bags and hoping that he would wake up.

"Good afternoon," Katie called out as she looked down at her watch to make sure that it was, in fact, afternoon.

"Hello, dear," Louise called back, walking into the room with Tom behind her.

"My name is Katie. I'm Mr. Marshall's nurse today."

"Oh, I know who you are, dear. I've seen you around. And, you can call him George. Only people who are scared of him call him Mr. Marshall." Louise spoke matter of factly, not intending to be funny.

Katie let out an unguarded chuckle and then quickly composed herself.

Louise looked at Katie in a way that Katie thought Louise might be annoyed. Katie became nervous that perhaps Louise heard about her outburst a few days ago or even that Louise was simply offended that she chuckled. Louise spoke mockingly, "So, I see you've got to experience a little bit of the pleasant George Marshall."

Tom chimed in, "I apologize in advance, miss. He can be quite a handful."

Katie relaxed and looked at Louise and then turned to Tom. "No need to apologize, sir." Turning back to Louise, Katie added, "And I'm sorry, ma'am. I didn't mean to laugh. Yes, I have gotten to know George a little bit. We have had some interesting interactions."

"Well, don't mind him. He's a bitter old man and I'm afraid that I haven't been able to do anything about it."

"Oh, no, quite the contrary." Katie started speaking excitedly, like she was about to let Louise in on a big secret. "Yes, we've had a few rocky moments, but we had a really good conversation yesterday. It's like he was a totally different person."

"It must be the drugs taking effect," Tom snidely said.

"Tommy…" Louise chided as she swatted at Tom's hand and missed.

"I don't know," Katie said. "He's not on anything that should affect him like that. You'll find that being here in the palliative care unit gives people time to think and reevaluate things in their lives."

"I'll believe it when I see it," Tom said.

"Well, I hope that you get to see it," Katie added and then turned white, wishing she could stuff those words back into her mouth. After an awkward pause, Katie said, "Well, I don't think there's anything I need to do here – I'll go now. Let me know if there's anything else that you need."

Katie left Louise and Tom in the room. Louise pulled up a small chair beside George's bed while Tom stood over by the window.

Louise stared at George. His face was relaxed. He was asleep, but he wasn't snoring. In fact, with the exception of the small rhythmic rise and fall of his chest, it was difficult to know for sure that he was even still alive. "He looks so peaceful, Tommy."

"Yeah, he does." Tom replied, not feeling quite as warmly about his dad.

"I suppose it won't be long." Louise said as she reached down and placed her hand on top of George's hand.

When Louise laid her hand onto his hand, George jerked a little bit and then slowly opened his eyes.

Louise looked at George and wanted to smile, but years of unreciprocated smiles trained her not to bother.

"Hi, Louise," George struggled to say, having trouble getting enough saliva to speak.

"Hi, George," Louise replied. She leaned over to the side and said, "Tommy's here too."

George slowly turned his half-open eyes up to Tom. Tom called out, "Hi, Dad."

With the little strength that he could muster, George squeezed Louise's fingers as she had wrapped her fingers around his hand. George slowly lifted his other hand toward Tom. His hand trembled as he raised it four inches off his bed, not too differently than the way it trembled when he was angry at Tom just a few weeks ago. This was not an angry tremble, however, it was an invitation. Tom was surprised, and he walked up beside his mom and took ahold of his dad's shaking hand.

George squeezed Louise and Tom's hands. Despite his weakness, he squeezed both of them hard and his entire arms started to tremble.

Louise began to cry – she wasn't used to much of any type of physical touch from George. Tom's eyes even teared up.

George opened his eyes fully and they also moistened as he spoke, "I'm so sorry."

Louise sniffled her nose and replied, "You can't help it, dear. It's just your body is about done – it's not your fault."

George closed his eyes and shook his head slowly and forcefully while maintaining his fierce grip. He opened his eyes a second time and his arms trembled again. "No," he gruffed. "I've been a terrible man. I'm so sorry."

Louise sniffled again. "There, there, George. It's OK."

253

George closed his eyes another time and again forcefully shook his head back and forth. He squeezed his lips together and contorted his face. "No," he said, reopening his eyes. He continued to speak, slowly and laboriously. "I've been miserable to you, Louise – I've been so mean. And Tom, I've been such a terrible dad to you. Neither of you have to forgive me, but I'm so sorry."

Louise hardly ever heard an apology come out of George's mouth and didn't know what to say. Her heart was filled with warmth and in an instant she was ready to forget fifty years of pain and misery. Instead of hurt, her heart overflowed with love for the man who held tightly onto her hand.

Tom was fully crying now as well, something that he tried not to do in front of his dad when his dad bothered him. He let down his guard today. Unlike so many of his hidden cries before, these weren't tears of anger or frustration. Yet, these weren't tears of joy or relief either. He rarely had an intimate moment with his dad and Tom couldn't decide if he should be happy or mad. Tom couldn't decide if he should be forgiving or if he should remain stubbornly obstinate.

Louise spoke, "I love you George. I really do. And I forgive you. I really do."

George coughed a heavy cough and released Tom's hand as he reached for his chest.

"It hurts," George said.

Louise, not wanting to let go of George's other hand, grabbed her handkerchief out of her purse with her free

254

hand and wiped George's mouth. "There, there. It's OK," she said, "Don't get yourself worked up. It's OK."

George, still holding Louise's hand, moved his other hand back away from his chest. He looked at Tom and said, "Tom, I've been really bad. Don't treat your family like I've treated you."

Tom, with a few tears still running down his face, replied, "I don't, Dad."

George continued, nearly oblivious to Tom's response. "And you treat Rachael right too, you hear? And those girls... you love them good, OK?"

"OK, Dad," Tom softly said, barely able to speak. Although George wasn't offering his hand to Tom, Tom reached down and squeezed his dad's free hand.

George closed his eyes and his breathing became more labored. Tom reached his other arm around his mom and the three of them embraced, Louise's hand in George's hand, George's other hand in Tom's hand, and Tom's other arm around his mother.

Over the next half minute, George's grip weakened and he fell asleep, seeming to breathe worse with every breath. Eventually Tom let go of his dad's hand and lifted his arm from his mom, but Louise sat in the chair beside George's bed, clinching George's hand with both of her hands, afraid to let go of this intimate moment and now finding herself reluctant to let go of her husband's life.

Over the next two hours, George's breaths turned into gasps for air. Louise didn't cry, but had perpetually wet eyes as she watched her husband drift farther and farther from life.

Finally, Tom suggested that they both take a walk to go to the bathroom and find a drink. Louise acquiesced. Standing up, she looked at her dying husband, and said, "It's OK, George. You can go. I love you." Tom put his arm around his mother as she released George's hand, and the two of them left the room.

Katie, who was sitting at the nurses station, saw Louise and Tom leave the room. She smiled at them when they walked by. Tom returned the smile while Louise wiped her eyes with her handkerchief. As soon as they turned the corner, Katie wanted to leap up and check on George still yet another time. Unfortunately, Sue was sitting beside her and had been bugging Katie to get some of her charts caught up. Frustrated and afraid she might miss something special, Katie sat at the desk and hurriedly did her work.

A few moments after Louise and Tom left his room, George cracked open his eyes and saw the little girl in a red dress standing beside his bed.

"It is almost time," the little girl said.

"I don't think I'm ready."

"Most people are not ready."

"I need more time."

"You have had all of the time that you need."

"I haven't spent my time well."

"You have spent your time just exactly as you have – you cannot change that. Well or not well. Good or not good. It is all about how the book ends, George."

Katie couldn't help herself and got up from her chair to at least walk past George's room. She peeked in and saw that his breathing was labored and that Louise and Tom were still out of the room. Katie aborted her walk-by inspection and instead went into the room to check on George and hope for something from the little girl. Maybe this would be the time that Katie actually saw the little girl. Maybe Katie would hear the little girl talk. Or, at the very least, maybe Katie would feel the little girl's presence. Katie recognized that George was in his last moments of life. As she quietly walked into the room, Katie saw George's mouth move, but she could not hear him speak.

George spoke to the little girl, "I don't know if they forgive me."

"Forgiveness can be a long process," the little girl replied.

Katie's hair stood on the back of her neck as she realized that, like with Lucille a few weeks ago, Katie was once again experiencing an interaction with the little girl. Katie watched George move his lips as he talked to the little girl, but Katie didn't hear anything that he said. His eyes were closed, but she could tell when George was speaking and she could tell when George was listening. Katie looked around the room over and over again, trying very hard to catch a glimpse of who George was talking to.

The little girl continued speaking to George. "We are not responsible for making people forgive us. We are only responsible to make it possible for them to forgive us. Many times, we will never know if people forgive us, and that is OK."

Katie watched George nod his head as he agreed with the little girl's words. Katie could only wonder what the little girl was telling George. Maybe she was telling George that it was time to die. Maybe she was telling George that everything would be OK. Maybe she was congratulating George on his recent, almost-too-late change. As she watched George's reactions to the little girl, Katie was shocked when she heard George talk out loud as he repeated the little girl, "Forgiveness can be a long process."

Very surprised, Katie asked, "What did you say, George?" Katie stared at George, frozen after he spoke. She saw that his eyes were closed and his breathing was terrible. He seemed asleep, but she actually saw his mouth move and she actually heard him speak those words out loud.

George didn't acknowledge Katie's question and she continued to watch him as his mouth moved again, but, like before, he didn't make any sounds. Katie tried to read his lips, but she couldn't tell what he was saying.

George asked the little girl. "How can I know? I don't want to leave here without knowing that they forgive me. Especially Tom... I want to know that he forgives me. Please, please tell me – how can I know that they forgive me?" George pleaded with the little girl, wondering if perhaps she had the power to grant forgiveness or even just the power read a person's mind and heart.

"You have to have faith," the little girl replied.

Again, as Katie stood in the room, watching George's mouth move, she heard him speak a second time out loud when George repeated the little girl, "You have to have faith."

Katie started to cry, not sure what was going on, but overwhelmed with emotion. Through her blurry eyes, Katie scanned the room again, hoping to see the little girl somewhere in the hospital room. She looked over by the window, hoping to see the little girl standing on the floor beside her. She looked over at the chair in the corner, hoping to see the little girl sitting there. She even looked up at the ceiling, hoping to perhaps see the little girl floating above George. Katie repeated George's statements in her head, "Forgiveness is a long process. You have to have faith."

Katie started thinking about Kyle and their marriage. Was the little girl talking to her? Was George talking to her? Katie shook her head, convincing herself that it was ridiculous to think that this little girl was speaking to her.

Katie chastised herself for her thoughts. She thought, "I can't believe this. There isn't some angel or ghost or other being in here telling me to forgive my husband. That isn't that way God works, is it? That isn't what really happens in life, is it? Is God here? Is God anywhere? Does God really do these things?"

Katie looked around the room again and then back at George. Through her tears, Katie's mouth seemed to be working a few steps ahead of her mind when she whispered, "I don't know if I can stand the long process to forgive. I don't know if I have faith anymore."

Katie didn't even know who she was talking to. Was she talking to George? Was she talking to the mysterious little girl in a red dress? Was she going crazy?

George didn't hear Katie speak and he continued his conversation with the little girl. His mouth moved, though yet again, Katie could not hear him say anything.

"I had another dream, just a little bit ago," George said to the little girl, who looked intently at George as he spoke. Katie couldn't hear anything they were saying.

"Oh, that sounds nice," the little girl said warmly.

"I think it might be my last dream."

"Yes, it will be your last dream, George."

"I saw Louise and Tommy. I saw Tom's family — Rachael and Elyse and Brynna. And I saw Lilly, too."

"That sounds like a very good dream, George."

"It was. It was a good dream."

"Tell me, George, did you dream in red again?"

"No," George replied, with a bit of pride.

Katie continued to watch George's mouth move. She cried and prayed out loud. "God, what am I supposed to do? How do I know it will work out? How can I be the wife I'm supposed to be? How can I believe it when I don't know that I believe it?"

The little girl responded to George with a hint of surprise. "Oh, that is really nice, George. Tell me, did you actually dream in white this time?"

"No," George said frowning, this time a little disappointed in himself.

Katie continued to pray and cry. "How do I do this, God? How do I go on? How do I be strong? How do I know this is real. How do I know that you are real?" Katie prayed out loud in anguish, unafraid of who might hear her and what they might think.

The little girl asked George, "So, if you did not dream in red and you did not dream in white? What color did you dream in, George? Did your reds and whites blend together, George? Did they swirl together like two types of ice cream on a hot, summer day? Did who you are and what you want to be collide into a beautiful new you, a mixing together of old and new, a mixing together of hurt and hope?"

George nodded his head slowly as the little girl spoke, affirming her questions.

The little girl smiled a genuine and big, beautiful smile. She asked George one more time, "So, if it was not red and it was not white, what color did you dream in?"

George spoke – this time was his last time. As his lips moved, he audibly said out loud and Katie heard him say, "Pink."

Katie balled as George said out loud this last, single word. George took in an especially deep breath, exhaled it, and then never breathed in again.

Chapter

18

. . . .

Katie stared at George, who looked somehow both lifeless and yet so full of life at the same time. She was numb, thinking about the totality of George's final words — not quite able to fully process his actual words, but rather the emotions she felt from hearing him speak out loud the words that he was saying to the little girl. In a feeling that was completely foreign, Katie felt like she had absolute clarity and peace about everything, though she didn't have a specific plan or general idea about what she was supposed to do about anything. Her peace was overwhelming and it calmed her spirit in a way that she imagined might only be possible when she, herself, passes from this world into the next.

Katie called the nurses station where Sue answered. Katie told her that George Marshall had just passed away and that his family was in the building, but not in the room. Sue said that she would call Dr. Moore and send someone to do a quick look for the family. Sue asked Katie if she was OK, and Katie was a little surprised to hear her voice answer back, "Yes. Absolutely yes."

Dr. Moore arrived a minute later where he officially declared George Marshall dead. Yet somehow, in the finality of such a call, Katie felt like George Marshall was more alive than he had been the last fifty or sixty years of his life. Katie didn't leave the room – she had no reason to stay other than not wanting to let go of such a special moment. Louise and Tom entered the room crying and thanking Katie for all that the hospital had done over the last few weeks. Katie accepted their thanks, though she processed little of what they said. Standing awkwardly for a moment while George's family cried beside his bed, Katie reluctantly left the room to let Louise and Tom have their final moment alone with George.

Like Trish had a notification on her phone for such things, she met Katie in the hallway and gave Katie a big hug.

"Hey there, girl. I'm so sorry. I know that cranky old man was starting to find a place in your heart."

"Yeah, well I guess I have a soft spot for just about anyone."

"Yeah, maybe that's part of your problem," Trish replied, turning her head slightly and casting a sideways look at Katie.

At first, Katie didn't quite understand what Trish meant, instead riding the incredible high of being totally outside of herself — separated from reality both physically and emotionally. Processing what Trish said, Katie snapped back to reality and replied, "I don't know, Trish. I know you're going to think I'm crazy, but I might be going back home tonight."

Trish bit her lip and tried to hide her disappointment. "Suit yourself, Katie. But listen, if it doesn't work out or if you come to your senses, you always have a spot on my couch."

"Thanks, Trish. You're a good friend."

Katie gave Trish another hug and then snuck off to the bathroom where she found an empty stall and pulled out her phone to text Kyle.

Katie wasn't sure what to type. It was just past five o'clock. On a normal day she knew that Kyle should be home by now. But, then again, she wasn't really sure what normal was anymore. She didn't know if Kyle would text her back now, later, or even at all.

Standing in the bathroom stall, Katie gave it a shot. "Hey, Kyle. How are you doing?"

Katie stared at her screen, hoping to see a reply. They had both tried to contact each other the last few days but could never seem to be able or willing to communicate at the same time.

Katie's heart skipped a beat when she saw texting bubbles dance beside his name. All at once she experienced a dichotomy of emotions – excitement that he wanted to text with her and fear that he might say something negative. She wasn't even sure what she wanted him to say. She, herself, was so uncertain about their future based on her mistrust of their past. Who was her husband, anyway? How real was he? Finally, Kyle's text came through.

"Hey there, Katie. I'm driving and almost home. I'll text you in a minute."

Katie frowned and sent a quick text back. "OK."

Katie wasn't sure what "a minute" meant. Certainly she could afford to hide out in the bathroom for a few minutes. After all, she just lost a patient. But, maybe "a minute" meant five minutes or ten minutes. Maybe he wasn't really "almost home." Maybe he was just trying to avoid her. Maybe he was buying time to think of what to say. Maybe he was shooting up with this mysterious Tony. Maybe she should just leave the bathroom and get back to work.

Katie sat down on the toilet and stared at her phone. Waiting impatiently, Katie thought more about the words that George said shortly before he died.

"Forgiveness can be a long process." Katie replayed the words in her mind. "What is forgiveness?" she thought. "Is it forgetting…? That doesn't seem possible. Is it a life without consequences…? That doesn't seem possible or even right."

Katie continued, "I don't think I can forget what happened. Kyle hurt me by his actions." She paused. "Why does it hurt me so much? It's not like he was doing it to hurt

265

me. He was doing it because *he* was hurting." She paused again. "But, it did hurt me. He wasn't honest with me. He didn't let me help him. I don't think I can forget that.

"But, then again," she thought, "maybe I don't need to forget it. No one can just forget something, so that must not be what forgiveness is." She paused again in her thoughts, mulling through her logic. "And forgiveness can't be something without consequences – there are consequences for everything in life. Kyle broke my trust – there are consequences for that. But, I suppose that doesn't mean he can't build my trust back."

Katie thought some more about George's words. She thought about him saying, "A long process." She reasoned, "Maybe it's not something I can just figure out right now. Maybe it's something that time will help develop, something that time will help mature."

Katie looked at her phone. She knew it would buzz if Kyle texted back, but she checked it anyway.

"What was the other thing he said," Katie thought to herself. "Oh yeah, 'You have to have faith.' That's a hard one. I always used to have faith. But that was when it was easy. Now it is hard. Life is hard."

Katie thought for a moment without forming new words in her head – she felt confused and like she was floating in a cloud of vagueness. After a moment of opaqueness, she continued, "How do I have faith? How do I know what is really what? Faith is so much of my roots, but how do I know that I'm still that same person and that my faith is still that same faith? Do I even want to have that kind of faith anymore? It seems so childlike and immature. That kind of faith doesn't feel like the real world. I don't think I can believe like that anymore."

Katie looked at her phone again – still no response.

Katie thought about George's last word. "Pink," she thought. "Why did George say that word? What did it mean to him?"

Just then, Katie's phone buzzed. Excitedly, she picked it up and read, "Hey, I'm glad you texted me. I was going to text you when I got home. I would really like you to come home this evening and talk – hopefully for good, but if not for good, then at least to talk. I think I'm ready to talk now. I'm so sorry I haven't been able to talk. It's been difficult figuring out what I think and feel, let alone to actually talk about it. I love you."

Katie was overcome with relief as she read Kyle's words. She wasn't exactly sure how to forgive Kyle and she wasn't sure she had a solid faith anymore, but she so wanted to see her husband and talk to him. And now, much to her surprise, she felt like she wanted to get things back on the right track. She didn't even know that's how she felt until she read his text. It was like a great weight was lifted off her shoulder. His simple, loving, and remorseful text was the permission she needed to want to love him again and to want to make their marriage work."

"OK, Kyle. I really want to talk to you too. It's been a crazy, crazy last few days and I really want to figure this all out. I love you, too."

Instead of hitting send, Katie read over her text. She wrote that last part of the text – "I love you, too" – without even thinking to do it – it was just a habit. But, as she stared at the words, "I love you, too," she decided that she might not have all the answers, but that it was true. She did love Kyle. She didn't know exactly what it meant. She didn't know what it would mean moving forward, but she did love him.

Katie hit send and waited.

"OK, I'll see you tonight. 8:00?"

"Yeah, that should be about right. I look forward to it."

Katie left the bathroom and went back to the nurses station. She almost felt like she might trip over her feet – her mind and emotions seemed disconnected from the simple process of placing one foot in front of the other. Sitting down at her seat, she could see the door to George's room. Just moments after she sat down, she saw Louise and Tom leave the room.

Katie sat at the station, catching up on her charts and preparing her notes for the next shift. She kept looking over at George's room. Ten minutes later she saw someone from downstairs go into his room or a few minutes and then take George out, covered from head to toe. That was followed by an aide who went into the room to clean it and get it ready for its next patient.

As the clock neared seven and just a few minutes before the next shift would begin arriving, Katie decided to go one last time into George's room, now cleaned and ready for its next patient.

She walked in and everything felt very odd to her. It was such a special, spiritual place just a couple of hours ago. Now it was a clean, empty hospital room that looked like every other hospital room on her floor.

Katie walked slowly around the room, inspecting everything – hoping that perhaps she might see the little girl in a red dress or that somehow she might recapture just a little bit of the divine encounter that she had so clearly felt a little bit earlier.

Katie walked over to the chair in the corner of the room. This wasn't the same room that Lucille passed away in a few weeks ago, but Katie remembered that Lucille looked over at the chair when she talked to the little girl. Katie stared at the chair in the corner of George's room. Katie tried to look at it with her eyes, with her heart, and with her spirit. Katie sat down in the chair and closed her eyes, hoping to feel something.

Seeing nothing and sensing nothing other than the warmth of the memories from moments ago, Katie got up and walked over to the side of the bed where she cared for George, where she hoped George would stay asleep, where she hollered at George, and where she cried with George. Katie placed her hand on the cold handrail, remembering the warmth of the moments she had with George these last couple of days.

Katie looked at her watch and said one last goodbye to George, though he was no longer in the room. As she walked to the door, she paused and turned back one more time, smiling as she left and a little heartbroken that it was over.

Just a little bit later, Katie got in her car and started the familiar drive to her house. She tried to form what she wanted to say and what she hoped to hear, but like so many other times during the last week, she had trouble playing out any conversation in her mind past the first sentence or two.

Partway into her drive, Katie realized that her inconsistent thoughts hadn't accomplished her hoped-for conversation planning and she gave up altogether. Wiping her mind clean, Katie started thinking again about George's final word, "Pink."

"What does it mean?" she thought to herself.

"Were there pink flowers in the room…? I don't think so. The water pitcher was pink. Was he thirsty…? I don't think so."

Getting closer to her home, Katie's thoughts turned to her own love for pink.

"Ever since I was little girl," Katie thought, "I have loved pink. My pink bicycle, my pink bedroom, my pink babydoll, my pink dresses. Mom would have to buy me the bigger packs of crayons just to make sure I got a pink one in it."

Katie thought about it some more.

"I suppose…. I suppose that pink is just who I am, or at least, who I was." At a stoplight, Katie reached her hand up to the top of her head and pulled out the hair tie that was holding her hair back. "Red." Katie stared at the hair tie. "I'm not red."

Katie tossed the hair tie onto the passenger seat and started driving. At the next red light, she opened her center console and found three pink hair ties. She grabbed one and put it in her hair.

A moment later, Katie pulled into her driveway. Parking the car, Katie sat there, thinking about all of the events of the last few days.

As she thought, the late June daylight still shown bright enough for her to see the pink flowers she planted last month along her sidewalk. She looked down at her passenger seat and saw the red hair tie sitting there alone, like it was an outcast.

All at once, a flood of emotions and realization hit Katie. Out loud she said, "Pink is the answer. Pink is the long process to forgiveness. Pink is the way back to my faith."

She pulled down her visor and looked in the mirror at the pink hair tie holding her ponytail together. Suddenly and unexpectedly, her out-of-this–world excitement from the victory of her revelation crashed back to earth. The pink hair tie didn't look right in her hair. Yes, pink was who she was and pink represented everything she knew to be true, but nevertheless, it looked foreign attached to her body. It looked like the eight-year-old Katie staring back at her in the mirror – the Katie who didn't know that life was full of death, that love was full of hate, and that trust was full of suspicion.

Disappointed and disgusted with herself, Katie reached up and pulled the pink hair tie out of her hair, letting her hair dangle free. She tossed the pink hair tie onto the passenger seat beside the red one. She paused and looked at both hair ties. Then, she picked up the pink one and put it in her pocket, leaving the red one on the seat.

Katie opened her car door, took a deep breath, and started walking toward the house. Before she could get to the front door, Kyle opened it and held out his arms, hoping that Katie would come into them.

Without hesitating, Katie jogged to the door and fell into his arms, crying. Kyle cried too, overcome with happiness to hold his wife again. Katie and Kyle held each other, both previously not realizing the essential need their bodies had to embrace each other. They stood there, temporarily forgetting days of hurt and sadness, their bodies and spirits renewed by their embrace. Without saying a single word, they were each committing from deep within themselves to the long and hard work of restoring their marriage.

Pulling just slightly away but still in his embrace, Katie said, "It's all about pink, Kyle. It's who I used to be and not quite who I am today. But I think I'm still a lot pink. I think it's still a big part of me. It's not all me anymore, but it's still a big part."

"Pink? What are you talking about Katie."

"All of it – I'm talking about all of it."

Katie and Kyle released their embrace and walked hand-in-hand into their house where they stayed up late into the night – talking, crying, hugging, and being together. Neither of them had answers. In fact, neither of them were really sure they knew the questions. Yet, they each vowed to work together – for better or for worse.

Chapter

19

A few weeks later, on a late Saturday night in July, Katie and Kyle had already been asleep for a few hours. They had spent their third Saturday morning in a row at the family meeting at the recovery center. Because Sue was kind enough to let Katie attend the meeting and come into work late, Katie's job hadn't even been getting in the way of their streak of three straight meetings. Katie and Kyle were proud of their three-Saturday streak and hoped to continue it, one week at a time.

Earlier on this Saturday evening, Katie and Kyle spent time with her family. Slowly overcoming the darkness she and Kyle created by facing their struggles alone, Katie was beginning to relive the joy and energy she received from spending time with her parents. She was invigorated by doing simple things with them such playing cards or making a Target run or even just sitting together on a porch swing.

Katie and Kyle's marriage wasn't perfect, but it was theirs and they were committed to fiercely protecting it. They couldn't change the terrible experience they had just gone through – it changed their relationship and their faith forever. But, they could embrace those changes and persevere through them as stronger individuals and as a stronger couple.

They both acknowledged that Kyle's addiction issues were bigger than either of them previously realized or could even currently comprehend. Despite the scariness of not understanding, they found peace in their ability to acknowledge and accept the uncertainty. Kyle still wanted to use, but he was developing tools to deal with those urges. Sometimes Katie still found herself thinking Kyle should be healed and over it all, but attending the family meetings helped her with her perspective, her expectations, and her willingness to support Kyle in ways that he needed.

Katie and Kyle knew they didn't have the answers for much of anything, but they were willing to keep on going. Tomorrow morning would also be their third Sunday in a row attending church together. They were even talking again about volunteering with the youth group.

On this particular Saturday night, while Katie and Kyle were hard asleep after their busy day, Madeline Ross stayed her first night in the palliative care unit at Southwest

Ohio Medical Center. Madeline spent the last few weeks as a patient elsewhere at SOMC, and as her condition worsened, her family and medical team made the difficult decision to focus on Madeline's final comfort rather than fruitlessly attempt to treat her terrible disease.

Madeline, it turns out, had not hardly had a coherent thought to herself or worthwhile conversation with another person in the nearly three years since her mind completely succumbed to dementia. For all she knew, Madeline could have been sleeping in her bed in her home, in a hammock in a beautiful forest, or even on a cot in a treehouse overlooking the African savannah.

But, on this particular Saturday night, Madeline Ross lied in a bed in which she had never lain – a strange bed in a strange room in a strange wing of the not-so-familiar hospital that she had come to think of as her home over the last few weeks.

Sometime in the middle of the night, Madeline woke up from her restless sleep. It wasn't uncommon for Madeline to open her eyes and look around in both the daytime and the nighttime, though most people reasoned that she didn't really comprehend what she saw.

However, on this night, in the cold hospital room with only the faint glow of an oxygen light providing just a little bit of light, Madeline felt an overwhelming degree of warmth. If she had lucidity enough to process her thoughts and emotions, then she would have realized that this warmth didn't come from outside of herself, but rather from within.

Who knows what Madeline understood as her eyes slowly scanned the possibly foreign, but yet possibly familiar environment. As she looked around the room, barely moving her head, the feeling of warmth overwhelmed her senses in a way that she had not felt in quite some time. In fact, for the first time in a long time, Madeline was becoming consciously aware that she was actually feeling anything at all.

As her gaze surveyed the room and continued around to the end of her bed, Madeline Ross's eyes froze when she saw the prettiest little girl standing there, wearing a red dress with her hair pulled back in a ponytail. Madeline didn't know how to react to the sight of the pretty little girl who was smiling back. Without understanding it, Madeline knew that the warmth she felt came from the presence of this little girl.

Madeline wanted to return the smile to the little girl, but in this particular instance Madeline couldn't quite remember how to contort her muscles into that particular gesture. Almost as if the little girl sensed the emotion Madeline wanted to express, a big grin spread across the little girl's face. The little girl looked deeply and affectionately into Madeline's eyes.

Madeline wanted to ask the little girl a question – at least she felt like she wanted to ask the little girl a question. In an unexpected way, Madeline's benign conscious abilities slowly came back to life. Madeline's eyes loosened their focus on the little girl as her brain began to focus more on her own inside rather than everything on the outside. She started to have thoughts and understandings that she didn't realize she hadn't thought or understood for a long time. For the first time in several months, Madeline understood that she was lying in a bed, Madeline understood that she was in a hospital, and Madeline understood that she was scared. She wasn't sure what she was scared of, but she could feel a heavy weight of anxiety and fear pressing down on her chest. Madeline didn't understand everything that was going on, but for the first time in a long time she could understand that she didn't understand.

As these old familiar thoughts and reasonings and emotions that had long evaded her rose back to life in Madeline's soul, she refocused her gaze on the little girl, who was continuing to smile at Madeline. The little girl's gaze – her very presence – calmed Madeline's resurrected whirlwind of emotions. Madeline liked looking at the little girl and Madeline felt an odd sense of peace from locking her eyes with the little girl's eyes.

Madeline's newfound mental capacities led her to wonder who this little girl was. Madeline didn't think that the little girl was her sister or her daughter or her granddaughter. Perhaps this little girl was Madeline's childhood friend, Anna, or even her cousin, Ruth. Madeline explored corners of her memory that had been closed for a long time. She could not figure out how she knew the little girl or even if she knew the little girl at all, though the little girl felt both familiar and new at the same time.

Madeline wondered why this little girl was here. Madeline wondered what the little girl's purpose was –

standing at the foot of her bed in the middle of the night in a hospital room.

Madeline determined that she was going to ask the little girl a question. Madeline dug deeply into her memories — trying to remember how to ask a question. What word should she start with? What word should she end with? Was she supposed to say "question mark" at the end of her query? How would the unfamiliar reverberations of her own voice sound to her own ears and to the ears of this pretty little girl.

With her mental faculties clearing and with her growing determination to investigate this little girl who was wearing a red dress, Madeline decided to risk it all and open her mouth. She was going to talk to this strange, yet comforting creature.

As Madeline cracked opened her mouth, ready to put forth the first words she had offered in nearly 18 months, the little girl took three steps forward, coming up beside Madeline as she lied in her bed. Somewhat startled, yet at peace, Madeline could not speak. The little girl placed both of her small hands on Madeline's bedrail and offered a renewed, loving smile as she gazed into Madeline's eyes. Madeline left her half-open mouth hanging without uttering its words.

After snapping out of her brief hypnotization by the little girl's advance, Madeline resolved yet again to ask the girl a question. Before Madeline could utter any words, the little girl in a red dress instead opened her own mouth. The little girl, looking intently and warmly at Madeline, said,

Joe Dodridge

"Hello, Madeline Ross. It is nice to finally meet you. Tell me, what color do you dream in?"

ABOUT THE AUTHOR

My name is Joe Dodridge and I live in Indiana. My full-time job is a high school teacher. I've taught school for 17 years and was a pastor for 10 years. I'm married and we have two children.

I write fiction books, Christian living books, and travel books.

Fiction by Joe Dodridge

Nicholas - The Legend Begins: a coming-of-age novel based on the real Saint Nicholas

Based on the amazing true story of the man our culture created into Santa Claus, this story has elements of action, adventure, romance, and faith. Don't read "Santa Claus" and think reindeer and elves. Instead, this novel is based on the true person and his true story.

Sofia with an F: a clean, romantic adventure

A clean romance with adventure, Sofia with an F is a short novel where a Hallmark movie meets *Oceans 11*. 25-year-old Sofia moved from the swanky Back Bay area of Boston to the hills of southern Ohio to pursue her graduate degree in art history. Little did Sofia know that she would meet a farmer named Braxton who would cause her to reevaluate everything she thought was important. Little did

Braxton know that Sofia didn't actually come to southern Ohio to get a college degree.

Christian Living Books by Joe Dodridge

You Are Chased by God: a personal Bible study through the book of Jonah

Understand and apply the book of Jonah to your life with this Bible study that you can use individually or in a small group.

Our Kids - Our Responsibility: weekly family Bible studies

If you're like our family, you've tried daily devotions and failed. This weekly family devotional goes more in-depth and provides an extra time just for parents.

Hold Your Breath and Jump In: a guide for the first year of college for Christians

This brief book is perfect for Christian college students to set their priorities and start college off right!